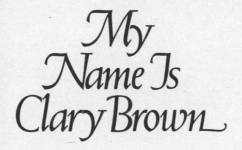

My
Name Is
Clary Brown

CHARLOTTE KEPPEL

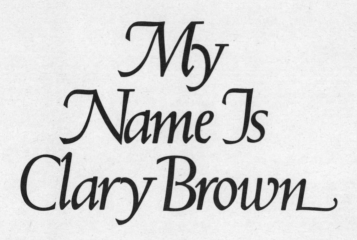

My
Name Is
Clary Brown

Random House
New York

Library of Congress Cataloging in Publication Data

Keppel, Charlotte.
My name is Clary Brown.

I. Title.
PZ4.K392MY3   [PR6061.E677]   823'.9'14   76-10195
ISBN 0-394-40677-X

Manufactured in the United States of America

2 4 6 8 9 7 5 3

FIRST EDITION

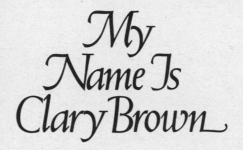

My
Name Is
Clary Brown

I

Diamond met the gypsy fortuneteller in Covent Garden. She might not have noticed her, for her mind was brooding on the coming brawl with the old man, but the gypsy saw her as she picked her way through the muck and mud to her carriage, and extended her hand, more in command than in greeting.

Georgy saw Diamond hesitate. She said quickly, "Now, Miss Diamond, don't be silly. You don't want to go talking to the likes of her. She's just a common tinker-woman—"

"So am I," said Diamond.

"Nonsense. Of course you're not. She's out for your money, and she'll just tell you a pack of lies. You come on now. His lordship don't like being kept waiting. It's all bad enough, God knows, without you making things worse." She added coaxingly, for she was a tactless woman, "If you come all nice and pretty and early, he might change his mind. I lay he still has a soft spot for you."

This, as she should have known, settled the matter. Diamond said, "His lordship can go to the devil. He's never in his life had a soft spot for anyone but his lordship, and I'm as glad to be rid of him as he is of me. Let him wait. Serve the bastard right."

And with this she turned her back on Georgy and walked swiftly toward the gypsy, who stood there impassively, waiting for her.

"Well, I don't know," said Georgy dismally, for all this was growing well beyond her, and she could not imagine what was going to become of them. She saw plainly enough that Diamond was not going to hurry herself. The old man would be furious, but then, he was so furious already that perhaps it hardly mattered. She trundled back gloomily to where James and the carriage were waiting, scowled, and climbed painfully into the seat, for her rheumatics always began to trouble her as the autumn came on.

James said, "Will Miss Diamond be long?"

"Oh, I've no idea," said Georgy.

"His lordship will not be pleased."

She gave him a look but did not answer. Her fingers itched to box his ears, but it really did not matter, nothing mattered any more; soon they would both be thrown out on the streets to starve. And so she fell into a muttering sleep. The coachman thought it was high time his lordship rid himself of such a couple, and wondered without much interest what the new sleeping partner would be like.

Diamond and the gypsy surveyed each other. Diamond saw a very old woman, with a filthy, walnut, wrinkled face; she was dressed in garish rags, a torn shawl about her shoulders and a cap on her grey hair, such as the Garden porters wore. The old woman saw a handsome girl of twenty-two, a little above the average height and dressed in discreet and expensive fashion, with jewels about her throat. (The old man had plenty of money and in such things was generous.) Yet the resemblance was there, in the aquiline features and the great dark eyes.

Diamond said with a smile, "Yes, we are both gypsies. I have Romany blood in me. Tell me my fortune, mother. Tell me all the wonderful things that are going to happen to me. Am I not going to meet a handsome man? Make him very handsome, won't you, and young, he must be young, mother, I'm sick to death of old men who only want us to warm their horrid feet on. And throw in three children. I want three children, and none of them will be in the workhouse." And saying this, she sat down on an old box that had held potatoes, spread her silken skirts about her, and extended both hands.

The old woman took the hands, but did not immediately look at them. Instead she gazed down at Diamond's smiling, excited face. It was a strange face, more beautiful than pretty, mobile as water, and striking. Mr. Garrick, who was a kind man and who had always liked her despite her appalling lack of talent, said once that with that face she should have played Cleopatra. But unfortunately, though the appearance was there, the ability was not; there were only three things that Diamond really did well. She moved beautifully, she could cry on demand with beautiful real tears that streamed down her cheeks, and she could scream in such a fashion that she could be heard three streets away. It was only due to Mr. Garrick's good nature that she ever had a part at all, and so she had played the maid who picked up Kitty Clive's handkerchief, now that she was too stout to do it herself; perhaps, with luck, a passing whore with two sentences and no virtue; and a member of a crowd when wailing and lamentation were required.

She could not, of course, read. The workhouse had not regarded reading and writing as necessary for a little gypsy brat who would never be more than a kitchen maid at best. But she had a phenomenal memory, and had listened many times to Mrs. Bellamy, whose blue eyes and golden curls sat oddly on the Egyptian queen but who spoke her lines with artistry and feeling; then she would go home and recite into her mirror, making only one mistake, which in the circumstances was remarkable:

> "O! withered is the garland of the war,
> The soldier's spear is fallen; young boys and girls
> Are level now with men; the odds is gone,
> And there is nothing left remarkable
> Beneath the visiting moon."

However, though she flung her head back, extended her hands and closed her eyes in a passion of grief, she saw when she opened them that she simply looked ridiculous, like a roupy hen about to lay an egg. And she swore and giggled and burst into genuine crying. It was too bad; it was as if it all lay inside her, yet she could never produce it when on stage. Mr. Garrick's star actress—silly, spiteful little George Ann Bellamy—who was always being abducted, and never crossed a field without falling over a shining serpent, could tear the heart out of an audience, but she, Diamond Browne, though she had the looks, a magnificent figure and a deep, husky voice, would never really act in a hundred years.

She wondered now if the old gypsy saw her as Cleopatra, if perhaps she would prophesy for her some magnificent career.

But the old woman stared at her in silence for a long time, her gaze moving over the delicate olive-skinned face with its full lips and eyes so dark as to be almost black.

"Well?" demanded Diamond, growing impatient. "Well, mother? Have you no wonderful future for me?" She added fretfully, "In Christ's name I need it," and thought of the coming interview with a sickness in her stomach. She had been bold enough in front of Georgy, but the old man had the power to frighten her, there was something so cruel in him, like a cat playing with a mouse.

The old woman spoke at last. She said, "You are going home."

"Am I?" Diamond looked crossly at her, for this was not what she had expected, this was stupid. She was prepared to cross the wrinkled hand, seamed with dirt, with silver, as was the custom, but this nonsense was not worth a penny. If she had a home at all, it was presumably Middleditch, and she had no intention of ever seeing Middleditch again.

"I see danger," said the old woman. "A little house. A child. Many children and all of them dead. And a woman with no face . . ."

Diamond was growing angry. She wanted handsome dark strangers, journeys across the sea, money, adventure, love. All this stuff about dead children, and women with no faces . . . She rose to her feet and began to rummage in her reticule; she would have to pay the old bitch something, but it certainly was not worth it.

The old woman seemed unmoved by this display of temper. She said, "You will leave him. He has never been any good to you, but at least he will send you home."

"I am not going home," said Diamond with a snap. "I am an actress, mother. I play in Drury Lane. That is Mr. Garrick's theatre. He says—he says I am doing famously. Not bad for a workhouse brat, is it? Besides . . ." She hesitated, then laughed. "Besides, I am an old man's darling."

And that was a silly way to put it, for his lordship regarded no woman as his darling, but the foolish phrase appealed to her.

Then the gypsy's next words wiped the smile off her lips. "You have made an enemy of him. Leave him. Go home. There will be another man."

"Ah!" said Diamond, appeased. This was more like it. "Tell me about him, mother. Is he handsome? Is he rich?"

"I do not know."

"If he isn't, he's no use to me. Where and when am I going to meet him?"

"Go home, girl, and you will find out."

"Will I meet him there?"

"Go home and you will find out. But have a care, child, have a care. There is terrible danger. Look after yourself, Clary Brown."

Diamond whispered, "What did you call me?" The color had receded from her face, leaving the high cheekbones sharp and clear.

The old woman had finished. She did not attempt to answer. She dropped Diamond's hands and extended her own, palm upward.

Diamond, still pale and shaking a little, muttered, "It's not worth a brass farthing what you have told me. How did you know my name?" Then, as if she did not want to hear the answer, she pushed a guinea into the clawlike hand—she must be out of her wits, but it was the first coin she found—picked up her skirts, and ran back toward the carriage.

Once she glanced back over her shoulder. The gypsy was gone. It was as if she had never existed. Diamond's pace slackened until she was almost trailing her feet. When she arrived at the carriage she climbed silently into her seat and sat there dreaming, her chin on her hands, not uttering one word.

Georgy was speaking. Georgy was always speaking. She was saying something about looking mopey and hair falling down, needed tidying, but Diamond did not answer, did not even raise her head.

Clary Brown. Dirty, ragged, starving little Clary Brown. Clary, the gypsy workhouse brat whom Mr. Vincent so detested, who was beaten and ill-treated, given the heaviest work to do, shut up once in a cupboard for five hours, sent bruised and striped and supperless to bed. But Clary Brown was gone, done, finished—beastly sniveling, stinking little wretch. She would never be seen again, and in her place was

7

Miss Diamond Browne, with the "e" at the end of her name, dressed in silks and satins, with perfume on her wrists and jewels on her bosom—Diamond Browne who had wanted to be a great actress and ended up instead in an old man's bed.

"I wish," said Diamond suddenly, aloud, "I did not have so quick a temper."

Georgy nodded vehemently to this, for sometimes brushes and make-up were slung at her head, though Diamond always apologized afterward, usually in tears, for she knew Georgy was a good friend, perhaps the one good friend she had. But Georgy did not say anything, for she knew her mistress was not talking about her, only of the old man who now summoned Diamond to his house, to tell her, as they both knew, to go to the devil and never trouble him again.

He had noticed her for the first time from his box in Drury Lane. She was playing the part of a maid. She had two lines to speak, but he did not listen to the lines, only looked at her face, from which his gaze moved slowly down. He was nearly always in that box, very upright, with a cold, handsome, lined face, and beringed fingers always at his snuffbox. He was perhaps about fifty, and to Diamond, then nineteen, he was as ancient as the hills, and it was an enormous shock to her to learn that he proposed to be her lover.

Kitty Clive, who played the female lead, nudged her when the note arrived. She had, of course, to read it to Diamond, who could not decipher a word of it. "I knew it," she said. "I saw his wicked old eye was upon you. He always likes them young. You could do worse. He's very rich. He is an old bastard, but in his way he treats 'em fair. I remember now. There was—" And she ran off three or four names on her fingers. Diamond stared at her in bewildered horror. She said at last, "But he's an old man."

"They are always the worst," said Kitty. She grinned at Diamond. Kitty Clive had no need of old men any more than Peg Woffington in her theatre heyday. Diamond loved Kitty very much, because the older actress had always been kind to the little country girl. When Diamond came off the stage after some minute part in which she had spoken a dozen words, and would ask tearfully, "Was I good? Oh, Kitty, do tell me, was I good?" Kitty always reassured her, though the rest of the cast was not so kind, and Mrs. Bellamy was smiling in a sneering way and muttering behind her hand.

Diamond said, her cheeks very pink, "I have never . . . I never thought of . . ." Then she cried out, almost in tears, "But he's old enough to be my granddad!"

Kitty looked at her thoughtfully, then, taking her by the elbow, led her to the far end of the green room where their conversation could not be overheard. She produced from the pocket in her petticoats a bottle which she made Diamond drink from; it was gin, and it made her choke and cough until the tears were succeeded by laughter.

"Now look, love," said Kitty, "you listen to me, there's a darling. I'm not playing the bawd. I can see you're a good girl, and it beats me how you've managed to remain so, with your looks. But just tell me this—what do you live on, Diamond? What do you eat on?"

"I don't know," wailed Diamond, the tears starting afresh, for she earned almost nothing by her acting. The small salary that Mr. Garrick paid her was really a charity, and she had no idea how long it would continue. He was a kind man, and sorry for her, but after all, he too had to pay his way, and a young woman, however decorative, who would never really act was a liability that one day he would be compelled to discard. There was never enough to eat; Diamond's waist grew smaller and smaller and her cheekbones more prominent. And it was only too true, she had never yet taken a lover, for she could not stomach the fumblings and whispered indecencies that young gallants were delighted to offer. But then, there was a reason for this, and because Kitty was her friend, she suddenly spoke of something that so far she had never mentioned to a soul.

"Mr. Vincent," she said in a flurry of words, the country accent of her childhood unconsciously returning, "he was the Master, he and Matron ran the workhouse. He—he used to get us into corners, I mean, all the girls he fancied. Matron knew about it, she didn't care, I think she helped him. She was an old bitch. I was only fourteen then, the first time. He tried to push me down, and I smacked his face and ran off. He beat me terrible. I remember it even now, and the old bitch looked on, she didn't try to stop him. After that he always treated me like I was dirt. Sometimes he tried again, but he saw it was no use, so he just did everything nasty he could. Once he made me walk down the street with a piece of paper pinned to my dress which said, 'Infamous Liar.' He was a terrible cruel man. The only thing in the world he loved was his little daughter, Maria, but he never saw us as children too. In the end I couldn't stand it any more, and I ran away. I was lucky he didn't catch me; I hid in a cart bringing vegetables up to London. He'd have killed me if he'd found out. He did dreadful things to us all, and one of the girls had a baby by him. Then he said she was a whore and threw her out on the street. The baby died. I remember she had to walk three miles to the funeral, carrying the coffin. After that," said Diamond, her good accent back again, "I found I couldn't bear men to touch me. I know it sounds silly, but when they started to kiss me, I somehow saw Mr. Vincent looking all red and swollen— his breath was horrid and he had great wet hands. It makes me so sad, I like men very much and they like me, but when they touch me— Oh, Kitty, I couldn't bear it, I couldn't. The very thought of it makes me feel sick. I suppose you think I'm gone in the wits."

"I think," said Kitty, looking grave and shocked, "you have no choice." She added, for once unlike her cheerful self, "What else can you do? You can't read or write and you're not the sort to become a night-walker—that would be worse than anything. I expect all this will pass. Try him out, Diamond. You can always say no." Then she said, smiling again, "Don't be so upset, love. We'll think of something. Mr. Garrick and me, we'll not let you starve."

"I have no choice."

They were almost the first words that Diamond said to the old man as she sat beside him in his fine carriage, with James —even then she disliked and mistrusted James—gazing remotely ahead, a faint, cynical smile on his lips. There had been a great many young girls in his lordship's carriage; they were all cheap drabs, and later on when they had developed airs and graces and fancied themselves real ladies, he would laugh to himself when they ordered him about in la-di-da accents.

"I have no choice," she said, and the shudders ran through

her as she spoke. She saw again Mr. Vincent's bloated face, felt the terror and disgust of him as he pinned her against the wall and tried with his powerful hands to push her to the floor. She glanced sideways at the old man as she spoke. He was handsome in his own vulpine way, he smelled of perfume like a woman, he did not look as if he would ill-treat her, and she could not imagine his doing anything so vulgar as to take her against her will. But he was cold, so cold, and she longed for warmth and tenderness, felt that if she found this, she could endure the rest.

The remark might well have angered him. They were strange words to come from a little village slut who played absurdly small parts so abominably, who was still raw and uncertain, who would have no idea how to eat at table, and whose clothes were deplorable. But her looks were so extraordinary, with the slanting black eyes and the thick straight ebon hair that always slid out of its pins. His irritation changed to amusement. Those looks, coupled with a voluptuous body—strange in so young a girl—interested him too much for him to ignore her. He laughed, a brief, sharp laugh, and asked her what the devil she meant.

She was dressed so badly, she was a laughingstock. Yet though her clothes were cheap and shoddy, they were not, he had to notice, vulgar. With her particular brand of looks she might easily have chosen garish colors, bright scarlets and orange and yellow, like the gypsy she so plainly was. But she had elected to wear a plain grey skirt with darns in it, doubtless somebody's castoff, a silk blouse washed to almost nothing, and around her shoulders a tawny scarf. She must have been freezing. It was winter. Probably she did not own a coat. He would never have taken her out to supper in such attire, but he had to admit that if she looked like a flower girl, she at least did not look like a whore.

She answered him with the directness that he was to recognize as part of her character. She learned in time to conceal it a little, but even then it slid out. "I have no money," she said. "I shall soon have nowhere to sleep, because I owe six weeks' rent. I do not choose to become a night-walker, and that is all that is left to me." She looked up at him as if these remarks were the most ordinary in the world. Then she added with great dignity, as if she were a lady and not a drab, "If you wish me to go, my lord, perhaps you will open the carriage door for me."

He surveyed her in silence for what seemed to her an eternity. During that silence she all but opened the door herself and ran for her life. The image of Mr. Vincent was printed on her eyeballs, the stink of him was in her nostrils. When at last he spoke, she jumped, her nerves so tense that she could not control herself.

Her remarks, if she had realized it, baffled him. He had never heard anything like this in his life. The innumerable girls he had requisitioned were flirtatious, brazen, coy or timid. None of them had ever told him that he was a kind of last resort, a refuge against prostitution. He was on the verge of opening the door and kicking her out. Then he looked down into those black eyes, noted the full breasts and minute waist, and smiled; he was in no way a kindly man, but he did have a certain sense of humor, and the novelty of this tickled him.

He said at last, "I want you to stay. I shall give you money. I'll see you have somewhere to live. Only, you will kindly do what I tell you, and the first thing is that you burn those . . . those things you are wearing. I could scarce call them clothes. I could never be seen with someone in such attire. Is that understood?"

She nodded and, as if this amused her, smiled. It was a strange, slanting smile, entirely provocative. It had beguiled Mr. Garrick into offering her a part, it had appeased angry landlords and debt collectors, and suddenly the old man wanted her passionately, knew that he would do anything and everything to have her.

She said, simply, "Yes, my lord," and this, until the final and disastrous scene, set the tone for their whole relationship. She did as she was told, and she did it well enough. As he himself seldom showed any emotion, he supposed he could hardly expect it in her, but this cool, detached acceptance never failed to surprise him, and in some odd way swelled his desire for her, as if somehow he must contrive to break that unnatural placidity down. He was, as he unbelievingly discovered, her first lover, and though he set James and the servants to spy on her, he could never find that she took any other, though her extraordinary looks brought all the young men ogling after her.

She never did him discredit. She learned at first glance, without being told. He did not, naturally, introduce her to his friends—either visiting her in the little house he had bought for such occasions or summoning her to his own when he was alone—but he knew that if he had, she would not have disgraced him. She soon discarded the burring accent of her childhood, she wore her fine new clothes with an air, and though she could neither read nor write, she seemed to possess a remarkable memory: once he had told her something, she never forgot it, and she never made the same mistake twice.

He never, of course, knew what was in her mind, but then, this did not interest him, he never thought of women as having minds at all. He had no idea how she mimicked him to Georgy, how sickened she was by his love-making, how sometimes when she was alone she raged and ranted at the humiliation of it all. And he never knew how much she detested the pretty little house in Highgate, where he installed his mistresses, one after the other.

"The bastard," she told Georgy—he never heard her using such words—"didn't even take the trouble to have it cleaned and cleared out."

The last occupant—Kitty, always a mine of information, told her she was a little dancer—had left behind a filthy brush, a few mildewed pots of cosmetics and some unspeakably dirty underclothes, as well as half-eaten pieces of rotting food and an empty bottle of gin. They were all there when Diamond arrived, and even the sheets on the bed had not been changed. The servants—there were three of them, chosen by the old man, and Diamond knew well enough that they were there not so much to wait on her as to report—grinned and shrugged when she rated them, as if this were the most ordinary thing in the world. Then Diamond flew into a grand, dramatic rage, and hurled everything out of the window, sheets and clothes included, and passers-by were surprised to find a filthy shift entangled in a tree, some tattered stockings entwined round the railings, the blackened sheets lying in the roadway.

"If I were a new dog in a kennel," declared Diamond in one of her celebrated screams, "he would at least change the straw."

She never mentioned this to the old man, though she supposed he knew about it—the servants would see to that—and presently, to all appearances, she and Georgy settled down well enough. She put on her beautiful new clothes, which enchanted her, she wore the jewelry he gave her, and the carriage was always sent round for her when she was wanted. She was even allowed to order it herself if she went shopping or took a drive in Hyde Park. Occasionally he took her to the theatre, and sometimes after this she would cry a little when she arrived home, for it was unbearable to watch the actors on the stage when she so longed to be among them.

Once or twice she managed to slip away to see Kitty. Kitty said, "You've lasted longer than any of the others. Perhaps he'll marry you."

"Oh no!" cried Diamond in horror. "No, no, no!"

"Why not?" demanded Kitty. "He's very rich. His wife is dead and there are no children. You'd be able to play him your way. You'd be his country wife and cuckold him with a handsome young man." And she quoted mockingly, " 'I have been toiling and moiling for the prettiest piece of china, my dear.' "

"No," said Diamond again, then fiercely, "I shall never marry." The slanting smile, a little bitter now, curved her lips. "I always call him my lord, Kitty, never by his name. It is the only way I can bring myself to endure it."

"I shall never understand you," sighed Kitty Clive. "You really are the oddest girl."

But then, though she remembered what Diamond had told her, she did not realize that when the old man made love to her, the stench and foulness and terror of the workhouse lay with Diamond like a noisome shadow. And it was Mr. Vincent who provoked that last unforgivable scene, when Diamond's calm was shattered so that she spoke what was in her mind, said the unpardonable things.

She knew at once that he would never forgive her. He said nothing at the time, only walked out of the little house she so detested. "Soon," said Diamond, when the tears and raging were done, and she had collapsed back on the bed, while Georgy, white and distressed, ran to bring her a hot posset. "Soon, Georgy my old woman, there'll be another doxy here to wear his bloody clothes, to sport his jewelry and have him fall on top of her. And," she said in a loud and furious voice, sitting up so abruptly that she slopped some of the posset onto the sheets, "I am going to leave her a note. At least," she added, "though I cannot write it, I shall get someone to do it for me. 'Dear Lightskirt—' That's how I shall begin."

"Miss Diamond!"

"I shall. 'Dear Lightskirt, all good luck to you. I will give you some advice as a friend—' "

"Miss Diamond, if you will please to drink your posset."

"I don't want my posset," said Diamond. "I want some gin."

"But . . ."

"I tell you, woman, I want some gin. And Madam Housekeeper shall bring it me. Why not? She is only a servant, and I am still in charge here, I haven't been kicked out yet." And with this Diamond tugged at the bell-rope so hard that she all but broke it. When the housekeeper at last appeared, she said coldly, in her most irreproachably genteel accent, "Kindly bring me a bottle of gin and two glasses."

The woman—how Diamond hated her, with her spying eyes and her hypocritical smile—was taken aback. She began, "Ma'am, there is no such thing in the house. If madam would like a glass of wine . . ."

"Madam would like a bottle of gin! And don't you tell me, you silly, spying old bitch, that there's none in the house," said Diamond in ringing tones that would have delighted Mr. Garrick—the only time she could ever act was offstage—"I know there is gin here. I've seen you drink it. You'll bring it at once, or it'll be the worse for you."

Poor Georgy was by this time trembling from head to foot, for she was in some ways a timid woman, with a vast respect for authority, always in awe of anyone whom she considered to be from a class above her. She watched in silence as the gin arrived five minutes later, delivered by the butler, whose face was icy with surprise and resentment—the housekeeper was having a fit of hysterics in the kitchen.

Diamond filled both glasses and forced one on Georgy, who took an unwilling sip and nearly spat it out.

"It's good for you," said Diamond. "It's what the common people drink, people like me. It's only fine ladies who drink ratafia and suchlike piss. You drink it down, Georgy, it'll make a man of you. You're going to need it. Soon we'll be out of this horrid house, and what we'll do then, I have no idea. Still, there's always Kate and her girls in the Garden, and after all, I am by now well trained."

"Miss Diamond, you mustn't talk like that!"

"Why not, pray? I talk as I please. But I didn't tell you the end of my letter, did I? 'Dear Lightskirt . . .' Where was I?"

Georgy gave it up. She sat down on the nearest chair, the glass in her hand, and gazed helplessly at Diamond, who, with her hair hanging over her face and her eyes alight with battle, drank down a gulp of gin, then declaimed, " 'He likes to go to bed, dear Lightskirt, at eleven o'clock precisely. He starts making love at ten past, and the whole business is over, thank God, by a quarter to twelve. He is not a very good performer, but then, he is old and needs encouraging. Besides, he drinks a great deal of wine.' "

Georgy closed her eyes.

"Then— I hope you're listening to me, Georgy."

"Miss Diamond," said Georgy faintly, "what has happened? Why are you behaving like this? What in the name of God did you say to him?"

"What did I say to him, the son of a whore? Oh God, God, God," cried Diamond. Then it was as if the hysteria suddenly left her, for she let her glass fall to the floor and burst into a violent flood of tears.

The old man could not endure scenes of any kind. She knew that well enough, for he had told her so at the very beginning. It seemed that this was the reason why her predecessor had lasted a mere seven months. Diamond did not find it difficult to control herself, for she could only endure the old man at all by retreating into the fastness of her mind— it was the shell of Diamond who spoke and smiled and submitted to his attentions. He seldom made any kind of conversation with her, though he sometimes told her of the people he had met, the dinner parties he had been to, and from time to time he criticized what she was wearing, telling her that a certain color did not become her, that the bodice was too high or too low, that her hair was untidy, that she needed a little rouge. Then he would pour her a glass of wine. It was always the overture to his love-making. Only once did he say "You are very beautiful," and it so astonished her that she flushed with pleasure, thinking that this was the first sign of warmth and feeling she had ever received from him. But her reaction must have frightened him; he never paid her any kind of compliment again.

II

That evening had started like innumerable others, yet from the beginning Diamond felt a little strange. In some way the ghosts of her childhood seemed to be surrounding her, as if the spirit of her Romany father had bequeathed to her the sight. She took the ritual glass of wine the old man offered her, but shivered with the cold, though there was a vast log fire burning.

She turned a little away from him—she could not bear to look at his hard, handsome face, knowing that soon it would be leaning over her. He did not notice. Such things did not interest him. He saw only that the deep crimson of her gown suited her well, that her hair was neatly piled up and glossy as silk, that the diamond necklace gleamed in the firelight on her soft olive skin. When she began speaking in her deep, husky voice, he listened to the music of it, which stirred him. It was only after a while that it dawned on him that she was saying extraordinary things, bringing up details of her past, acting as if she were a human being in her own right, not simply his possession.

"It was Captain Ringham who sent me there," said Diamond. Her voice was slow and drowsy. "Captain William Ringham. One day I know I'll see him again. If I were a man, I should shoot him. I'm sure it was he who put me in the workhouse, after he had hanged my pa. He knew how unhappy I was. He must have known. And I managed to get away to see him, I begged him to take me away, anywhere, so that I need not go back. I told him about Mr. Vincent, but I don't think he believed me. He simply sent me back. That was why I ran away. Sir Francis would have been kinder, I wish I'd gone to him. His wife was my friend. I think she was my only friend.

She was a dear, sweet lady. She was an actress too, you know, but I suppose it was not suitable for Sir Francis's wife to remain on the stage. I remember her very well. She used a great deal of make-up. The villagers sometimes laughed at her, but I think they were really fond of her, she was always good to everyone. I would like to meet her again, to say thank you. When I met her she was not very young, and she had lost her looks. Perhaps that was why she made up so much. I believe once she was very beautiful. She built a little theatre for us. We were never allowed to use it, but I used to creep in sometimes. It was then that I knew I wanted to go on the stage. But Mr. Vincent and Captain Ringham—"

Then she broke off, becoming aware that the old man was staring at her as if he could not believe his ears. She swung round, staring straight at him. She saw that his expression was one of astonished distaste, as if a pet kitten had suddenly leaped at him and raked its claws through his cheek. He looked at her almost with incredulity, and Diamond, reading his expression and emerging from her unhappy dream, for the first time in the whole of their acquaintance disastrously lost her head and her temper.

She knew that she had no business to speak like this. It was not, as one might say, part of the bargain. That had been made plain from the beginning. In his own way he had treated her well enough. He never ill-used her, he saw that she wanted nothing. She was wearing clothes that she had never in her wildest dreams thought she would possess; the little house, for all she hated it, was warm and comfortable; and at Christmas he always formally presented her with a small piece of jewelry. But he had never, apart from that one brief moment, said a personal word to her. He had never laughed with her, petted her, shown the least affection. And Diamond had often wondered how one could perform the intimate act of love with no love involved; the greatest compliment he ever paid her was to offer no criticism.

"I've done it," she had told Georgy afterwards. She knew that she had stepped irrevocably over the line. She studied that handsome, disdainful face. His wife, so they said—for a great deal of gossip came to her ears—had died of neglect. There were no legitimate children to carry on his name, and the nearest relatives fawned on him for his money and spoke hideous things of him behind his back. Nobody seemed to love him and he loved nobody. The only emotion she had ever seen him display was when one of his favorite race horses had won and brought him in an enormous sum of money.

Perhaps if she had apologized . . . She did not. She exclaimed, "Why don't you ever treat me like a human being?"

He did not answer. His face was twisted now with anger and contempt.

But she could not stop. "You have never once," she said, "asked me about my father or my childhood or what sort of life I led. I didn't mean to talk of Mr. Vincent and Captain Ringham, I know they are nothing to you—"

"Nothing!"

"But they are to me, they are part of me. Are you not interested at all?"

"No." He was looking for his hat, which he had thrown down on a chair. When he came at such a late hour, it was a convention that the servants must not see him. This was entirely absurd, for both house and servants had been bought for his mistress, but Diamond knew that she was expected to let him in and played out the little play religiously, though at the beginning it made her laugh.

She was too upset now to care what she said. It was over anyway, nothing mattered any more. She cried out, "Then you should be interested." She had never used such a tone to him. The thick black hair was beginning to come down. She looked wild and distraught. She said fiercely, "I know I am your whore, but we have known each other for nearly three years now, and—and we are like people in a play. We strut on the stage, pulling faces, then the play is done and the curtain comes down. It's not real. It's so cold. Oh," cried Diamond, acting beautifully now, "your world is such a cold world. There is no love in it. I think there is no love in you. Have you ever really loved anyone, my lord?"

This last impertinence was too much, she knew perfectly well it was, and the expression on his face was so dreadful that she was frightened back to her senses. But of course it was far too late. She fell silent, staring at him, the tears shining in her eyes, but the thoughts crawling in her mind were two-fold. One part of her was thinking, *I shall never have to go to bed with him again, thank God, thank God,* and the other, wild with panic, *I am going to be thrown out, I'll have to fight to live again, I won't know where my next meal is coming from, I shall have no money for my rent. What in God's name am I going to do?*

He did not so much as say goodnight, and she felt she could hardly blame him. She heard the front door close and the sound of the carriage wheels trundling off. A lesser person would have slammed the door—Diamond felt that in the circumstances she would have crashed it off its hinges—but he shut it very quietly. And she sat there, feeling crushed and frightened, like a naughty child, with the silence of the house about her.

He waited for three days before summoning her for the final interview. By this time Diamond had recovered something of her spirits, for she was never one to be set down for long. "I'll go back to Mr. Garrick," she told Georgy. "I am sure he will do something for me. After all, my voice is better now. I pronounce more correctly, Kitty told me so. And I daresay I can keep some of the clothes. I could always sell them, they are so lovely."

"There's the jewels," said Georgy hopefully.

Diamond looked down, frowning a little. She said crossly, "I don't know. I daresay they are for the next one. I am not a thief, Georgy. Besides, he'd have me hanged. I'm sure he would love to see me swinging at Tyburn."

Then the full dramatic horror of this overcame her, and she burst into wild tears for the dozenth time—she saw herself riding on the cart, standing there pale and beautiful, her long hair flowing in the wind, so that the avid crowd was hushed and people wept at the piteous sight.

Georgy said prosaically, "You are making a play of it, Miss Diamond. Now if you'll only say you're sorry, cry like, go down on your knees—"

"What!"

"It's the sort of thing gentlemen like."

"Well, it's the sort of thing I do not like," said Diamond,

blowing her nose. The tears stopped instantly, and she did not cry again. When she was shown into the old man's drawing room, where he was awaiting her with the air of an executioner, her eyes were dry and wide, though her stomach felt as if it had been dislodged and was slowly sinking down.

It was very quiet and well-bred. There were no reproaches or recriminations. He simply looked at her as if she were some distasteful creature crawled out of the gutter, and said calmly, "I imagine you must know why I wish to see you. We will come to the point immediately. I think it is time you went back where you belong."

Diamond thought for one shocked moment that he meant the workhouse. She said nothing, only sat down on the footstool by the fire. It was her customary place, and she instinctively spread her skirts wide, as she always did, so as not to crease them. He had not asked her to sit down, but she had no intention of standing before him like a schoolboy due to be whipped.

He said in the same tone, "I have been making inquiries. There is a vacant cottage which my agent has now purchased for you."

"Where is that?" asked Diamond, bewildered.

"Surely I made it perfectly plain. Middleditch, of course."

"Middleditch!"

"That is your home, is it not? I trust you will agree that I am treating you most generously. I have no doubt you would be delighted to spread the rumor that I have thrown you out without a penny, but I have no intention of giving you such an opportunity."

Diamond, for all she was dazed and incredulous, could understand this perfectly well, better than he would have appreciated. Until she met him she knew nothing of the *ton* except as people in the boxes, who could afford to pay the enormous sum of five shillings for the privilege. Captain Ringham, the detested Captain Ringham, had plenty of money and the Hall was a fine house, but he was hardly in the aristocracy. As for Sir Francis Axenford, he was someone she hardly knew at all. But this she had seen happen before; his lordship belonged to the old school where gentlemen pensioned their discarded mistresses off. It was not that he cared a damn what happened to her. She could starve, for all it would trouble him, go on the streets, be knifed in a back alley, end in Bridewell. But he could not endure the idea that she might spread stories against him; it would be an insult to his pride. You took your pleasure, but you paid for it. It was a kind of antique code. There must be a great many small cottages dotted over England, with discarded ladies living in them—only, why did he have to select Middleditch for her? Why must he send her back to the one place she never wanted to see again?

You are going home. The old gypsy had said that. She had said, *Go home, girl.*

Oh, I don't want to, I just cannot bear it, whispered Diamond to herself. But she did not speak aloud, only rose to her feet to stand by the mantelpiece; she could not take this humiliation at a level so far below him. She was wearing a dress he had bought her only two weeks before. It had cost thirty pounds and was made of some new fashionable material called soupir-étouffe lutestring. The name meant nothing to Diamond, but she knew it was beautiful. The old man was generous and he was entertained by her obvious delight in new clothes. But there again it was his pride—if he had a toy, it must be the best-dressed toy in the world. Around her neck was a string of diamonds, bought because of her name, though she once admitted to him that her name was not really Diamond at all.

She moved so beautifully as she rose to her feet that for a second the desire flickered within him. There was no denying that she was a most handsome girl and, astonishingly, more ladylike in her appearance than many fine ladies. But then, it was the way of the world for whores to behave like ladies and ladies like whores; after all, it mattered to the one and not at all to the other. The flicker subsided. He could not be expected to tolerate a creature who suddenly burst into so tedious a squawl about, God save us, her childhood. He said coldly, "The cottage is ready for you. You will go tomorrow. James will take you and your maid down. I shall be giving you a sum of money which, if you are careful, you should be able to manage on for at least a year. After that, naturally, you must deal with everything on your own. I daresay you will not find it so difficult. You have no reason to complain of me. But there is, of course, one condition attached."

"One condition?" repeated Diamond, too dazed to do anything but echo the words. Her cheeks were flushed. She understood well enough what he meant when he spoke of her dealing with everything on her own; he assumed there would be a succession of lovers. She looked at the old man, thinking how strange this all was, how unexpected. She was only twenty-two, yet she felt a hundred years older than the little workhouse brat in her shabby, ridiculous clothes. She thought of those clothes, the old grey skirt Kitty had found for her, the washed-out blouse. She had told the old man that she had burned them, but this was not true. To her they were the last link with her real life as Clary Brown, and she had bundled them into a small portmanteau which she kept on top of her wardrobe. Now perhaps she would have to wear them again. Her eyes moved sideways in reflection. She had just realized who the next bed-warmer must be. Her name was—oh, what was it now?—Fanny, yes, Fanny. Fanny was a round little blonde, rather like Mrs. Bellamy, with blue eyes and golden curls, who tripped onto the stage from time to time, helping heroines dress or undress themselves before hiding behind screens. Well, good luck to Fanny, and she would certainly get someone to write the little note for her so that she could stick it on the mirror.

She said again, "What is the condition?" And she added, almost derisively, "My lord."

His name was Harvey. It seemed to her a silly kind of name, like a surname, not a proper name at all. She had never once used it. She wondered what he would have said if she had done so.

He said very stiffly, "The condition is that you never under any circumstances approach me again. If you do so, whatever the reason, I'll have you thrown into Bridewell. If you don't think this possible, you don't know me at all."

Diamond thought it was very possible. She said nothing. It was all like acting in a very bad play.

He went on in his normal tones, "I have a document here

to that effect. You will sign it. You can put a cross for your name, which I shall write underneath."

She exclaimed in sudden temper, "I can write my own name, thank you!" And indeed she could do so; Kitty had instructed her. It took her a long time, with her tongue sticking out, and the letters meant nothing to her, but she could do it, and at the beginning was so proud of her achievement that she scrawled her name everywhere: on the leaves of books, on odd scraps of paper, and even once on the white wall above her bed.

She saw his eyebrows meet. But he only said, "Very well," and this disdainful acceptance infuriated her so that she cried out, "I shall be glad to go."

"And what do you mean by that?" He was rummaging in his desk, not really listening to what she was saying. But her next words made him turn, the long, thin mouth down at the corners, the eyes narrowed. When he looked like that he was frightening; she could well imagine his throwing her into prison and leaving her there to rot.

She said, nearly in tears, "I've never really liked it here." The Middleditch accent, as always in emotional moments, swam back into her speech. "I don't like nothing about it. Oh, I know you've treated me fair in your own way—"

"Thank you," he said, tight-lipped.

"But it's not my way," said Diamond. As she spoke she pulled the diamond earrings off and began to undo the clasp of the necklace. "It's not my life," she said. "I don't think I'm made to be a whore. I'd rather do the making, if you know what I mean. Oh, it was all right for a time, and it was lovely having nice things to eat, and pretty clothes, and I liked sitting in your box. It was glorious, I felt like a queen. But you see," said Diamond, well away by now—Georgy would be almost fainting, and the old man was flushed with amazed fury, for never once in his whole existence had one of his mistresses presumed to address him in such a fashion—"I'm what they call independent and I don't think I really like men. At least I don't like it when they start clutching me, it makes me sick. It's too like Mr. Vincent— But you won't let me talk about him. It don't matter really. And now I shall be able to come and go as I please, I can even walk. Walk! I like walking, you know, and in your world it's like having no legs, you even take a carriage to cross the road. It'll be nice to walk again, and not having your horrid servants sneering at me when I use the wrong knife or don't speak to them proper."

"Have you finished the sermon, pray?" He was angrier than he could remember being for a long time, he was shaking with it. But some of the anger was because when she talked like this—the intolerable impertinence of it!—she looked so damned handsome. It was preposterous. She was a slut and a whore and as common as dirt, but with her face so flushed and that black hair falling down she was quite beautiful, and in comparison, Fanny, who would certainly be more amenable, seemed somehow like a cheap little doll.

She heaved a great dramatic sigh. She said, "Yes! Only I had to say it somehow. You don't ever think of me as human, but I am. I suppose I'm what the world calls a bad girl, and I'm a horrid actress, I know that, sometimes I cry like anything when I think of it—but I am human too, and you don't want me to be human, you can't bear me talking of myself—"

He said savagely, "I find it intolerable. I shall be thankful to be rid of you." He held out to her a long sheet of paper. His hand, half concealed by a lace ruffle, was shaking. "You will kindly sign this," he said. "James will call for you early tomorrow morning. The money will be handed over to you when you arrive. Sign, please, since you say you are capable of doing so, and then go. The sooner all this is over, the better."

"This cottage," said Diamond. "Will I like it?" The diamond necklace and earrings gleamed on her open palm. It was a small hand and well tended. Once the nails had been as black as coal, but by now she had learned better.

"It is a matter of complete indifference to me whether you like it or not," he said. "You are extremely fortunate that I am so generous. After the way you have just spoken, most men would simply throw you out of the house." He added, so angry that his words fell over each other, "Do you have the effrontery to complain about the cottage? You are nothing but a workhouse brat. You are lucky to have a roof over your head at all."

"I suppose I am," said Diamond. It was, perhaps, a kind of victory that she should have compelled him to speak in such a fashion, for normally he was cold and composed, but she felt almost sorry for him. He would never forgive her for such a display, but he would find it equally hard to forgive himself.

"Of course," he said, "you have grown accustomed to luxury. You may, by the way, keep all your clothes. That should comfort you. As to the cottage, it may not be as grand as my home but it will still be better than the workhouse."

"Yes," said Diamond, "it will be better than the workhouse."

Then it was as if his temper died. He returned to his normal urbane self. He had the document in his hand, and he smoothed it over his knee. He reached for the quill pen that lay on the escritoire beside him.

Diamond looked around her. What she had said was true. In a fashion she was glad to go. She had grown used to this Park Lane mansion, but she had never liked it and she did not like it now. The room was beautiful, high-ceilinged, with fashionable silk paper on the walls. The furniture was old and heavy and polished until it resembled a mirror, so that wherever one was, one saw one's own face. The silver and porcelain were worth a fortune, and the walls were covered with family portraits that all looked the same—cold, humorless and arrogant, as if love had withered on the family tree. Diamond had often wondered what it must be like to be married to such men. Could any wife survive?

Then she took the paper from the old man's hands.

He said very formally, "I shall read it out for you."

"Does it matter?"

"Of course it matters. Are you gone in the wits? You should never sign anything without reading it through." He put on his spectacles. "It is quite short. This is what it says—"

"Oh, I don't give a fig what it says," said Diamond. "You'll not deceive me, my lord, because it wouldn't do you any good if you did. All you want is to be rid of me, and now you are, so why worry over a silly bit of paper that I probably

27

won't understand anyway. Besides, you could always read things that ain't there. Let me sign it. I don't really care. And here are your diamonds."

This time he was not angry, only taken aback. Certainly, never in his career had one of his ladies offered to return his jewels. He had been prepared to ask for them. Now, as she dropped them into his hand with a carefree gesture as if it did not matter, he looked almost silly in his bewilderment and, for the first time, very old.

"I don't want them," said Diamond, who seemed entirely to have recovered her spirits, "not where I'm going. You say you're sending me home. Well, I'd look precious silly walking through Middleditch with all that lot on me. They'd probably think I'd pinched them. You give them to Fanny. She'll love them. They're very pretty."

She did not notice his renewed anger, for she was engrossed in writing her signature. She was not writing "Diamond Browne," but was penning, with the utmost difficulty and several blots, "Clary Brown." It took her nearly ten minutes. Then she triumphantly handed the paper back to him.

He looked down at it. It was quite deplorable, and the signature sprawled all over the page. Then he glanced up at the strange, beautiful face with its small, elegant, oriental features, and was possessed of an unprecedented desire to strike it across. But he only said in his dry voice, "Why have you signed like this?"

"It is my name."

"I thought you preferred to call yourself Diamond."

She was backing toward the door as if this were her exit line. She moved beautifully, like Ophelia, like Cleopatra, like Lady Macbeth, whom she had seen performed by Mrs. Pritchard during her last visit to the theatre. Her face was in shadow. She said, "When I say goodbye I am Clary Brown. That is how I want you to remember me. Will you remember me?"

"I shall forget you," he said, "the moment the door closes behind you."

This was not true. It was said to hurt and it did. Diamond's eyes suddenly filled with tears. It was not that she loved him or even liked him, but she had known him for three years, they had slept together—he could at least have said goodbye in a more kindly fashion. She stood there against the door, and for that moment they looked at each other across the vast, finely appointed room. Then he swung round to tug at the bell-rope. "James will drive you back," he said.

Diamond did not answer, and it was as if this immobile silence were more than he could endure. He took a step toward her, impelled by God knows what reason, and at this she gave a little whimper and ran, slamming the door behind her. He was not to know that in that one moment he was no longer my lord, the old man in his fine clothes. He had seemed a brutal middle-aged man, breathing like a bellows, his face red and blotched, his hands grabbing at a terrified little girl in her black workhouse overall. He only thought she must be drunk or mad; he shrugged his shoulders, thinking that he was well rid of her. It was a pity he had kept her so long, it had doubtless given her ideas above her station.

He stood by the fire for some time—it was a cold autumn—then poured himself a glass of wine to help him recover his composure. He rang the bell again, to tell his footman to go to the theatre to reserve a place in his favorite box. He would forget about Diamond, who did not matter, who had never mattered; he would invite Fanny to his carriage.

But he felt oddly cold and lonely, as if the ghosts of people he had almost forgotten were creeping out of the shadows. His wife, dead for seven years, an illegitimate daughter he had never seen, and others, men and women who had stepped across his life, been with him briefly, then vanished when he had no more use for them. The document still lay between his fingers. He glanced down and saw again that abominable half-illegible signature. A child could have done better. Clary Brown. What a name! *When I say goodbye I am Clary Brown.* Then he swore, tore the paper in two, and threw the pieces into the fire. The diamonds lay on the escritoire, waiting for their new wearer. He bundled them into one of the drawers. They were fine diamonds and perfectly matched; they deserved better than an illegitimate bitch from the workhouse.

By the time he went upstairs to change, Diamond arrived back at Highgate. James had been smiling and sneering and nodding to himself throughout the journey, but she did not even notice. She stormed into the house, where Georgy, pale and shaking, was waiting for her, prepared for hysterics, tantrums, tears, even perhaps a swoon.

Diamond did not swoon. She flung her hat and gloves on the nearest chair, and herself after them, her legs sprawled out, her face flushed and defiant.

Georgy exclaimed in horror, "Miss Diamond, you're sitting on your hat!"

"Damn my hat," said Diamond, then, "It's all over, Georgy."

"Oh dear, oh dear," wailed Georgy, "what is to become of us?"

"You are a silly old faggot," said Diamond, "and I'll tell you what is going to become of us. We are going back to my old home village of Middleditch, to some dirty old cottage provided by his confounded lordship. We are pensioned off so that for at least a year we shall not starve. What I do then, I cannot think, but it don't matter. I only wish I had said no to him and thrown his beastly charity back in his horrid old face."

Georgy knew nothing about Middleditch, for she had first met Diamond in the cheap lodging house near the theatre, but she now saw a brief gleam of light in the black despair that had engulfed her, and she began to smile.

"If I had the guts," said Diamond, "I'd turn it down. Oh, Georgy, how I wish I could turn it down, say, 'Thank you, my lord, to the devil with you, my lord, I hope your damned cottage goes up in flames and you with it, you keep your charity for them that wants it.'"

"Now, Miss Diamond, that's silly, and you know it is. I'm only glad his lordship has been so generous."

"Generous!"

"Well, so he is. At least we'll have a roof over our heads. What do you imagine you could do if you had nowhere to go?"

"I don't know," said Diamond, and her face fell into wretched, sulky lines. She said wearily, "Oh, I've been spoilt. I know it. I could never go back to the old life unless I had to, and I don't know what I'd do then."

And it was dreadfully true. She could not endure the thought of returning to her former life. She remembered the times when she had nothing to eat, when she could not go out in the winter cold because she had nothing to wear. She remembered the ugly scenes with the landlord when she could not pay her rent, how she had to barricade her door for fear that he would come and throw her out. The only food had been a mutton pie in a pie-shop, and perhaps a glass of porter, and at nights she had often lain there, shivering with cold and fear because of the other lodgers who scratched and pushed at her door, who shouted drunkenly and fought and yelled obscenities on the stairs outside. Sometimes Mr. Garrick would give her a tiny part—preferably a weeping one, for genuine tears were her great asset. This would mean a guinea for her, and she would at once buy some food and stuff herself with it until she could eat no more. Then next day she had gone hungry again. And so it went on while she had become thinner and shabbier and more and more depressed and exhausted. There were, naturally, a great many young men who offered to take her out, but Diamond soon made it plain that when she had eaten her meal the play was over. The word soon went round that she was cold and virtuous, and the offers grew so rare they almost ceased altogether.

"I cannot do it," said Diamond, and her own words appalled her, for she had always believed herself capable of dealing with anything. But she was a clear-sighted girl, and now she saw only too plainly that two alternatives lay before her: one to find herself a man to protect her, and the other to go back to Middleditch.

"I don't know what my pa would say to me," she said on a sigh, then more briskly, "This is our last night here, Georgy. We are being transported tomorrow."

Georgy gave a great shriek of horror. "The packing!" she wailed, and began to run round like a decapitated hen, for she invariably went frantic in any emergency.

"Yes, the packing," said Diamond unkindly, "and I am going out. I want to say goodbye to Kitty. She has been my best friend."

They left early in the morning. There was not, after all, so much packing to do, for all the furniture belonged to the old man. The jewelry Diamond set out methodically on the table—"I'm not swinging at Tyburn for any old lord," she said—and the clothes all fitted into one large box. Diamond carried with her the little portmanteau, and when Georgy asked her what was in it, she replied, "Middleditch."

Georgy was a little frightened. She adored Diamond and would have gone to the stake for her, but sometimes she did not understand her at all. Her mistress was prettily dressed in a fashion that delighted her, for she took a childish pleasure in the fine gowns and was only sorry that the diamonds had to be left behind. In her fur cape and the little feathered hat she looked, Georgy thought, every inch a lady. How his lordship could bear to part with her, Georgy could not imagine. It did not seem in any way wrong that a handsome young woman should find herself a protector. Georgy hoped that Diamond would soon find herself another one, younger perhaps, who would look after her to the end of her days. But there was a strained look on the young face, as if she were somehow away, and so cold and remote did she become that even James, prepared to be as insolent as he dared, took one look at her, then handed her into the carriage without a word.

The little house they had lived in waited for its next tenant, only this time the bed was stripped and there were no dirty clothes left lying on the floor. It was entirely impersonal. The empty rooms were cold, the furniture had no character. But on the dressing-table mirror there was a piece of paper stuck to the glass.

"You must write it for me," Diamond had told Kitty Clive, sitting on the floor at her feet in the green room that she loved so much and which she might never see again. It was during the interval, and she had been watching the play from the wings. Kitty, with her air of childish simplicity, had sung in her true, sweet voice:

> *"What woman could do,*
> *I have tried to be free,*
> *Yet do all I can,*
> *I find I love him,*
> *And though he flies me,*
> *Still—still he's the man."*

32

Oh, how I would love to feel like that about someone, thought Diamond, flushed, smiling, yet near tears. Oh, I wish I could be on the stage again, with the pit cheering me, the center of attention, everyone loving me . . .

When Kitty came back, dressed in her stage clothes and with make-up on her face, Diamond flung her arms round her, saying, "You were so good— Oh, Kitty, how I shall miss all this, how I shall miss it!"

"Find yourself another gentleman," said Kitty cheerfully, "only make it someone younger this time."

"I don't want another gentleman."

"They all say that. Your old beau is in his box tonight."

"I saw him, and I took precious good care he didn't see me." Diamond shuddered a little, for she was already going back in time, and when she saw the old man in his box, using his lorgnette and eying Fanny, who had a tiny role of ten words, she felt as if this were three years ago, when, in her dreadful clothes, she had ben summoned to the carriage.

I have no choice.

She said to Kitty, who had produced a farewell bottle of gin, "Does it not seem to you a strange kind of life? So cold, so cold. To make love with different girls, to take them into your bed, and to feel no love, no affection, nothing, and when you've finished, throw them out and whistle up the next. Oh, Kitty, it freezes the marrow in my bones. And he has all the money in the world. I am beginning to think I will never love any man, but he has certainly never loved anyone in his life."

"Oh fiddle!" said Kitty, who did not follow one word of this. Then Diamond began to laugh, and presently, what with the gin and the emotion of the parting, the two of them were giggling helplessly like a couple of schoolgirls.

Diamond said, "I want you to write a letter for me."

"To *him?*"

"Oh lord, no. What would I be writing to him for?"

"To say goodbye, perhaps." For Kitty, with her kind heart, was a sentimentalist, and it seemed to her perfectly natural to write a last word of farewell.

Diamond looked at her expressively, but made no comment. She said, "It's to the next one—what's her name?—Fanny."

"Diamond, you're clean out of your wits!"

"No, I'm not. Go on, Kitty. It's only a note."

"I've never heard anything like it in my life," said Kitty helplessly, but she found a pen and a sheet of paper, and wrote down neatly the two lines that Diamond dictated to her.

It was this note that was stuck on the mirror. Neither Diamond nor Georgy could read it, but both of them studied it as if they could, Diamond nodding her head as she did so. "I only hope," she said, "that the old cow downstairs leaves it. After all, it's quite friendly, so why not? I couldn't be jealous of her, poor little slut. She doesn't know what she's letting herself in for, but perhaps she doesn't mind, she looks a little simple to me."

The note ran: "Dear Fanny, I'm the one before you. I wish you luck. He's not so bad really if you don't cross him. He don't like scenes. I hope you get lovely clothes and jewels. Your Friend . . ."

And it was signed with a flourish by Diamond herself: "Clary Brown."

❧ III ❧

The journey to Middleditch took six hours. The roads were appalling, the rain was pelting down, and the countryside looked bare and desolate. They stopped at an inn for luncheon, and Georgy, who had never eaten out before, put away her meal with a happy appetite. Diamond, usually so hungry, could manage little but a glass of wine. Her face was pinched and pale, so that she looked almost plain.

On the last lap of the journey Diamond talked non-stop; it seemed to Georgy as if she were talking to herself.

"I remember it so well," she said. "There was the little stream where my pa and I used to go. We had our hut there. It was just a few wooden boards nailed together, really, with the stream a few minutes away. It was pretty, Georgy, with lots of flowers; my pa liked flowers and he knew so much about them. He was a good man, for all they said such dreadful things about him. They had no business to hang him, just for a rabbit. After all, they couldn't expect us to starve. But it was that Captain Ringham— I look forward to meeting him again. I'll wear my very best clothes, and I swear he'll not recognize me. I don't look like a workhouse brat now, do I? Do I, Georgy?"

Georgy thought she looked as if she were running a fever, yet knew that this was no moment to say so. Certainly her mistress in her fine wool traveling gown looked anything but a workhouse brat, though it was a pity her hair was falling down again, and she was talking so fast and wild, she did not seem like herself at all.

She said, "No, Miss Diamond. You look lovely."

"I'll get even with him," said Diamond. "I'll find a way. Oh, believe me, I will, I'm good at finding ways. I know there's danger. The old gypsy said that. But it'll be danger for him, the bastard. He don't know what a bad enemy he's made. I daresay he never thought to see me again. 'I'm Clary Brown,' I shall tell him. 'Don't you remember me, Captain Ringham, sir? You hanged my pa, Captain Ringham. You put me in the workhouse. You didn't even listen to me when I told you about Mr. Vincent. I'd like to cut your throat, sir, if you please, sir, if you'll pardon the liberty, sir. You know what a wild, savage lot us gypsies are.' "

"Miss Diamond, don't talk so!"

"I'll talk as I please. There was a little boy—I've forgot his name. He was Captain Ringham's stepbrother. Philip. That's right, I'm sure it is. He'll be—let me see now—he'll be about eleven or twelve. I don't think I'd recognize him. But I'll tell you something, Georgy. I'll not let on to the captain who I am. I'll make eyes at him, I'll show him all my fine clothes, and he'll think I'm a lady with lots of money. Then perhaps he will ask me to dinner, he might even try to kiss me. Then I'll tell him. 'I'm Clary Brown.' That's what I'll say. What do you think he'll do? Oh, Georgy, what do you think he'll do?"

"I think you shouldn't talk like this, Miss Diamond. After all, it's a long time ago."

"Six years. Only six years."

"Well, that's a long time, and he may be married now. He might even be dead. He'll not remember any of this. What's the point of raking it all up like this? You're a fine lady now, Miss Diamond, you're a famous actress. There's no use in reminding him you was in the workhouse. I don't see any sense in it, none at all."

"You don't understand anything, do you?" said Diamond.

"Not when you talk like this, I don't."

"You're a poor, silly old woman," said Diamond, and took Georgy's hand briefly in her own. "Well, we'll leave Captain Ringham for the moment, and Philip don't interest me, he's just a baby. Well now. There's Sir Francis. Sir Francis Axenford. Now, there's a fine gentleman for you. I think I could fancy Sir Francis, for all he's old enough to be my father."

Georgy was beginning to smile, but Diamond's next words dashed her hopes.

"It's a pity he's married," she said. "It wouldn't make all that

36

difference, not from what I've seen of fine ladies and gentlemen. They seem to go with each other's husbands and wives as if they were playing a game of change partners, but I liked her. She was good to me, I would never want to do her any harm. That's Lady Caroline," explained Diamond. "She was kind and gentle, I don't think she'd hurt anyone. I remember one day when I was so cold and hungry, she took me into the little theatre she'd built for us, and she fed me bread and chicken, as much as I could eat. That's the kind of lady she is. It's odd the things one remembers. I think it worried Sir Francis that she put on a deal of rouge on her cheeks and lips. One day there was a kind of harvest festival, and we were invited. We all sat at a long table in the fields, and Lady Caroline was at the head, with her cheeks bright scarlet. Sir Francis jumped to his feet and came over to her, whispering in her ear, and she took out a handkerchief and tried to rub it away. But she was always gentle, and she looked very sad. I never thought she was really happy."

Diamond fell silent for a moment, and the cessation of her voice brought Georgy—who had been nodding off—suddenly awake.

Then Diamond started again. "She said she had been on the stage when she was a girl. I asked her to recite something for me. She said, 'It doesn't matter any more. I'm finished, Clary.' That's what she said. I suppose she meant her acting career. I think Sir Francis didn't like the thought of his wife on the stage. But she said she'd recite something for me, and she asked me what I'd like. I didn't know what to say, Georgy. I didn't know one thing about plays and I couldn't read. I only knew the theatre was lovely and that somehow I felt at home there. My pa said I'd be an actress. I told him all about it. Then she began to speak. She had a beautiful voice, Lady Caroline. She did a bit from *Romeo and Juliet*. She told me the name, but of course I'd never heard of it—I didn't know about it till I came to Drury Lane. I'll do it for you, Georgy. It won't be half as good as her, but it'll show you what I mean."

James heard some of this monologue. He thought privately that his lordship was well shot of this one; she was mad, with her long speeches and her odd looks. She made him uneasy. He longed to say something insulting to her, and in a way it would have been safe enough, she would never be able to report him, but somehow he did not quite dare. The strange words she was now declaiming in that droll tone of voice pricked the hair on his head; he did not like it at all.

"*When he shall die*
Take him and cut him out in little stars,
And he will make the face of heaven so fine
That all the world will be in love with night,
And pay no worship to the garish sun."

Diamond, as she spoke, fell instinctively into a dramatic pose, and Georgy nodded off again, for it had been an exhausting day and what was being said meant nothing to her.

"I look forward to seeing Lady Caroline again," said Diamond after a pause, during which she half waited for applause from the pit. She added, almost in bewilderment, "She is the one person in Middleditch I want to see from love." Then she said, after another long pause, "Except Miss Falconer. She was the schoolteacher. She was kind too."

At last she became silent and gazed out on the grey September afternoon, as if a little awed by the somber landscape, the trees that were turning brown and gold, the isolated farmhouses. Middleditch was not a cozy village set in a pretty countryside, and at this season of the year it wore a forbidding air.

Georgy slept, snoring a little, and James drove grimly on, wishing he were back in London. This was not the first doxy he had taken to some distant cottage, but he could not remember anyone as strange as this Miss Diamond, nor had he ever taken a bleaker journey. He was a town man himself, a Cockney born within sound of Bow Bells. He loved the noise, the dirt, the bustle, the crowd, and deep in his heart he utterly despised not only the light ladies he had to take to and from his master's house, but the old devil himself, who had no family, no friends, nothing but his damned money, and who picked up from the gutter the stupid bitches he wanted in his bed. He'd get himself the pox one day, and serve him right. He was mean as hell with his servants, and only paid off his women because he was afraid they might cause a scandal.

James, like Diamond, had summed up his master's motives correctly enough; he knew even better than Diamond that the generosity within his lordship's heart would go on the point of a pin and with room to spare. Still, it was a job, and not entirely lacking in interest to an inquisitive man who enjoyed the vagaries of human nature. One day James thought he might enjoy a small, profitable sideline by making use of some of the information he had acquired. Valets and coachmen did this more often than the quality ever suspected.

Diamond exclaimed suddenly in a hoarse, choked voice, "This is Middleditch. Georgy, wake up. Georgy! This is Middleditch. This is my home."

Georgy, slumped over herself, jerked up her head, a snore stifled in her throat. She looked blearily out the window. God knows, there was nothing to write home about. And even Diamond, who should have known it, whispered, "I did not remember it so small."

They were now driving through the village's main street, which was the only street, with a handful of cottages on the hillside. One of these was their destination, and James knew which one it was because the old man had carefully primed him. "If you bring her back to London," his lordship had said, "you will be instantly dismissed without a reference, and your family will be thrown out on the street. Make sure her boxes are taken in. Don't give her the money until everything is done. Don't listen to any arguments or entreaties or excuses. I want that cottage door shut, with the pair of them inside, and you well on your way back. If she don't like it, that's her business. It is not yours or mine."

James saw with fury—he had been driving since dawn—that he would have to carry the boxes up the hill. There was nothing but a rough path leading to the cottage, and a fine ramshackle-looking old affair it was too. Miss would not like that at all, not after all that grand living. No doubt there would be hysterics and tantrums, but the Lord willing, they'd take place after he was gone.

In all this he did Diamond an injustice, but then, he had never begun to understand her. At that moment she was staring, half in bewilderment and half in delight, at the small, blackish street they were driving through.

She clutched at Georgy's arm. "That's the Rose and Crown," she said. "I wonder if the Armstrongs are still there. My pa used to have a tankard there sometimes when he had the money. But she didn't like it, she said she didn't want no dirty gyppos in her inn. Oh, and Mrs. Rigg's shop. How I wanted to buy some ribbons! My pa said he would get me some one day, but we could never afford it. I'll buy them now. I'll buy . . . I'll buy twenty yards, Georgy, of each color, then I'll put them round my neck so that the ends trail behind me, and I'll walk up and down the street, singing, 'He promised to buy me a bunch of blue ribbons.' Oh—oh! There's the woods where my pa went a-hunting, and way back, you can't see it from here, is Axenford, where Sir Francis and Lady Caroline live. It's a lovely house, very old. And on the near side, on the hill there, you can just see it, is the Hall. That's Captain Ringham's. It's quite small, really. Perhaps I could burn it down—"

"Miss Diamond!" said Georgy, more from force of habit than anything else.

But Diamond was too excited to listen to her. She said wistfully, "It would make a fine blaze. But he's not worth being hanged for. I'll get my own back in some other— Stop, James! You must stop." Her voice changed. "That's the work-house. Just by the woods. I think it's closed. It looks as if there's been a fine blaze there, a real blaze. They can't blame me for that, Georgy, you old croaker. Do you see it? And you too, Mr. James. You look. I daresay a fine chap like you has never seen a workhouse before, though you never know what you'll come to, when you're old and nobody wants to employ you." She leaned forward as she spoke, and prodded James between the shoulder blades.

He swung round indignantly, wanting to slap her for her impudence—you never know what you'll come to, indeed!—then his eyes turned unwillingly to the great black ruin on the outskirts of the woods.

There had been a fine blaze indeed. The building, black and grim, was gutted, the windows gaping, the great iron door, which had shut with so ugly a clanking sound, swinging in the late September wind. Diamond stared at it in silence, then turned back to James, who had reluctantly slowed down and was waiting, his lips compressed, for her order to proceed.

"Do you see that, James?" said Diamond.

He muttered, "It's not much of a place. You say it was a workhouse. I don't see why we have to look at workhouses."

"I lived there, James. I lived there for three years. I was thirteen when I came. They hanged my pa for stealing a rabbit, and Captain Ringham put me there. I suppose you could call it my home. It ain't much now, but it was like hell to me, with all the demons thrown in. I wonder who Mr. Vincent is tormenting now."

Georgy wailed, "Oh, Miss Diamond, can't we go on? I'm tired and cold, and my rheumatics is hurting me cruel. You'll have all the time in the world to go over workhouses, though the good Lord knows why you want to, but let's get on now, for pity's sake, and get a nice hot drink inside us and a bite to eat."

Diamond said in her most ladylike voice, "Drive on, James."

He answered with happy malice in his voice, "There's no driving to the cottage, ma'am. It's way up the hill. You can see it there on the left. I can go on a few yards more, then you'll have to walk. His lordship said I was to carry your boxes for you." And he nearly added the rest of it, only stopped himself just in time.

Georgy, who was not after all a young woman, burst into passionate lamentations, but Diamond, to James's disappointment, indulged in no hysterics. She jumped down from the carriage, and said briskly, "Don't be stupid, Georgy. It's not far, and I'm sure James will give you a hand. I'm going up now. You can both come after me."

And with this she picked up the little portmanteau and set off up the hill, moving, as James had to see, with the agility of a young goat. He looked at Georgy, and for a second there was almost agreement between them, though he despised the old woman even more than her mistress, and was furious at having to carry her luggage, her not even being a lady.

Georgy perhaps read his thoughts. She stepped down awkwardly, nearly falling headlong as she did so; it was true what she had said about the rheumatics, and the long, cold journey had not improved them. Then she said with great dignity, "Get the boxes down, my man. You'll have to give me a hand. I can see it's rough going." Then she exclaimed, "I can't think why his lordship couldn't find us something lower down. I don't fancy running up and down hills at my age. But I don't suppose he even thought about it. People are so inconsiderate these days."

James could have answered that his lordship did not give a damn; all he wanted was to be rid of his encumbrances. But he silently lifted the cases down, thanking God that there were so few of them, and taking the old woman's elbow, hoisted her ungently over the stones and gravel that made up the path. It was a slow and uneasy progress, with the wind tugging at their clothes and the cold biting their toes and fingers. It was still only autumn, but it was as if winter had already set in. James wondered if they would offer him a glass of wine, and decided it would never enter their fat heads. He could only hope that the next one—silly little blond piece she was, with as much brains as a carrot—would end up somewhere more approachable.

Diamond was in the kitchen when they arrived. It was, as Georgy had feared, a miserable kind of affair. It had not been cleaned for years, there were no curtains at the window, and the range was choked with grease, rust and dust. It would take hours to get a fire going, and she was freezing cold. There were, of course, no provisions, and she was thankful that she had had the foresight to bring food with her, including a roast chicken and three bottles of wine, all lifted from the Highgate kitchen when the housekeeper's back was turned. Georgy had never learned the quality's way of drinking wine with everything and often by itself, but now the thought of those bottles warmed her a little. It was lucky she had not left the matter to her mistress, who never troubled her head with such material things.

James dumped the boxes down. He, too, thought the place deplorable. It was not fit for a pig to live in. He was not displeased, yet his eyes moved all the time to Diamond, who, far from being hysterical, wore a strange, preoccupied air, almost as if she were happy. She had already rolled up her sleeves in preparation for making the place more habitable.

He said, "If there's nothing more you want, I'll be getting back, ma'am." Then he added, as if it were not important—he had been hoping that Diamond would ask him—"His lordship asked me to give you this package. If you wish to count the money in it . . ."

She looked at him, shaking her head. It was almost as if she were trying not to smile. She did not even look at the package. He threw it down on the kitchen table, shrugged his shoulders, and made for the door. As he stepped onto the path—it would be the devil to manage at night, especially in bad weather—he turned, to see that Diamond, her arms akimbo, the black hair blowing across her face, stood in the doorway.

The lamplight was behind her. Someone had provided oil and wicks; they were the only things there to make any kind of welcome. Perhaps it was a neighbor, though the nearest cottage was a couple of hundred yards away and even higher up the hill. She stood there, framed in the soft glow, and she looked so lovely and so strange that James, who was after all a man as well as a coachman, found his breath taken away.

He was never afterwards able to explain what happened. He was never to mention the business to anyone, certainly not to his wife and children in their small tied cottage at the back of his lordship's mansion. He had always despised the old man's whores. He believed fervently that loose women should be whipped at the cart's tail and thrown into Bridewell, and Diamond, more intelligent and less easily bullied than most of them, had sometimes aroused a fury in him that made him long to beat her to the ground.

He stared at her now, a broad-shouldered young man with precious little in the way of scruples and a hearty contempt for the world that employed him. He believed that one day men like himself would come into power, and people like his lordship who lived on money handed down to them would be drowned in the Thames. Yet now he looked at this little doxy from the workhouse, and he burst out in a hoarse voice that he barely recognized himself, "Why don't you come back with me? This ain't no kind of place for a young lady like you. Leave the old woman here. I'll find you somewhere to live. His lordship will never know." And it was almost at that moment as if he had her in bed with him. The blood raced through him so that he felt quite dizzy, and he stretched out his hands toward her.

She backed into the cottage. Her face in the lamplight was

43

white. She did not answer him, only gave a gasping cry. The next moment the door was slammed in his face, and James came instantly to his senses, detesting her as much as he had wanted her, furious at the rebuff, furious at his own stupidity. He swore savagely, swung round and blundered down the path to where the horses stood waiting.

He was not to know that in the dusk of late afternoon she had not really seen him at all. The old terror of a man's passion engulfed Diamond and she ran back into the kitchen, burst into frantic tears, and flung herself down on the one chair, a rickety affair that creaked beneath her weight.

The tears restored Georgy more than anything else could have done. She at once became her normal, bustling self. Miss Diamond talking strangely of workhouses was something she did not understand, but Miss Diamond frightened, in tears and in need of comfort, was something she did. She forgot all about the rheumatics, the cold, the filthy cottage, the steep path, the nightmare of it all. Miss Diamond was tired, Miss Diamond needed food and drink and warmth. She opened the basket and put a cold chicken, bread, fruit and a bottle of wine on the table. In a moment she had carved off a lavish section of breast, poured out the wine, and set the food on plates that were also stolen from Highgate, together with knives and forks and glasses. Immediately the tears were done, she and Diamond were gobbling up the food as if they had not eaten for a week. And Georgy, who was after all a market woman accustomed to difficulties, had somehow got a fire burning in the sitting room with the wood that was stacked up on the floor—who had troubled to do this?—and for all it was dirty, dreary and in no way home, the cottage had become theirs. They were part of it.

"Oh, I do feel better," Diamond exclaimed after a second helping of chicken, two slices of bread, an apple and most of the wine. "And do you know," she said to Georgy, "I am glad to be home."

"Tomorrow," said Georgy, "I will clean the place up, and we will buy some things for it and make it look pretty." She glanced down at the package. She had no idea how much was in it, and probably it would not last long, but it would at least provide some comforts for them. There was a great deal that could be done with this cottage, however terrible it had seemed at first sight.

Diamond heard the footsteps coming up the path. She went a little pale, for the day had been full of shocks for her, but then she saw that poor old Georgy was frightened to death, and this pulled her together. She said briskly, "I think we have callers. Perhaps," she said, "it is Captain Ringham come to welcome me home and put me back in the workhouse."

"Don't open the door," whispered Georgy as someone struck a great rat-a-tat-tat on its surface. But Diamond at once rose to her feet, crossed the small hall, and flung the door open.

Georgy heard the silence. It was broken by a deep masculine voice. "Captain Ringham at your service, ma'am. May I come in?"

✧❦✧ IV ✧❦✧

It was at this point that Georgy fainted dead away. It was natural enough. She was an old woman, she had undergone a most exhausting journey, and this grim little cottage, so bare of proper furniture, so cold despite the fire she had now got going, was a sad contrast to the house she had just left. Diamond had hated the Highgate house, but to Georgy it was paradise, something she had never even dreamed of in her life. It was warm and clean and comfortable, there were servants to wait upon her, and hot food that she neither had to buy nor prepare. And added to this, she even received a small wage. Now it was all over, and what she longed for was her bed. To learn that the gentleman at the door was the wicked bogeyman who had sent her darling Miss Diamond to the poorhouse was the last straw. The color peeled off her normally rosy face, her rheumaticky legs crumpled beneath her, and she collapsed on the floor with a crash that rattled everything about her.

She could not know this, but her dramatic swoon was a godsend to Diamond, who stood there, staring unbelievingly up into a face that she had never forgotten, and had secretly prayed, despite her defiant words, that she would never see again.

It was a handsome and forbidding face. It was, Diamond thought within her dazed and horrified mind, a hangman's face. It seemed to her that Captain Ringham had not changed at all, as if the passing of six years had not laid a finger on his countenance. There was scarcely a trace of grey in the brown hair that he wore countryman's style, unwigged, and there seemed to her neither kindness nor charity in his look, though he had apparently called upon her to see if she required any help in her new home. For a second she forgot that she was no longer Clary Brown, that it was unlikely he would recognize the sniveling, furious little girl, with her dirty, unkempt hair, bare feet and ragged workhouse clothes, in a handsome young woman of twenty-two, dressed in the height of fashion, and one who, as he would certainly have heard, was an actress on the London stage. For that second, which seemed to her an hour, Diamond lost all the poise she had acquired; she had thought proudly that now she could cope with any situation, treat her enemies with the disdain they deserved.

She had always known that one day she must meet her enemy, and she had planned a grand drama within her mind. Dressed in one of the old man's silks, she would sweep past him, speaking in the high chill voice that the *ton* adopted, perhaps even make him fall in love with her so that she could kick him away.

And now she simply stood there, as white as poor Georgy, with not a word to say, her mouth a little open.

She saw the great dark brows meet, then, as he began to say, "I fear I have alarmed you, ma'am," Georgy, with a sense of timing that Diamond herself had never achieved, had crashed to the floor. They both spun round and ran into the kitchen.

Georgy lay flat on her back on the floor. Diamond exclaimed, "Oh, my poor old woman!" But Captain Ringham without a word picked her up as if she were a baby, the full twelve stone of her, and carried her into the sitting room, where he looked about him to see where he could set her down.

There was almost nothing. The old man might pension off his lightskirts, but it was no concern of his that they should be comfortable. There were a couple of hard-backed chairs, a table with a lamp upon it, and along one side of the room an old sofa that had certainly seen better days. Diamond had not so far climbed the steep stairs that led to the bedrooms; she assumed there would be some kind of bed, but even of that she was no longer sure.

She looked despairingly at Captain Ringham, almost forgetting in the emergency that he was her worst enemy. He made a kind of appalled grimace at her, then laid Georgy, now beginning to stir, upon the sofa. He produced a flask from his pocket and set it to her lips. The brandy made her splutter and choke, but it brought her to her senses and she began shakily to try to sit up.

Diamond, now kneeling beside her, took her in her arms and tried to make her lie back again. "It's all right, old lady," she said urgently, "it's all right. You lie quiet now, and in a little while you'll be as right as rain. You're exhausted, that's all, and when you've had a rest . . ."

Georgy said indistinctly, "I'm fine, Miss Diamond. There's nothing wrong with me. I daresay the gentleman would like a glass of wine."

She had forgotten in the shock of the fall that this was the wicked man who so frightened her mistress, and she was anxious to make a good impression on someone who might be their next protector. But the heavy fall and the excitement of it all was too much for her, and she fell back again, feebly pushing away the flask that Captain Ringham was once more holding to her lips.

He straightened himself and looked at Diamond. He said, "What kind of place is this for two women? I instructed one of my men to leave you oil and wood, and he told me the cottage was uncleaned and empty, but I believed you would bring your own furniture down with you. Surely, ma'am, you cannot stay here. What has happened? I could not quite believe it when they told me this cottage was sold to a young London lady. It's been untenanted for years, but naturally I assumed—" He turned his head.

The fire burning well, thank God, made a long black shadow of him, and Diamond, who had by now somewhat recovered herself, looked at him with a kind of shuddering amusement. The shudder was provoked by her last memory of him, but the amusement was there too, for certainly this was no place to play the fine lady, and her skirts were trailing in a dust that lay like grey mold on the bare floor.

She said in her best actressy voice, "I will trouble you, sir, for a glass of your brandy, and then, if we can find chairs to sit on, I will explain." She wrinkled her brow. She might be the world's worst Cleopatra, but she could always act in private life, and already her fertile imagination was composing a fine story to account for all the strangeness. "Your name, sir," she said, "is . . . ? I'm afraid I didn't quite catch it. The wind outside . . ."

"Captain Ringham," he said. "Captain William Ringham. I live in the house on the hill, beyond the woods, with my young stepbrother."

Diamond, all the devils in the world at work within her, slanted her eyes at him. They were fine eyes, her most striking feature, large and long-lashed. They gazed up into his grey ones, and as she spoke she began to dust at one of the chairs with her glove. He exclaimed impatiently, took out his handkerchief, and swept an appalling cloud of dust onto the floor.

"Do you have glasses?" he said.

"I should very much doubt it," said Diamond, then remembered that Georgy had produced a couple for the meal and went into the kitchen to look for them. There were indeed half a dozen, as well as assorted cutlery and plates. It was enough no doubt to hang her at Tyburn, but it was unlikely that the old man would trouble himself with something that to him would be so insignificant, even if the housekeeper reported it to him. Georgy did not possess her fears or her scruples. They were not kitchen glasses either, for she had a keen eye for good things; they were the glasses brought out for the old man on his visits when he took his pre-love-making wine with her.

"At least," said Diamond grandly, returning with the glasses in her hand, "this is something that has not been stolen."

It was not the most fortunate remark in the circumstances, but by this time the story was so running in her mind that truth and fiction were becoming confused, and she almost believed her own lies. As she sat there on the high-backed chair, a glass of the captain's brandy in her hand, she felt as if past and present were intertwined, for when she looked into the dark face shadowed in the firelight, the bright little smile slipped from her lips and the hand holding the glass began to tremble.

"Don't send me back," she had begged. It was the day before she ran away, only at that moment she could not visualize any kind of escape. She was wild and distraught, sobbing, her hands pleating at the black overall that they all had to wear. "Oh, sir, you can't send me back. He's a devil, he'll kill me. You don't know what he's like, you don't know . . ."

She thought he hardly listened to her. His eyes would not meet hers. He was a tall man, well over six feet, and to little Clary Brown, undersized then and underfed, he seemed a monstrous giant. He said in a strange, urgent voice, "You must go back. I know you don't understand, but you must. Where else can you go? You have no family."

Then she screamed at him, "You killed my pa!"

He did not answer. He looked at her, almost in bewilderment, and half moved out his hand. She thought he was going to hit her, and jumped away. She burst into a wail of rage and terror and misery.

"You did! You know you did. You hanged him. You strung him up to choke to death, and he was a good man, he never did anyone any harm. What did he do? He took a rabbit for our dinner. A rabbit!"

His face suddenly twisted. He looked away from her. He said abruptly, "I know nothing of that."

"Of course you do. It was you who did it—"

"I tell you, child, I know nothing about that. But it's over and done with. I want you to go back like a good girl. It will only be for a little while, I promise."

But she did not believe him. She cried out, "You're a black, bloody-minded old devil, I hope you go straight to hell, I want to kill you."

And as she said this, she flew at him, her nails aiming at his face, but the man with him dragged her back. Then she turned and ran. Her last words were, "I'll kill you yet. You'll see. I'll be even with you, Captain Ringham, if it's the last thing I do, yes, even if they hang me like my pa. It would be worth it, just to send you to hell. Oh, how I hate you. I hate you, I hate you, I hate you—"

The next day she ran away.

And Diamond Browne, Miss Diamond Browne, late of Drury Lane, London, was remarking in a clear, genteel voice, "So good of you to call. It really has been very unfortunate. Especially as I was so excited about returning to Middleditch."

His eyes moved about the cottage as she spoke. He saw that the front door had come open. He rose to his feet and kicked it shut. "You need a stout padlock," he said. "I'll get it done for you." He sat down again and continued to stare about him as if he could not quite believe his eyes. Georgy, what with the brandy and the excitement, had fallen asleep. Diamond felt now that the cottage was entirely her home, but she had to admit that it was deplorable. This bleak and filthy room must seem to him more like the workhouse.

But then, he would have no real idea of what a workhouse was like. A workhouse was only for the dirty little brats of hanged poachers, gypsy sluts like herself who were of as much importance as a cockroach.

Suddenly he concentrated his gaze on her. "Did you say returning to Middleditch?" he asked.

"Yes," said Diamond, furious with herself at her stupidity. It was not so easy to lie, after all. She took a quick sip of her brandy. Her hand was still shaking, but he surely would not notice in the dim light, or if he did, he would put it down to exhaustion. "Oh," she said, "the first time I was here, I was just passing through, of course. I came to see a friend. You must know her. She is an actress like myself. I have acted with Mr. Garrick, you know. At Drury Lane . . ."

He did not answer any of this. She could not help feeling that he was not as impressed as he should be, but there was something else, a tension that for no known reason frightened her. Though after all, what she was saying was mostly true, except for the passing through, except for all the brilliant lies that were to come later. But she did not like his silence, it unnerved her, and her next words came out in a rush.

"I am speaking of Lady Caroline Axenford," she said, "the wife of Sir Francis. They live in the house that is just called by the family name. Axenford. I saw it as I drove through. I hope when I am more settled that I may call on Lady Caroline. She was once very kind to me."

Then for the second time she could have cursed herself. This remark, which came out instinctively, was more of a giveaway than he could possibly know, but it really betrayed nothing serious. It was simply a warning to herself to be careful and never to drink too much brandy.

Captain Ringham said abruptly—had the man no manners at all, no sensibility?—"Lady Caroline is dead."

The words plummeted into Diamond's mind, knocked all the lies and fabrications out of her. She exclaimed, unaware that in the shock the rough burring tones of the little village girl had returned to her voice, "Oh no! Oh no! She can't be. The poor lady . . ."

And for that moment she forgot about Captain Ringham, did not see the strange look he turned upon her, only beheld again the pretty lady who wore too much rouge, who had acted for her in the little theatre, and who had fed her to bursting point so that for the first time she was no longer sick with hunger.

It don't matter any more. I'm finished, Clary. That was what she had said. *I'm finished.* And Diamond could still see that sad, worn face, with the scarlet painted on so crudely that her gaunt cheekbones stood out like poppies, and remembered how, even as a child, she had wondered that a fine lady should make up so inartistically, slap the paint on as if she were a doll, and outline her beautiful mouth in scarlet so thick that the color ran like blood.

The tears were trickling down Diamond's face. Lady Caroline had been so kind, and surely she was not old, though to a child she would appear so. She dragged herself back to the present, and asked, "Why did she die? Did she have some terrible illness?"

Captain Ringham answered in a dry, rough voice, as if he did not care, as if it all mattered not a damn to him, "How should I know? You must ask Sir Francis."

"She cannot have been very old," said Diamond. "She must once have been so pretty."

He rose to his feet. He seemed enormous. Then she knew that he still had the power to frighten her, and she hunched herself a little on the chair, drawing her petticoats about her as if his shadow were dangerous and evil. He said, "Death is no respecter of youth or beauty. If it interests you, ma'am, she went away to die."

"What do you mean?"

"I know no more than I am telling you. Her ladyship went on a visit to her sister in London, and there she died. We never saw her again."

"Oh, poor Sir Francis! He must have been heartbroken."

To this, Captain Ringham said nothing, and she thought again that she had never met a man so lacking in feeling. But she was still chilled with the shock of it all, and she, too, stood up, on the pretense of setting her glass down on the table. She said in a bright, brittle voice, "Oh well, these things happen. It is very sad. I loved her very much, you know. It was one of my reasons for coming here. Of course," said Diamond in the same tone, "my arrival has not been very fortunate. My agent, you know. I should never have trusted him. I'm afraid he has stolen the money I gave him. So many lies— I have no patience with liars, and I am sure, sir, you are the same."

He exclaimed, his voice rising, "But this is disgraceful. The fellow must be brought to justice. This is almost a hanging matter."

Yes. A hanging matter. Steal money, and you hang. Steal a rabbit when you're starving, and you hang. She said harshly, "You believe in hanging, do you not?"

"I believe in justice."

"I wonder," said Diamond, her face turned away from him, "if justice really dangles at the end of a rope."

He was silent for a second, then he said, "You are a very strange young lady. You tell me your money has been stolen and, I gather, your furniture, yet you do not seem to approve of the villain's being punished. I am, after all, one of the justices here. But this is entirely your business, ma'am. If you choose to be robbed and do nothing about it, I am delighted to leave the matter." He looked once more round the room. "However, you must admit that this place is hardly suitable for you or your maid. I think the best thing to be done is for me to send my carriage round, and bring you to the Hall. There are several spare rooms, for I do not keep a large staff, and my housekeeper will be delighted to cook you a decent meal and see that you are comfortable until we can get this cottage in order. As it is, it really is no place for you to stay in. It is cold and damp, and the front door does not latch properly. You cannot possibly spend the night here. In my house you will be comfortable and looked after. It is no trouble to me, for I am often out seeing to my tenants and estate, and tomorrow and the day following I shall not even be in the house. You will be able to do as you please, and in the meantime I will arrange for a little furniture to be brought here, and see that the place is cleaned up."

"You are very kind," said Diamond faintly, and it was true, this impossible and horrid man was indeed kind. Why he should do so much for what he would regard as complete strangers, she could not imagine. She knew suddenly, and bitterly resented it, that despite her youth and strong body, she was most desperately tired. The thought of a warm room, a bed with clean sheets, and a sustaining hot drink served on a tray, was something she could hardly resist. But she would not and could not accept such an offer from her enemy. She had a wild desire to say something like, "Why, sir, do you always invite workhouse brats to your home? I might soil the fine furniture, I might pocket some of your silver. I am just a common gypsy girl and you could never trust me."

But she simply said, forcing the words out, "Thank you, but I could not possibly take advantage of such a generous offer."

He said indifferently, "As you please," and then she was furious that he had not made some show of persuasion; it was as if he were secretly relieved that she was not coming.

She knew this was unreasonable, but was too tired to care. She said in a choked voice, "I do appreciate your offer, but I feel this is all my fault. It is my home and I must get used to it. Tomorrow it will seem much better, and if one of your servants could perhaps help us, as you suggested, I am sure it will look beautiful and cozy in quite a short while."

As she spoke, she could not stop herself from looking at the cobwebs on the ceiling, the filthy floor, the windows so begrimed that she could not see through them. She all but cried out, "Oh, please take us away, I can't bear it."

He had turned toward the door. "I will send someone round in the morning," he said, "with the furniture and some provisions."

"Oh, but—"

"I run a farm, ma'am, and a dairy. It makes no difference to me. This is the country, not London town. Here we try to help each other."

Diamond said in a clear voice, "Then I am going to ask you for something."

He looked astonished, as he well might, but said, a faint wariness in his voice, "By all means, if it is something within my power."

"I would like a rabbit," said Diamond. "If there is one thing I love above all others, it is a rabbit fricassee. Oh," she said, clasping her hands in a manner normally alien to her, "it is something I have looked forward to. It is the kind of thing we never have in London."

He must, of course, think her completely insane. But he said calmly enough, "With the greatest of pleasure. Here we tend to look on rabbits as vermin; they infest my crops and eat half my best vegetables. I will see you have your rabbit, Miss Browne. Indeed, I will go further. I will make you a present of a rabbit every week during your stay here, and if you wish, till the day you die."

"Thank you," said Diamond, and something in those choked syllables must have startled him, for he shot her a swift, baffled look. He made no more comment on the subject of rabbits, only said, "There is one thing, ma'am, that I must ask of you."

"What is that?" asked Diamond. She had turned a little so that he could not see her face.

"I must ask you and your maid on no account, no account whatsoever, to go out alone at night."

"And why not, pray?" demanded Diamond, affronted, for she had never been a missish girl. This was her home, and if she could walk alone in Covent Garden on her way to and from the theatre, she could surely cross Middleditch a hundred times without any harm happening to her.

He said grimly, "You must not."

"But you can give me a reason, Captain Ringham. It sounds so absurd."

He said, "If you have any sense at all, which I am beginning to doubt, you will listen to me and do as you are told. Do not, Miss Browne, go out alone at nights. Don't start prying in the usual way of females. I can see well enough that you are of the prying kind. Don't be. I beg of you. For God's sake, let ghosts lie."

Diamond said in a whisper, "What makes you say that?"

But he ignored this, and went on, "If you wish to make a call or go on some errand, I will gladly lend you my carriage, as I see you do not appear to have one of your own. But walk abroad by yourself, you must not."

"I do not," said Diamond coldly, "recognize your right to tell me what or what not to do. What business is it of yours if I go out alone or not? I shall do precisely as I please. You have been quite helpful to me, and I am grateful, but that does not give you the authority to dictate to me."

Then he shouted at her in such a voice that the dust flew in a cloud around him, "You are the most damnably silly bitch I have ever met!"

"Captain Ringham!"

"And don't play the fine lady with me. It doesn't impress me at all. Keep your dramatics for Drury Lane, ma'am, as that is where you belong. Go your own self-willed way. Walk abroad. Dance cantrips beneath the moon if you want to. Only, when you land yourself in trouble, as you certainly will, don't come whining to me for help, for you'll get something you won't expect. I have enough to do without looking after stupid young women who think they know better than anyone else." He flung open the door as he spoke. The wind had risen, and it roared in, sweeping out his greatcoat behind him. Then he turned. He spoke more quietly. He said, "You will probably prefer not to listen to this either, but I suggest you set your table against the door. It doesn't matter to me if you have your throat cut, but at least I'd prefer to believe it was not my responsibility." He added, "As I am one of the justices here, your murder would involve me in more work than I have time for."

And before Diamond, now gasping with anger, could say any of the innumerable things that were choking her, he shut the door, which instantly blew open again. But he did not turn back. She heard his footsteps going rapidly down the path.

Georgy's voice, a little plaintive, said, "That is a very bad-tempered gentleman." She added wistfully, "He's so handsome."

"That," said Diamond in a weak cry of fury, "is a bastard." She whirled round on Georgy, who was sitting up, rubbing at her eyes. "We're going to eat rabbit," she said. "Rabbits here are vermin; they eat all poor Captain Ringham's vegetables. They have to be shot down. But if a poor man steals one for his dinner, he's a thief and he's hanged. If Captain Ringham shoots a rabbit, it don't matter, it don't matter at all, because he's a gentleman. I hope you can cook rabbit, Georgy, for we are doomed to have one every week. My poor pa died for a rabbit, but we shall be eating them, eating them till we're sick of the sight and smell of them. And now, my old woman, if you pinched another bottle of wine, I'm going to get drunk, for otherwise I'll not sleep a wink tonight in a village that is dangerous to walk about in. It is full of devils like Captain Ringham, and by God, I swear I'd be safer in one of Old Kate's brothels in the Garden. And tomorrow we'll be furnished by Captain William Ringham, fed by Captain William Ringham, protected by Captain William Ringham, who talks of slit throats but who don't know that one day it's his throat'll be slit, and by me. Stir yourself, you lazy old hulk, and let us celebrate."

But as poor Georgy, grumbling and still half asleep, began to set out the wine, Diamond pulled the table along the passage and set it across the door.

Soon Diamond, exhausted, overwrought and a little drunk, began to talk in a high, breathless tone, almost as if to herself.

"Lady Caroline is dead," she said. " 'Cover her face; mine eyes dazzle; she died young.' Not so young, oh, not so young, but still young enough to live. Did you hear him saying she was dead? Such a pretty, kind lady, though she used too much rouge. Why do all the good people die, Georgy? Can you tell me that? I swear she never did an unkind thing in her life, and she was so gentle and sweet, even to a nasty, dirty little gyppo brat who was nothing to her, and now she's dead, while people like that Captain Ringham will go on for a hundred years. And my pa is dead too, Georgy, and he was a good man too, even though they say gypsies are always bad. And I want some of that cheese, Georgy. I don't know what's the matter with me, but I can't stop eating. Perhaps I'm breeding—"

"Miss Diamond! How can you say such things?"

"Well, I'm not breeding," said Diamond, almost sulkily.

"I can tell you that, my old woman. I may be all kinds of things, but breeding I am not. Perhaps Captain Ringham will make sure that I am breeding."

"Miss Diamond," said Georgy in more normal tones, "you are overtired and you should go to bed. You are talking too much. Come upstairs with me now, and we'll see what the beds are like. No, Miss Diamond. You don't want any cheese, it'll give you the bellyache. Drink up your wine now, like a good girl, and come upstairs with me."

"Georgy," whispered Diamond, "what's that?"

"What's what? You're half asleep, my lamb."

"No! There is something. Listen . . ."

Georgy's hearing was not as acute as that of her mistress; besides, she was still a little fogged with exhaustion and the shock of her fall. But then she, too, heard it, and she went quite white, her hands clutching at the table.

It was a kind of high chanting, faint, as if in the distance, almost like a hymn. It carried in waves on the high wind, advancing, then retreating. It was a sweet, ugly sound, and Diamond listened, very still, her eyes dilated. At last it ceased, but she remained without moving, and then, very faint, there was a scratching at the door.

Both she and Georgy turned their heads. Neither of them uttered a word. It seemed to Diamond that the door, securely blocked by the heavy table, moved a little, as if someone or something were pushing at it. Georgy, whose face was now ashen, began to whimper, but Diamond instantly laid a hand across her lips, shaking her head. Then she rose softly to her feet, and from her reticule produced a pistol, which she cradled against her, the muzzle pointing toward the door. Her hands shook so that the pistol trembled, but nonetheless she stood there, her finger on the trigger, until the silence indicated that whoever it was had gone away. There was no sound of footsteps, but then, the sopping earth would smother them. The wind still thudded against the cottage so that the very windows rattled.

Georgy said at last, in a croak, "Where did you get that, Miss Diamond?"

"His lordship gave it me."

"What did he do that for? Ladies don't need pistols."

"It seems to me," said Diamond in an unsteady voice, "that ladies need them very much. And I know how to use it, too. I don't say I shoot very straight, but anyone who broke that door down would get a nasty shock. I could hardly miss, could I? Oh yes, my old woman. It's true what I say."

Georgy sighed, for it was sometimes hard to know when Miss Diamond was speaking the truth. It had to be admitted that she told a great many stories, and in one of her dramatic moods, could make almost anyone believe her. But undoubtedly she had a pistol, and if it was not the old man who had given it her, how could she have come by it? Even Georgy could see that it was expensive, with its little pearl handle. It was obviously meant for a lady, and equally obviously, Diamond knew how to use it. That trembling hand might not be much use in a duel, but it would prove lethal to an intruder.

Diamond said, "It was when we first met. He liked me then. I don't think he loved me, I don't think he has ever loved anyone, but he told me London was a dangerous place and I should always carry it around with me. I always did. I think," said Diamond with sudden savagery, "it is a very good thing I do. But what has happened to Middleditch, Georgy? What is going on here? It used not to be like that. Captain Ringham says I am not to walk abroad at night. Of course I shall pay no attention to him. I'm not going to be told what to do, especially by that bastard. I'll walk where I please and when I please, but I won't be alone, this little fellow shall go with me."

"Miss Diamond—"

"And if anyone threatens me, I shall shoot him dead. Like this. Bang!"

"Miss Diamond, will you please go to bed."

"Oh, you are a tiresome old bitch. I don't know why I put up with you." Diamond was pointing the pistol at the door and apparently about to press the trigger. She whirled round on Georgy. "I do what I please. Why should I go to bed? I'm not tired. I wouldn't sleep a wink anyway." Then a great yawn engulfed her, and she said meekly, "All right, Georgy. I'll go to bed. If there is a bed . . ."

"Well, that we will just have to see," said Georgy. She was far more tired than her mistress, but it was plain that Miss Diamond was in the state where she would at any moment burst into tears, and there would be no peace until she was warmly tucked in.

She started climbing the steep little staircase, and Diamond followed behind her, trailing her hand on the dusty banister. There were two rooms upstairs, and an attic. Georgy opened one of the doors. There was a bed there, and nothing else. It was a common trestle bed with a straw mattress, a couple of blankets thrown across it. There were no pillows. The bed in the other room was the same. The old man was certainly not overindulging his castoffs; as Diamond remarked, the workhouse could have done better. But by now she was too exhausted to care, and presently she was tucked up in the blankets by Georgy, a clean handkerchief underneath her head and a candle on the floor beside her.

Yet tired as she was, she could not sleep. The cottage creaked and rattled in the wind. The moon outside, with clouds scurrying across it, made strange shadows, and once she was sure that she again heard someone trying the door downstairs. She jumped out of bed and padded across the uncarpeted floor to Georgy's room. She crept in beside her, snuggling against her as if she were a child again, and Georgy, half asleep, put out an instinctively protective arm to comfort her.

Then they both slept. But Diamond, just before she toppled into exhausted slumber, said in a clear, loud voice, "Why is he doing so much for us? I don't like it. It's not natural. He don't know us, and I swear he don't like us, either. Why? I don't understand. I must understand."

But Georgy either did not hear or preferred not to answer, and in a little while there was a profound silence. Neither of them stirred again until the daylight flooded through the window.

V

Naturally, in the morning light the fears receded. Diamond ran downstairs in her shift, despite the cold, then wrapping herself in a shawl, moved the table and flung the door wide, while Georgy raked up the fire and put a kettle on the hob.

"I'm going for a long, long walk," said Diamond, breathing in the cold, hard autumn air.

"You'll have to get dressed first," said Georgy, frowning at her. It was not right that a young lady should wander about barefoot, wearing only a shawl and shift. "You feet will get cold."

"My feet are tough," said Diamond, then, smiling, extended one foot for Georgy to see the hardened sole. "I walked barefoot all my childhood."

"I don't think you should go walking. The gentleman asked you not to."

"Oh, even Captain Ringham said nothing about going abroad in the day. What harm could possibly come to me? I daresay we imagined it all last night. We were both dead tired and there was a high wind; it could only be the wind that rattled against the door."

"There was that singing," said Georgy from the kitchen. She was not as happy as her mistress, who looked quite restored, her eyes shining and the color back in her cheeks. But Georgy was old and she was still tired, and the cottage, seen in daylight, looked even worse than the night before. It would take her the whole day to clean it, and there was not even a decent chair to sit on. It was fine for young bones, but Georgy's rheumatism pained her badly, and she yearned passionately for the little Highgate house that Diamond so despised.

"The wind in the trees," said Diamond firmly. But she

flinched as she spoke, because it had undeniably been singing, and no known wind chanted perceptible words. It seemed to her as she looked about her that it had come from St. Joseph's Church, on top of the hill. And why St. Joseph's should hold a service at midnight she could not begin to understand, nor why the chanting had so heathen a sound.

"I'll go and ask him," she said, forgetting that Georgy could not have the slightest idea that she was referring to the parson. "I remember him quite well. A nice old man with a beard. His name— Now, what was his name? Oh, I've forgot, but I remember how on Christmas Day he came to the workhouse with his wife and children, and they brought us all little cakes. We liked that much more than sermons, Georgy. Georgy! Are you listening to me?"

"Miss Diamond," snapped Georgy, appearing in the hallway, very cross and dusty and with a handkerchief tied round her head, "I am trying to get the kettle boiling, and the stove's smoking, and everything's so filthy I can't even set a cup down. I got better things to do than listen to your chatter, and you ought to be getting some clothes on. If you want some breakfast, you'll kindly come in and shut the door, because the draft is putting the fire out, and the whole place is as cold as charity as it is."

"As cold as charity," repeated Diamond reflectively, but she did as she was told, and presently was drinking three bowls of hot chocolate and eating some rather stale rolls without butter.

Georgy said, "What about furniture? We need some desperate. We can't live like pigs. This ain't no better than a midden. What you going to do about it, Miss Diamond? His lordship's given you some money, so you'd better spend it. Perhaps Captain Ringham— Didn't he say he was sending round some things? I can't quite remember, that fall muddled my head."

"Don't you talk to me of Captain Ringham," said Diamond, rising to her feet.

"Well," said Georgy, whose memory of last night was blurred and who no longer saw the captain as a sinister enemy, "he's a gentleman, Miss Diamond, and two females on their own can't do without a gentleman. What did he say? Don't you remember?"

"He said a great many things," said Diamond, adding fiercely, "Gentlemen always do." She gazed round her. The cottage did not depress her as much as it did Georgy, for it was all part of the adventure, but she had to admit that it was not attractive. No doubt Georgy would soon sweep the dust away, but the uncarpeted floor was cold and depressing-looking, the two hard-backed chairs uninviting, and certainly there must be some curtains at the windows, and sheets and pillows for the beds. Diamond did not possess much home-making talent, for she had never had the opportunity, and she could not visualize herself hemming little pieces of pretty material or setting artistically arranged bowls of flowers on the table. She only thought without much interest that it would be all right in the end; perhaps kindly neighbors would come to the rescue, or perhaps the parson, whose name she still could not remember, would persuade his wife and children to rally round.

She decided she must dress. Halfway up the stairs she called down, "Never mind, old Georgy. I will go for my little walk, then when I come back I'll bring in something for our dinner and—"

Georgy now did remember something. She said hopefully, "Captain Ringham said he'd send us a rabbit." She was beginning to see the captain as a savior. She had completely forgotten the horrid things her mistress had recounted, and in her matchmaking mind, thought that he might become the new protector. He was, after all, a handsome man and apparently unmarried.

Some forty minutes later Diamond was downstairs again, parasol in hand, prepared to go for her walk. She stood in the kitchen doorway, half laughing. "How do I look?" she said. "Come on, my old woman, tell me how I look. Tell me I look beautiful. Tell me I'll take Middleditch by storm."

Georgy gaped at her, enchanted. Her mistress was always unpredictable, and why she should dress herself up as if she were going to Ranelagh, she could not imagine, but certainly Diamond looked magnificent, dressed in the newest gown that the old man had bought her, with her fur cape about her shoulders and the little hat tilted over one eye. Diamond might not be able to hem curtains but she knew how to dress her hair and wear her clothes. She looked entirely the fine lady and the village of Middleditch would surely be overcome.

Georgy hoped that Captain Ringham would meet her, but had the sense not to say so. She simply said, "You're beautiful, my darling. I doubt Middleditch has ever seen anything like you."

Diamond said in a hard voice, "Oh yes, Georgy. Middleditch has seen something like me six years ago, but I'll lay a hundred guineas they'll never know it. They kicked the workhouse brat into the gutter, but they'll doff their hats to me, and their wives will say I'm not respectable." She began to laugh. "It's true, isn't it? I'm not respectable. I'm an old man's darling, or perhaps I should say an old man's castoff. Never mind. I'll soon find myself another beau, perhaps a nice nut-brown farmer's boy who'll roll me in the hay, or maybe some elderly gentleman who's got no more strength in him and needs a bed-warmer."

Georgy tut-tutted, for she did not like this way of speaking. She made no answer, only went back to cleaning the kitchen range and stoking up the fire, while Diamond, singing softly to herself, stepped out onto the muddy path, holding her skirts high so as not to soil them. Middleditch was not going to see her with a dirty dress.

She came out into the main street and stood still for a moment, leaning in a genteel fashion on her parasol. The parasol was ridiculous in such weather, but it was pretty, and it seemed to her a symbol of the world she had left, perhaps forever. She knew perfectly well that she looked absurd in her fashionable clothes, but she knew, too, that she looked beautiful, and it was desperately important that Clary Brown should be obliterated by this fine lady she had become.

The villagers were all abroad. It was nearly ten in the morning and most of them had been up since five or six, as she had done in the workhouse. But then Miss Diamond Browne was a fine lady, used to wicked London hours. She met the curious, appraising glances, smiled, inclined her head. Mrs. Rigg, who ran the local shop, was just as she had always been. She had snapped crossly at the little urchin girl, told her to go away at once, never offered her so much as a sweetmeat, though some of them had fallen to the floor and would only be swept away. But now she gave a little bob, and Diamond was delighted, wanted suddenly to tear off her hat and burst into song. However, she simply said "Good morning" in her most cultured voice, and Mrs. Rigg sidled up to her, saying, "Excuse the liberty, my lady, but I think you are my neighbor."

"Oh, indeed?" said Diamond, twirling her parasol and looking bored. "I have only just arrived, and I fear that I have come before my belongings. I trust we did not disturb you."

"Oh no, ma'am, never, ma'am. Indeed, if you'll pardon the liberty, ma'am, I was distressed that you should come to such a place. I—I hope I was not intruding, but I did tap on your door to ask—"

"Oh, so it was you? We were a trifle exhausted, and it seemed late for callers." But how relieved Georgy would be, and Diamond was relieved herself. Perhaps there was some equally simple explanation for the chanting.

"Oh," cried Mrs. Rigg, "I'm afraid I took a liberty. I am so sorry."

"That is all right, my good woman," said Diamond, but the look in her eye must have briefly betrayed something else, for Mrs. Rigg looked even more frightened and backed away, saying in a tremulous voice, "I'm sure, my lady, you are used to the London shops, but if there is anything in my stock that catches your fancy— I could of course send off to one of the neighboring towns. I hope I am not taking a liberty, but I should be so pleased to help."

I'd like a handful of sweets, you old toady. I'd like a pretty ribbon for my poor, greasy hair. I'd like a kind word, a smile. It wouldn't be a liberty. Perhaps even to be asked in to warm myself at your fire. But no, dear Mrs. Rigg, no. It's, "Get away from my window, you little brat, there's nothing here for the likes of you. I know your sort, you gyppos are all the same, you'd steal anything once my back is turned."

Diamond said indifferently, "Perhaps one day. Thank you so much," and turned away with a sweeping gesture, flicking her parasol as she did so. She saw out of the corner of her eye that Mrs. Rigg was gaping after her, no doubt estimating the cost of the material, wondering perhaps if she could imitate the beautiful hat and sell it to the local gentry. Diamond remembered that she had not been born in Middleditch, which perhaps explained her servile attitude, for the villagers were not, unless her memory betrayed her, so easily impressed. But now, as she continued to walk up the street—so interested in everything she saw that she forgot to be elegantly languid and swept along at a brisk pace—she found that she no longer wanted to laugh; there was instead a bitter taste in her mouth. Did fine clothes and a pretty well-washed face make such a difference? What kind of person would kick aside a wretched child desperately in need of comfort, yet fawn and smile and speak of liberty—liberty indeed!—to a lady who, from her appearance, must need nothing.

At least Mr. Armstrong was no toady. She passed him coming out of the Rose and Crown, a small, thick-set man. He had once been something of a boxer, and as was well known, deferred to neither man nor beast. The only person who could keep him in order was his wife. She was some five inches taller than he, and could deal with drunken customers as capably as her husband. The Armstrongs had objected to Diamond's father drinking in their place. But then, they were prejudiced people, they probably objected to everyone.

Mr. Armstrong looked at her now, touched his hat, and walked stiffly on. Diamond thought it was a pity she could not stride into his parlor and demand a tankard of ale, but even fine ladies could not so defy convention. She wondered what Mrs. Armstrong would say if she did, then turned up the hill toward St. Joseph's Church.

It looked exactly as she remembered, with the cemetery in front, the headstones bearing the names: Ringham, Axenford, Armstrong, Falconer, Cowling—those who lay there dead and whose descendants walked outside. But there was no Romany Brown. Romany Brown lay in an unmarked grave in unconsecrated ground at the back. He lay with a broken neck, and no one had ever laid a flower over him, except for a ragged little girl who, finding nothing by the banks of the stream, had stolen a wreath from another grave and set it on his, with a stone upon it to keep it down.

Diamond, her face sad, thought that she would never be able to find his grave, for the patch of unconsecrated ground was nothing now but grass growing tall between the pebbles;

perhaps the malefactors lay there laughing and linking hands, making a mockery of the saintly-good with clean white headstones above them. She decided she would ask Mr.—Walsh, Walker, Wall? That was it, Wall. She would ask Mr. Wall about him, make up some story. He could be the father of her maidservant or something of the kind. He could once have told her mother's fortune. And even as she thought of this, the tears came to her eyes. She shook her head angrily and held her head high as she pushed open the churchyard gate. She would stay there for a while by one of the graves, to calm herself.

As Diamond sat on a gravestone, the tears would no longer be repressed. They poured down her cheeks, and it was as if she were weeping for a wretched child called Clary Brown, though Clary was gone, and by the grace of God, would never come back. Clary had starved, Diamond was well fed. Clary shivered in rags, Diamond wore silks and furs. Her pa was dead, his sufferings were done, there was nothing to cry about, yet she continued to sob until the bitter cold bit through her fur cape and brought her to her feet again, dabbing furiously at her dripping cheeks.

She blew her nose, gave her cheeks a final mop, and gazed round her at the churchyard, where sometimes in the old days she had crept, to be by herself, to beguile herself by looking at the inscriptions that she could not read. She still could not read them. Miss Falconer, who was the one other person who had been kind of her, would be very cross indeed. "You must learn to read, child," she had said sternly on the day when she presented Clary with a picture book. "I know you don't understand how important it is, but for a female on her own it is absolutely essential. If you are going to make anything of your life at all, you must read and write. If you don't, you will regret it more than you imagine." And she had even offered to give her lessons, but Diamond, then ten, could see no point in it and had never turned up. There was always something much more interesting to do, like watching fox cubs playing or picking berries off trees. She saw now that Miss Falconer had been perfectly right, but it was too late to start learning, and after all, she had not done too badly, she had made something of her life.

Then, preparing to climb the steep church steps, she saw that the cemetery had changed, was not entirely as she remembered, for now it was untended. In the old days it had been neat and orderly. The grass had been removed from the graves, the headstones were cleaned, the path between the crosses kept clear. Now the grass grew unchecked, the headstones and crosses were dirty, their inscriptions half obliterated; some of them even leaned sideways, great chips gouged out of them. The path was overgrown, and people apparently discarded their litter here, for there were small piles of torn paper, vegetable peelings, pieces of wood. It was as if the dead were no longer cared for, whether they had died by hanging or neatly in their beds. Diamond remembered that there had always been some old man or other whose duty it was to keep the graveyard tidy. He was usually someone friendly, willing to chat, and she had often sat there, listening to strange stories of departed people now six foot deep in the ground. But no one had used a brush or spade here for years. The neglect was somehow chilling, for if one did not trouble about the dead, why should one trouble about the living?

It was strange that Mr. Wall had let this happen; he was always a conscientious man. And looking round her, she remembered for no particular reason that ugly chanting she had heard in the night. The scratching at the door had apparently been Mrs. Rigg taking a liberty, but the chanting was inexplicable and somehow seemed allied with this barren, desecrated ground.

Diamond, still standing there by the untidy graves, said aloud, "It wasn't like this before."

Or was it? She was sixteen when she ran away, and she had spent three years imprisoned in the workhouse, only managing to creep out on rare occasions. She had never spoken to anyone except poor Lady Caroline, who was now dead, to Miss Falconer, and to the few people who visited Mr. Vincent for various business or charitable reasons. She might not have noticed things as a child.

A smooth, rather high-pitched voice broke in on her meditations, and she swung round, angry at being caught in such foolishness.

"Ma'am," said the voice, "if you continue to stand here, you will surely catch your death of cold. It is a bitter day, so unseasonable. If you are wishing to see our church, it is open, and I shall be delighted to escort you round." The voice broke off with a giggle. This was presumably a nervous habit, but it jarred Diamond. It seemed somehow obscene. "I am afraid," he said, "you are noticing how badly kept the churchyard is. It really is quite deplorable, and it grieves me very much. I must speak to Sir Francis about it. I find it impossible to find anyone who will work here, and you will appreciate I cannot do the work myself. I am not very strong, and my clerical duties take up all my time. But this path— Oh dear. I am sorry you see it like this. It makes such a bad impression."

This was certainly not Mr. Wall with his round red face and thick beard. This parson, as his collar proclaimed him to be, was a tall, willowy man with a smooth face and curiously white-lashed eyes that gave him an almost naked appearance. Diamond did not like the eyes, the high voice or the giggle, but she came up to him at once and extended her gloved hand. "I am Miss Diamond Browne," she said. "I arrived here yesterday. I am hoping to spend a little time in your village—to recover my health," she added, aware that there was nothing unhealthy in her appearance, and that it might seem odd that a delicate lady should choose to sit in a biting wind admiring disorderly graves.

"My name is Revill," he said, taking her hand lightly in his. The strange naked eyes moved over her, and as they did so, Diamond felt suddenly naked too, as if they were stripping her of her fine clothes. "Perhaps if you have visited Middle-ditch before, you knew the last incumbent, poor Mr. Wall? Pray come into the church, madam, and after that, perhaps you would care to take a glass of wine with me. I like to become acquainted with my parishioners. The vicarage is a few steps higher up the hill. Such a hilly place, this—I hope it will not prove too much for you in your delicate state of health.

You are bamming me, said Diamond silently, and she did not like it, any more than she liked Mr. Revill. But she only said in what she hoped was a frail-sounding voice, "Oh, I am accustomed to hills. And I should so much like to see the church again. I have such happy memories of it."

And that was a black lie, like most of what she had already

uttered during her few hours in Middleditch. But Mr. Revill was not to know that, and doubtless he hoped that this rich-looking young woman would be running to give money for the preservation of the Norman arch or the sixteenth-century chancel, or whatever it was one preserved in churches.

Diamond very much did not want to drink wine with him, she did not want to set foot in his house—though surely there could be nothing safer than a vicarage, and no doubt there would be a Mrs. Revill to chaperone her. She permitted him to give her a hand up the steps, though she could have leaped up them nimbly enough. Now that she stood within St. Joseph's Church, she had moved into the bitter heart of her memories, so that she spoke no more lies, indeed she did not speak at all, only put a hand up to her throat.

They had come here every Sunday morning and every Sunday evening, a procession of sad, starved, white-faced little girls, in their black overalls, black stockings and boots, black tattered shawls to cover their heads. During the week they went barefoot, the boots were only for the Sabbath day. For most of them it was their only outing. They came, wind, rain or snow, and the local children jeered at them as they trudged silently along the path that led from the workhouse to the church. "Charity bitches!" they would yell. "Workhouse sluts!" And the bravest of them would throw stones. Once Diamond, in a black rage, threw a stone back, only it was not just a stone, it was a small rock, and it hit the ringleader on the head and knocked him unconscious. For this she was terribly beaten and locked up without food for three days, but even through her cries and tears she knew it had been worthwhile, and that particular boy never threw stones again.

She could see the pews now where they had sat, three pews at the very back of the church. They walked in procession, clutching their prayer books, and they stood up, sat down, knelt like puppets. They never listened to one word the parson said, except for a specially chosen girl who changed every week, and she had to tell the rest what the sermon was about; this had to be related to Mr. Vincent on their return, for all he and the Matron accompanied them and knew about it perfectly well. When the service was over, they walked back again to their Sunday dinner, the only meal at which they ever had any meat, or their Sunday supper, which was nothing but bread and drippings and a glass of water.

Diamond, the tears stinging her eyes, could even smell them, smell the reek of wretchedness, hunger and unwashed bodies. She looked down at her soft woolen dress, and the hand that unconsciously stroked the fur of her cape became a thin, dirty little claw, red with chilblains. Then she grew aware that Mr. Revill was watching her intently, and because she was disconcerted, said, "I believe I'll accept your offer of wine, sir, for I am most dreadfully cold."

And indeed she was cold, for the church was unheated. But it was the memory that chilled her, and she knew she could no longer endure the little church with its stained-glass windows, its effigies of early Axenfords and its odor of enforced piety.

Mr. Revill exclaimed, with his nervous giggle, "But, my dear lady, you should never have come out in such weather." Diamond knew perfectly well that he did not give a damn, and cursed herself for uttering such stupid words. However, it was too late to do anything about it, and ten minutes later she was sitting by a roaring fire in Mr. Revill's study, a glass of wine in her hand.

There seemed to be no Mrs. Revill. Perhaps that was too much to expect from that smooth face and high voice. The fire was magnificent, but the room was dark, with books from ceiling to floor, except above the mantelpiece, where an enormous crucifix hung. Diamond disliked the atmosphere, but told herself she was growing fanciful, she must stop seeing evil everywhere—and what could be more sane and healthy than a clergyman's study in a country vicarage?

She said, "I hope Mr. Wall is well. I gather he has retired."

"I fear Mr. Wall is dead."

Oh God, thought Diamond, is everyone who was in any way kind to me dead? She was too curious to let the matter lie. She said, "I am really sorry. He always seemed such a healthy man. But then, I suppose, he was quite old. What exactly happened?"

"It was a most unfortunate business."

"What do you mean?"

"It is hardly a tale for a young lady's ears."

Nothing could have provoked Diamond's curiosity more,

yet the words sent a shiver through her. She said, her eyes very wide, "What happened? You are making me imagine the most terrible things."

"Nothing could be more terrible than the truth," said Mr. Revill, and despite herself, she once again had the impression that he was enjoying himself, though his face was solemn and his voice subdued.

She waited in silence, sipping at her wine. She had always believed she could deal with anything, but she now had the feeling that it was all swimming away beyond her control. She had only spent a few hours in Middleditch—God knows, she had never expected to come back—and already she had learned that two of her friends were dead. And Captain Ringham, whom she hated, was only too much alive; he was her enemy, as perhaps Mr. Revill was too. The dramatic part of her nature rose to this challenge, but she could not help wondering what was going to happen next. At least it was not boring. People who said the countryside was dull had no idea what they were talking about; they should come to Middleditch and find out.

She wondered when she could decently take her leave. She was a fool to have come here. In a few moments she would go, and then she would do the one thing she had longed to do from the very moment Middleditch was mentioned: walk along the banks of the little stream where she and her father had spent such happy times. Never mind that it was late September, that it was cold and the wind blowing strong, this was something that would be worth all the trials and difficulties that had pursued her. The shadow of a dreadful death could not obliterate this small oasis where little Clary Brown had loved life, when she had held the hand of Romany Brown and talked to him of everything that came into her mind.

"Will I be rich?" she had asked him once. They never had any money, and to Clary Brown, being rich meant nothing except always having enough to eat and perhaps living in a great big house like Axenford. She did not think of fine clothes because she did not know them, but she did think of jewels because they were pretty, because she had seen them sparkle round Lady Caroline's throat. "I would like diamonds," she said. "Lots and lots of diamonds."

Her father said gravely, "Then you will have to be very rich indeed."

"Are they so expensive?" she had asked. She was ten years old. She had no idea of money, because, like fine clothes, she had never seen it. Her father earned odd shillings by mending things, making wooden toys, doing odd farm jobs, like hop-picking, setting snares, gathering strawberries. There was never much work. People mistrusted gypsies, and Romany Brown— with his long black hair, brown skin and aquiline features —looked what he was. Clary believed that diamonds would cost at least a shilling, perhaps two; such a sum to her was wealth unimaginable.

"Very expensive," said her father.

"How much?"

"Oh . . ." He hesitated. He knew the price no better than his daughter. "A hundred pounds perhaps."

"A hundred pounds!"

"At least." He grinned down at her. She was no beauty in those days, with her long, tangled hair and the dirt chasing the freckles from her face. "You'll have to find yourself a gentle-man, girl."

"Would he buy me diamonds?"

"He might. Depends on the gentleman."

"When I'm grown-up," said Clary, "I shall call myself Diamond. It's a nice name. Don't you think it's a nice name, Pa?"

He shrugged. "Clary suits me."

"Oh, Clary's just dull. I shall call myself Diamond Brown."

She smiled at the memory, for indeed she was Diamond Browne and diamonds had been bought for her. Then she realized what Mr. Revill was saying—perhaps the warmth and the wine had made her drowsy, for she had not been listening to him—and the smile was shocked off her face.

"He was murdered in the church," said Mr. Revill solemnly.

"Oh, good God!" exclaimed Diamond, and though she was no girl for the vapors, she went pale, as if the heat of the fire were making her dizzy.

"They crucified him before his own altar."

Diamond sprang to her feet, as if somehow she could not take such horror seated, and Mr. Revill made a half-apologetic gesture, motioning her to sit down again. But she did not, only stared at him, one hand clutching the mantelpiece. She whispered, "But who could have done such a terrible thing?"

"We never found out. It was a most shocking business," said Mr. Revill, and gave his nervous giggle. Once again, unbelievable as it was, she could have sworn that he was amused by what he was saying. But his face was grave and mournful, and he added in the kind of voice that no doubt he employed for the sick and dying, "My dear young lady, I have distressed you—"

Diamond said with some acerbity, "That is hardly astonishing."

"I should never have told you. Forgive me. Let me pour you out another glass of wine."

"No. When did this happen?"

"A year and a half ago. That is why no one will work in the graveyard. They all say it's haunted. They talk of black magic. This is a strange village," said Mr. Revill, looking at her intently. "I do not feel that it is a place for a young and beautiful lady like yourself. How long are you planning to stay with us?"

"Indefinitely," said Diamond, raising her chin haughtily. She was sure there was some hidden menace in Mr. Revill's voice, and somehow this restored her courage. She was damned if she was going to be frightened by this strange, giggling creature who called himself a clergyman. As he began to walk toward the door, she said in a missish little voice, "It is pretty here. Though it is a most shocking story. But murders happen everywhere, one cannot be driven away by such things. I am very sorry—" Her voice cracked a little. "I liked Mr. Wall. I think he was a kind man. But you are surely not suggesting that I could be in any danger?"

"I see you have great courage," said Mr. Revill, opening the door for her. He did not, she noticed, answer her directly. "But I should be careful, Miss Browne. I think you should never walk the village at night."

"So Captain Ringham has already told me," said Diamond, and saw to her surprise a sudden look of fury pass across Mr. Revill's smooth face. It seemed that he liked Captain Ringham as little as she did. This should have been a bond

74

between them, but she could feel only a positive revulsion and dislike.

She said goodbye civilly. The old man had instructed her in the courtesies of life, and these she had absorbed, together with long words that would not ordinarily have been in her vocabulary. No one could have faulted the little workhouse brat in her soft speech, her turns of phrase, the genteel way in which she extended her gloved hand. "I see I have made a fine lady of you," the old man had told her once, his voice ironic. "I observe and I remember," Diamond had answered. "I may never have been a good actress, my lord, but I never forget anything, and I imitate like a parrot." And this frankness amused him—it was on that day that he bought her the diamonds.

She sailed down the hill. Mr. Revill watched her from the door. Once, when she looked back, he waved his hand. She could see that his face was convulsed with amusement, and he was seized with a fit of silent laughter that shook his shoulders up and down.

✥ VI ✥

Diamond reached the little stream some fifteen minutes later.
She found that she was still very frightened. The memory of
Mr. Revill made her feel quite sick, and there was something
about his study that worked in the recesses of her mind, something odd that disturbed her, that she could not understand.
She sat down on a stone by the bank, not thinking of her fine
clothes, only thankful to be away. She had meant to make this
a day of exploration, to stop at the burned-out workhouse by
the woods, but now she felt she could not face the blackened
ruin with its ugly memories.

Here, surely, by the river, the kindly ghost of her father
would protect her. The wind had died a little, and the bank
was sheltered by the bushes at the back. In the odd way of
things seen in retrospect, everything was far smaller than she
remembered. She had visualized a rushing stream; this was a
mere trickle that threaded its way through the pebbles at the
bottom. There were a few flowers on the bank and plenty
of blackberries—she reached out to pick herself a handful and
stuffed them into her mouth as if she were Clary Brown again
—but she could see no signs of the thick clumps of violets that
used to grow there, there was not even one leaf. What had once
seemed to her a forest was now nothing but a few small trees,
and there was not a trace of the wooden hut her father had
built.

But it was peaceful, no sound but the gentle murmur of
running water and the sighing of the wind through the
branches. Her fear and shock began to subside, and the shivering stopped. It was as if the ghost of Romany Brown had
risen from his dishonored grave and sat himself beside her as
he had done so often in life. His long legs stretched out, his

hands in his pockets, he had talked of people and the world around them, told his small daughter about the animals and birds who lived their secret life around him, and showed her how to set traps for small creatures who might provide their dinner. And if there were a dinner—sometimes there was not —he would bake it on hot stones. Diamond thought that for all the grand food the old man had given her, she had never tasted anything so delicious again in her life.

"Oh, Pa," she said aloud, "I do love you so. I wish you were alive again, even if it meant being Clary Brown."

And she shut her eyes tightly, feeling the warmth of him beside her, sensing the smell of him, a compound of earth and sweat and tobacco, a lovely, warm, human smell that the perfumed quality might despise but which signified for her all happiness and love. It was almost as if his hand, rough and strong, clasped her own, and she leaned back to set her head against his shoulder. For that moment there was no more pretense, no more lying. It was as if she were stripped of her fine clothes and dressed once more in the rags that were all she had possessed.

A man's voice said gently, "Miss Browne—it is Miss Browne, is it not? I don't wish to alarm you, but the temperature is near freezing. It looks as if it might rain, and really, this is no place to sleep. I fear you might never wake up again." There was a hint of laughter in the voice, which was a pleasant one. "Permit me the freedom of the country and take my arm. I will escort you back to your cottage, where I am sure your maid will be only too eager to make you a hot drink. Indeed, if you press me, ma'am, I will drink with you. You may not be cold, but I assure you I am."

Diamond opened her eyes and sat up very straight. She was hardly distinguishing herself on her first day back home, and the intruder was perfectly right. It was very cold, and her foot had gone to sleep. She looked up at Sir Francis Axenford, and bestowed on him a smile of genuine pleasure. Here at last was someone kind who was still very much alive. She recognized him immediately. Six years had in no way changed him. Here there was nothing sinister, nothing bad-tempered, only a large, loose-limbed man of perhaps fifty, a little stouter than when she had seen him last, but good-looking in a lined, kind way, with amused eyes, a smile that made gentle fun of her and a voice that was soft and deep.

She had heard that he sang well. Lady Caroline had told her. "My husband has the most beautiful voice," she said. "I believe that is why I married him. I told him when he proposed that he must sing to me on my wedding night, that I would never lie with him unless he made love to me in grand opera."

Young Clary Brown had thought this the last word in wit and daring, and had laughed so long and loud that her ladyship laughed too, saying, "I should not speak to you in such a way. But you are only a child, and I daresay you do not understand."

And after that she had looked very sad, which astonished Clary—but Diamond was not thinking of her at this moment, only delighted that she had at last met a friend. She let Sir Francis take her hands to pull her to her feet. And then, tottering with the cold, she decided that this was one person to whom she would tell the truth. She could not spend her entire life in a lie, and she felt sure that she could trust him.

He took her arm, and they walked swiftly back toward the cottage. He asked, "May I inquire how long you will be staying with us, Miss Browne? You see that we know all about you already."

"Do you?" said Diamond, with a little sideways smile.

"Oh, yes indeed. There are no secrets in a small village. From the moment your man appeared, inquiring about the cottage, we all knew that a famous London actress was coming here, straight from success at Drury Lane. I am only sorry that I have never seen you act, but though Londoners believe that we have nothing to do, we seldom have a minute to ourselves. I have not been up to London for—oh, at least three years."

"You have not missed much," said Diamond, a little disconsolately.

"Why, is London so changed, then? I have always thought of it as one of the most splendid cities in the world."

"I am not talking about London, Sir Francis. I am talking about my own acting."

He smiled at her. "I think perhaps you are being too modest. I cannot believe that Mr. Garrick would employ anyone who was not a seasoned actor."

"Oh," said Diamond, with a little wave of her parasol, "he is a most kind-hearted man. I have two advantages, sir, and I know that better than most. I have reasonable good looks . . ."

"You are very beautiful," he said gravely, and he spoke as if he meant it.

"Am I? Perhaps." Then she laughed. "I also am impertinent. I will try almost anything. I am not easily set down."

"That I can imagine."

"But it's not enough. Not nearly enough. I shall never act again," said Diamond.

"I think you are acting now."

"And what, pray, do you mean by that?"

"You are acting the little ingénue. You are doing it very well," said Sir Francis, adding, "And I do not believe one word of it."

Then Diamond burst out laughing again, and he laughed too. It was in this style that Georgy, running out to greet her mistress, saw them, and she was smiling too, as if she were quite restored. When she saw that Diamond had a gentleman with her, she made them both a dignified little bob and started back into the house. But as she retreated, she could not resist saying, "There is a great surprise for you, Miss Diamond," and the thought of what awaited her mistress so completely overcame her, she was convulsed with giggles, and she ran into the kitchen, her apron over her face.

"Georgy," said Diamond, stepping into the cottage and motioning Sir Francis to follow her, "is my most faithful friend, but sometimes she thinks she must behave in a horrid, toadying kind of fashion, just to prove I'm a lady. After all—" She broke off with a little gasp, then called out in a roaring voice, "Georgy!"

Georgy came out of the kitchen. She had recovered from her giggles and was mopping at her eyes. "Oh, Miss Diamond," she said, "isn't it wonderful?"

"It's a miracle," said Diamond.

And so indeed it was. There were curtains at the windows, there were rugs on the floor, there were comfortable chairs and a chaise longue, and everywhere great bunches of late-flowering roses, and chrysanthemums, newly picked from a

79

garden. Diamond turned to Sir Francis, holding out her hands. "Is it you who have done all this?" she said. "It's so beautiful. It's really my home now. I don't think I shall ever leave it."

He was about to reply, but Georgy, forgetting to behave in the way that she considered proper, cried out, "It's that Captain Ringham."

Diamond said, "Oh. Of course. I had forgot." The joy died in her face. She touched one of the armchairs. "No doubt," she said in a remote, chill little voice, "his housekeeper had no more use for it. And I do not care much for the curtains, such a cheap material."

"I think," said Sir Francis, who had been viewing this pantomime with barely concealed amusement, "you do not care much for Captain Ringham."

"I hate his guts," said Diamond with vigor and with venom, and this was too much for Georgy, who made a shocked face and fled back into the kitchen, from which came a warm, spicy smell of cooking.

"Shall I tell you a secret?" asked Sir Francis.

"Please. And we will have some wine. Georgy! What are you cooking? And bring us some wine. A great deal of wine."

Georgy reappeared, looking cold and reproachful. She said austerely, "I am preparing a rabbit stew."

"I detest rabbit stew," said Diamond.

Georgy longed to tell her mistress that she was behaving abominably. The captain had been so generous. Indeed, he had arrived only a few minutes after Diamond had left, bringing with him three men from the estate and a cartload of furniture. Within a couple of hours the cottage was transformed, even to fresh linen on the beds.

She had said, "You can't give us all this, sir," but he had answered without a smile, "There's nothing I'll miss. Keep it until you have better."

It was not perhaps the most gracious of remarks, but after all, he had been kind. No one else had offered to help. What was the matter with Miss Diamond to be so bad-tempered, to be dwelling on the past so? Why even the rabbit stew, filled with fresh herbs and vegetables from Captain Ringham's garden, smelled delicious.

But when she returned with the wine, Diamond was laughing and chatting. And certainly this was a fine-looking gentleman, obviously very smitten. Georgy at once placed him in the role of new protector.

Diamond poured the wine. This, too, was a gift, if not an altruistic one. Mr. Armstrong, deciding that the new young lady was plainly wealthy and might prove to be a good customer, had sent over half a dozen bottles with his compliments, together with a French brandy and a Spanish sack.

"I do not like Captain Ringham either," Sir Francis was saying, making a little resigned gesture with his hands. He wore, as Diamond noticed, a square black ring on one finger, marked with curious signs that she could not understand. "Indeed, Miss Diamond, as you are now part of Middleditch, you should know that we are scarce on speaking terms. We have already had various disputes about rights of way and footpaths, for our estates, as you may have remarked, adjoin, and there have been a number of regrettable incidents. Only the woods separate us, and the boundary has never been completely defined, but a little good will could easily overcome that. I hope I am not so litigious as to rush to the law if someone steps on my private land, but when this occurs over and over again, and Captain Ringham rides over it, destroying crops and frightening my deer, then I feel I am entitled to complain. There was a case in point a few months ago— But I must be boring you. This cannot possibly be of interest to you."

"It is of the greatest interest to me," said Diamond. She was sitting in one of Captain Ringham's comfortable chairs, the rug was soft beneath her feet, and the scent of his roses perfumed the room, but she chose to push out of her mind that all these things were his gifts. Her face was cold and contemptuous with dislike.

"It concerns young Philip," said Sir Francis. His expression was somber. "You have heard about the boy?"

"I understand he is Captain Ringham's stepbrother."

"That is so. The late Mr. Ringham married twice, but the second wife was a poor sort of girl who caused much dissension in the family. Philip is her son, and she died giving birth to him. There is, I'm afraid, bad blood in him, and I suppose it is to his half-brother's credit that he has adopted the boy as if he were his own. I sometimes think that in other circumstances he would already have ended on the gallows."

"But he's only a child," exclaimed Diamond, a little shocked. She held no more brief for Captain Ringham's stepbrother than for the captain himself, but the thought of hanging a twelve-year old boy appalled her.

"In our world," said Sir Francis with a grim smile, "it makes little difference. Oh, don't misunderstand me, Miss Diamond. I am not advocating the rope for someone so young. I am only saying there is a wickedness in him—I cannot give it a milder name—and Captain Ringham makes no effort to control him, even urges him on."

"But what did he do?"

"He broke the leg of one of my race horses."

"Oh no!"

"Yes. He took him from the stables and rode him barebacked through the woods. The animal got tied up with some branches, and threw him. Master Philip came to no harm, but my horse broke his leg and had to be destroyed. I could even overlook such behavior," said Sir Francis, his voice harsh and his face dark with anger, "if he had come to me and told me what had happened. But he simply ran off home, leaving the animal there in agony. If one of my gamekeepers had not discovered him, he would have lain there till he died."

"I think that's shameful," said Diamond, her voice trembling with anger.

He looked at her, gave her a rueful smile, and briefly laid his hand on hers. "I see you have a tender heart," he said. "But you will understand that this has hardly improved my relations with Captain Ringham. Naturally, I at once went to see him. I told him what had happened. He laughed—"

"Oh, I cannot believe that!"

"Neither could I. But that is what happened. And a great deal more besides. I fear I entirely lost my temper and threatened to horsewhip the boy. And I would have done so if I had had the opportunity. Since then, as I said, we do not speak to each other except through our agents, and that involves a long list of complaints of trespass and damage and poaching, and God knows what else. And if that were only the worst—

But I cannot tell you everything, Miss Diamond. I have no wish to frighten you."

"Perhaps," said Diamond, regarding him steadily, "you are about to tell me not to walk abroad alone at nights. Captain Ringham has already given me such a warning."

"Has he indeed!" said Sir Francis. "He is a clever man." He rose to his feet and stood against the window. She could no longer see his expression, but his voice was stern. "Then perhaps you had better listen to both of us. There are evil things that happen here, Miss Diamond. Graves are desecrated —and other things, including murder. I don't know. But there was a workhouse here—"

Diamond stiffened. She stared up at him, silent.

"For young girls. Some of those girls vanished. Perhaps they simply ran away. But the master, Mr. Vincent, grew frightened. I don't think he cared much about the girls, but people began to talk. He was, after all, responsible, and the disappearances became so numerous that he could no longer ignore them. Whether he protested, no one knows, but suddenly the workhouse was burned down. There seemed to be no reason for the fire. I believe Mr. Vincent lost his only daughter. It has never been rebuilt."

Diamond had, God knows, no happy memories of the workhouse, but this shocked her so much that for a moment she could not speak. It had been her home, in a fashion; to learn that it had been completely destroyed was almost as if her own past had been wiped out. She said at last, her voice low and shaking, "It had a theatre at the back."

Now it was he who fell silent. He looked at her.

"It was your wife who had it built. I'm sorry she is dead. She was the most kind-hearted lady."

He still said nothing. He looked down so that his face was hidden from her.

"I lived in that workhouse," said Diamond. "I was one of the girls who disappeared. Only, I ran away—to London. My name is not Diamond. My real name is Clary Brown. You see, Sir Francis, I am not real. Nothing of what I say is true. Except this. I am a workhouse brat called Clary Brown, and your wife was one of the few people who were kind to me. I have never forgotten, I never will forget. Please, sir, tell me how she died, if it don't hurt you too much to speak of her. And tell me where she's buried so that I can put some flowers on her grave. It's not much to do for her, but I never forget kindness," said Diamond, the tears beginning to trickle down her cheeks, "and when I knew I had to come back here, one of the things that made me happy was the thought of seeing Lady Caroline again. And now I shall never see her, never."

And with this she put her hands over her face and began to cry in earnest. She felt Sir Francis's hands on her shoulders, but could not raise her head. The hands remained there, and he spoke very softly.

"Dear Miss Diamond," he said, "I will always love you for so loving my poor wife, and if it makes you feel any happier, I know who you are. I knew from the beginning. Do you think it makes any difference to me? Stop crying. Please stop crying. I am your friend. Surely you must know that."

Diamond raised her head at last. She rubbed at her eyes. She said in a childish kind of way, "How did you find out?"

He was now kneeling beside her, and took both her hands in his. He said, "Shall I offer you my handkerchief and say, 'Blow,' as one does to children? After all, I am old enough to be your father."

But she only repeated, "How did you find out?"

"I think I might have known anyway. I have a good memory for faces, and yours is a remarkable one. But you told me yourself. I heard you speaking aloud when you were sitting by the stream."

"Oh no," said Diamond, like a child caught out in wrongdoing, and she flung her hand up to her mouth.

"You said, 'I wish you were alive again, even if it meant being Clary Brown.' Who were you speaking to, Miss Diamond?"

"I was speaking to my pa." Diamond blew her nose energetically, but her eyes were still shining with tears. "We used to walk there when I was a little girl. He was the kind of father children dream of. He knew all about animals and plants and birds, and he told me wonderful stories. We never had any money, and sometimes we didn't have anything to eat either, but it didn't matter. And then one day—" She stopped, her voice choked.

He said gently, "I remember. Do not distress yourself, Miss Diamond."

"They hanged him. For stealing a rabbit, just like the one that's cooking in the kitchen. Captain Ringham said rabbits are vermin, and he has offered to send me one every week, but it was Captain Ringham who had him hanged. My father never did anyone any harm, but he was a gypsy, and folk here don't like gypsies. I am a gypsy too, and I am proud of it. One day I'll tell Captain Ringham." Then Diamond, after another pause, went on in her most refined voice, "Oh, I must be boring you so. Do pray forgive me. Let me pour some more wine."

He did not answer this. He rose to his feet again, twisting his fingers against the palm of his hand as if he were deliberating. She could not see his face, for he was looking down. She went on, "Will you not tell me about your wife, if you don't mind too much? I would like to know. I hope she didn't suffer."

He said quietly, "I fear she did. I think sometimes it is always the good people who suffer. You remember her well, Miss Diamond?"

"Oh yes, I do. And of course, her little theatre. Mr. Vincent did not approve of such things, he didn't want us to enjoy ourselves. We were never allowed to use it. I used to sneak in sometimes by myself, when no one was looking, and pretend I was a great actress. I suppose it was burned down with the rest of the building."

"No. By some miracle it survived. If you remember, it was right at the back, overlooking the woods. The fire must have broken out in the front of the building."

Diamond said in a small, hard voice, "The children—did they manage to get out?"

"Some of them did. Others, I fear, died in the blaze."

"But Mr. Vincent, I gather, escaped. He would," said Diamond fiercely. "I expect he knocked the children down and stepped over their bodies to get to the door. He's the kind that survives."

Sir Francis looked at her oddly. "He did and he did not."

"What do you mean?"

"You will see. Why don't you ask Captain Ringham?"

"What has he got to do with it?"

"I don't think this is the moment to discuss the matter."

"You mean that he started the fire?"

"I didn't say that. One day I'll tell you about it. My dear wife died shortly afterwards. You asked me how she died."

"If you'd rather not discuss it . . ."

"I should like to tell you. You will remember perhaps—though there is no reason why you should, you were only a child—that she liked to use her ceruse box. She suffered from some wasting disease that made her very thin, and she felt she had grown so ugly. She said her face was a skeleton face with all the bones showing."

Diamond remembered that wasted face with the bright red on the cheeks, the overvivid mouth. She looked at Sir Francis, her eyes wide and horrified.

"They say—I do not know much about such things—that rouge contains a mixture of lead that can destroy the skin. My poor Caroline used too much, and it bit into her face. Toward the end she was most dreadfully disfigured and in the utmost pain. The doctors here could do nothing for her. At the very end we decided she should go to stay with her sister in London, to see if the town physicians could perhaps find a cure. I even arranged for her to see someone who attended on the royal family. But it was too late, and she died within three days. Perhaps it was merciful. But I never saw her again," said Sir Francis, now looking directly at Diamond. "The last sight I had of my dear wife was when she was in her coffin. She does not even lie in St. Joseph's Church."

"Poor Lady Caroline," said Diamond, and instinctively pressed the palm of her hand to her own unrouged cheek.

"Well," he said quite briskly, "enough of that. I did not wish to burden you with my unhappiness, but I know how fond you were of her and I felt you were a person who should know what happened. She loved you too. I know that. She said you were a most gifted child, and intelligent above the ordinary. She was sure you would go on the stage, like herself. Sometimes I wonder of all this was not my fault, for she so loved acting, and she gave up her career when she married me. Perhaps if she had stayed in the theatre— But we none of us know these things, and there is no point in dwelling on what is past."

"Do you have any children, Sir Francis?"

For the flash of a second his face altered. It was as if a spasm contorted it. In that moment the friendliness and good nature vanished, leaving something ugly and despairing. Then again he looked as he always did, so that Diamond believed she must have imagined it. She thought reproachfully that this was a question she should not have asked. Georgy was only too right, she spoke too often without thinking.

But he answered, simply, "No," then as if he thought this might sound snubbing, added, "We both wanted children. It was a great grief to us that there were none. It is, after all, the only way to stay young. But now let us talk about you. How long are you staying with us, Miss Diamond?"

"Oh, I don't know," said Diamond. "Perhaps I may stay here forever. Middleditch is the only real home I have ever known."

"It would make us all happy if you did stay. Perhaps one evening, when you have settled in, you will come and dine at Axenford. I do not entertain much these days," said Sir Francis, "but my housekeeper would be delighted to see me do so, and if you will forgive my egotism, I suspect it would do me good not always to dine on my own. Indeed, you would be doing me a favor. I would of course send my carriage for you."

"I should love to come," said Diamond, and managed to prevent herself from saying that she was perfectly capable of walking the quarter of a mile or so that would take her to his house. It seemed that she must play the fine lady whether she liked it or not. How Pa would have laughed!

"There is one thing more," said Sir Francis, now at the door. He looked very grave in his kindly way. It was plain that he was genuinely concerned for her, and Diamond was so touched by this that she nearly wept again.

"No," he said as if reading her mind, "I am not asking you not to walk abroad on your own. I think it would be wiser if you did not, but I fear you are a most headstrong young lady, Miss Diamond, and would not even listen to me."

"I am used to walking," said Diamond. "In London fine ladies seem to have no legs at all, but I used to walk with my father for miles and miles without tiring, and I sometimes think that if I always go in carriages, I shall become fat and horrid like some overfed lapdog."

He said, smiling, "I don't think that will happen for a very long time, if ever. No. It is not that, though I warn you I shall keep an eye on you. You were a friend of my wife's, and therefore my responsibility. It is simply this, and you must try not to misunderstand me. Captain Ringham—yes, I will mention the name, and you are not to look so angry—has apparently been kind and generous to you, but I must beg you not to trust him too much."

"I don't trust him at all," said Diamond.

"You are very direct. Perhaps— I do not know. Sometimes people change, but in his case I doubt it, and I am frankly bewildered that he has taken so much trouble to make you welcome."

"So am I," said Diamond, making the kind of face that Georgy deplored.

He burst out laughing. "You are quite impossible. What can I say to that? Then we'll leave Captain Ringham out of it. Perhaps you will reform him altogether. I can only hope so. No one will be more delighted than myself to have a neighbor who is no longer an active enemy. But there is something else I must say, and perhaps it concerns Captain Ringham too, though I am not certain. This is a strange village, Miss Diamond."

"That I have already discovered."

"What have you discovered?" asked Sir Francis sharply.

Diamond was about to ask him about Mr. Wall and his dreadful death, even to say that she disliked Mr. Revill very much. But something stopped her. Her father had said to her once, "Never confide too much in people you do not know. Keep things to yourself. If you overconfide, you put yourself in people's power, and then they start to order you around. Always leave something unsaid."

It had already struck her as a little odd that Sir Francis had made no mention whatsoever of Mr. Wall and his horrible death, but then, he had talked of so many alarming things that he might think any more would send her running back to London. But her father's advice had always been useful, so she rallied her wits about her and said, "I have discovered that people who are cruel and brutal to workhouse children become prodigious civil to ladies dressed up in fine clothes. I have discovered that when you look as if you have money, you can trample on the world, but if you look poor, the world tramples on you. I think that is horrid. You must agree with me."

"None of that is peculiar to Middleditch," said Sir Francis dryly.

"Oh, perhaps not. But I still find it disgusting that someone like Mrs. Rigg, who drove me away from her shop window when I was starving, now bows and becks before me and would let me buy up everything on credit."

"You are quite a philosopher, Miss Diamond."

"I think," said Diamond with sudden fierceness, "I am just angry. They hanged my father, Sir Francis, and really, all they hanged him for was being poor. If you snared a rabbit and took it home for your dinner, no one would say a word. When I was in the workhouse, hardly anyone spoke kindly to me. Now they cannot make enough of me. When they learn that I do not really have much money, they'll all run to kick me into the gutter."

"That is not quite what I meant!"

"I'm sorry. I think," said Diamond, "that coming back here has been something of a shock. I'll not speak like this again. I am getting used to it all already."

He still looked disconcerted. Perhaps country ladies did not speak so. Kitty Clive had once said to her, "You speak your mind too much. It's a good, quick mind, Diamond, and it's a pity you cannot read, but you must try not to sound as if you know everything. The gentlemen still prefer geese, you know. They don't like clever females, they're frightened of them."

Sir Francis was speaking again. "I want to ask you," he said, "not to be too inquisitive."

"I don't know what you mean," said Diamond.

"I beg of you," said Sir Francis very earnestly, "not to interfere in things you do not understand."

"But I—"

"It's dangerous. Please, Miss Diamond. I do feel responsible for you, and as I have already said, there are strange happenings here. I hope that one day we will find the culprit, but in the meantime let me emphasize that you could be in extreme danger. Will you promise me not to peer or pry? Your very life may depend on it."

"I promise," said Diamond, though she was by now so consumed with curiosity that she was longing to pry to the best of her ability. Sir Francis did not really know the feminine temperament; he could not have said anything that would provoke her more. But she smiled charmingly at him, put on her most docile expression, and hoped she looked as if she would spend most of her days reclining on the chaise longue.

"And," he said, opening the door, "if you find anything that disturbs you or seems in any way strange, you will get in touch with me immediately. Is that understood?"

"Of course," said Diamond. She was not quite sure why she was lying, but as soon as Sir Francis was gone, she put it all out of her mind and went instantly into the kitchen, announcing that she proposed to eat a mountain of rabbit stew.

ꙮ VII ꙮ

Diamond did not repeat much of the conversation to Georgy. The sinister happenings indicated by Sir Francis would terrify the old woman. Diamond herself was a little frightened, and she tried to calm herself by rearranging all the new things in the cottage. Certainly, though they were gifts from the detested Captain Ringham, it was wonderful to have the place so well set up. She wandered idly about, moving furniture here and there and back again, smelling the roses and full of rich rabbit stew.

"You say his poor wife is dead," said Georgy, for this piece of news had been imparted to her.

"Yes," said Diamond, and added fiercely, "I swear I'll never put rouge on my face again."

Georgy did not follow this at all, for of course all actresses put rouge on their cheeks, but she said hopefully, "Such a good-looking gentleman. So tall and so kind—"

"Now make up your mind, old woman," said Diamond, seizing a rose from one vase and sticking it into another one filled with chrysanthemums, where it looked entirely ridiculous. She said, "You want me to settle myself with another gentleman, don't you?"

"Oh, indeed I do," cried Georgy, clasping her hands to her plump bosom. Ladies with protectors were rich, carefree, with fine clothes and carriages and lots of money. She longed to see her young mistress set up in some vast mansion, with an army of servants that she herself could order about.

"You're nothing better than an old bawd," said Diamond derisively. "And I tell you, you'll just have to decide which one it's going to be. This morning it was Captain Ringham, which God forbid, and this afternoon it's Sir Francis. I don't know how many gentlemen there are in Middleditch, but if there are any more, I daresay you'll be pushing them onto me. I cannot run a harem of gentlemen. Which one is it to be? The lucky fellow!"

"I think Sir Francis might marry you," said Georgy hopefully.

"Captain Ringham is also unwed. And Sir Francis must be all of fifty."

"I think Sir Francis looks kinder. What does age matter? He might die in a few years and leave you all his fortune."

Diamond began to laugh helplessly, and a vase of Michaelmas daisies was knocked to the floor, the water spilling all over the rug. This brought Georgy running, clucking with dismay. "The new carpet too— Miss Diamond, you should be ashamed of yourself, you're worse than a child." And the question of her future was temporarily forgotten, though certainly Georgy would return to it, it was something permanently in the old woman's mind.

Diamond had once said to Kitty—oh, she missed Kitty, she missed the whole atmosphere of the theatre, the chatter, the smell of greasepaint—"Do you think I would make a good wife? Would I like being married?"

"You'll have to forget that workhouse man first," said Kitty.

"I sometimes think I'll never meet anyone who could make me do so." Even as Diamond said these words she was back in the nightmare, with Mr. Vincent trying to crush her against him. In London, she had only endured the old man by a sheer effort of will. She had told herself that she was acting in a play, it was not real, it was like being murdered on the stage. Somehow she had removed herself so that it was only the shell of Clary Brown who lay beneath him and suffered his embraces. At the beginning, when he left her, she had vomited in disgust. After a time this ceased, but always when it was done, she felt unclean and revolted, and sometimes she was so exhausted that she could not even sleep. She never derived anything but nausea and torment from his love-making, and sometimes was amazed that he should not recognize this. If he had, he would surely never have come near her again. Sometimes she wondered if love and kindness might have rid her of her obsession, but then thought in dull depression that even if she fell in love—which so far had never happened to her—she would still be haunted by Mr. Vincent's putrefying ghost.

"I don't think," she said to Georgy, "I shall ever fall in love. Sometimes I even believe I'll never go to bed with a man again."

But Georgy paid no attention to such nonsense. What would a pretty girl like Miss Diamond be doing without a man? Indeed, she was already picturing her as Lady Diamond Axenford, with all the village bowing and becking before her. She did not say this, however, only primmed up her mouth as she scrubbed the rug and put the flowers in another vase.

Diamond slept badly that night, for all there were pretty curtains at the window and fresh-smelling linen on the bed. The wind had dropped, and there was no strange sound of singing from the church. Yet, as she tossed and turned, trying to pay no attention to Georgy's snores next door, she could only think, in a bewildered, resentful fashion, that this was no longer the village of her childhood. Then, until her father's cruel death, when the evil of the world was let loose upon her, it had seemed to her quiet and peaceful and sweet, with no tales of ladies dying from too much rouge, or old parsons murdered in their own church, and workhouses being burned down.

In the light of day she felt better, and really, the cottage was most charming. She was determined that morning to lay a ghost, and once again she dressed herself with great care, and and presently sailed forth, wearing a rather larger hat and a crimson wool dress that showed off to perfection her dark eyes and hair.

Georgy stood at the window, a duster in her hand, gazing after her young mistress who tripped so gracefully down the rough path, who had such an air to her that even small boys gaped at her in admiration.

Diamond was making for the ruined workhouse. She was too disturbed at the thought of seeing it again to trouble about making an impression on the village. She did not even hear Mrs. Rigg's soft, humble greeting, nor notice that curtains moved at the windows of the cottages she passed. When the deep, cracked voice spoke to her, she whirled round, startled. She was furious at such a self-betrayal, but the warnings of Sir Francis and Captain Ringham had made more impression on her than she wished to admit.

However, there was nothing alarming in the minute, upright old lady, with her snow-white hair and a face so wrinkled that it resembled a withered leaf. She hardly came up to Diamond's shoulder, but the eyes, of brightest blue, were fierce and keen, and the voice firm. She used a stick that she leaned on heavily, but there was a fighting independence in her stance that Diamond saw at once, liked and admired. But she did not at first recognize the woman, and she said as civilly as she could, "I beg your pardon, ma'am?"

"Well, it's Clary," said the old woman. "Such fine clothes too— But I'd be willing to wager you still can't read."

The color rushed to Diamond's face, and for a moment she resembled the little girl she had once been. Then she recovered herself, though her cheeks were still pink, and laughed. "You are Schoolmistress, aren't you?" he said as she might have done six years before. "You're almost the first person to recognize me. Most of the village hasn't the least idea who I am."

Miss Falconer replied, "Ah, but they look at the fine dress and the well-brushed hair under that ridiculous hat. I do not, young Clary. I look at the face, and it's the same face, though I must say it's a trifle cleaner than when I saw it last. So you have come back to us, have you? And are you leading a life of shame?"

"Miss Falconer!" Diamond, a little disconcerted, found herself stuttering, then began to laugh. The old woman—she had been old then, she must now be in her eighties—had always treated her like a human being, and there was a quality to her that had earned her pupils' respect and kept them quiet. Even now one felt that she could quell an insubordinate class, though she was so frail, a breath of wind might have keeled her over.

"So you do remember me after all, young Clary. Don't worry, child. Your secret is safe with me. I've never been a gossip," said Miss Falconer. "If you wish to play the fine lady, it makes no difference to me. Come inside, girl. That's my cottage there, though I daresay you'll not remember it. I'm too old to stand about in the cold, and I think you can spare me a few minutes. Why, I'll even offer you a glass of wine. Is that not what they do in high society?"

And so speaking, she limped across the street to a small cottage Diamond did not remember at all, pushed open the unlatched door, and motioned her to go into the parlor.

"So many books," said Diamond, astonished, as she looked about her. The air smelled of dust and parchment and leather, and she had to step over piles of books to reach a chair. She even had to push a couple of volumes off the seat before she could sit down. In the middle of the books sat a large cat, and Diamond, who liked cats, finding them civil, undemanding animals, held out her hand to it. At once it sprang onto her lap.

"So many books indeed," said Miss Falconer, apparently searching for the bottle of wine, and finding it at last half submerged under volumes of poetry. "And you, you poor, ignorant girl, cannot read one of them."

"I'm afraid that's true," said Diamond penitently, and she picked up the nearest book to hand and opened it. The pages were covered with what to her were simply black marks. Suddenly she longed to understand them. It seemed absurd and wrong that someone had spent his lifetime producing this, while to her it made less sense than the pattern of the stars in the sky.

"That is Hobbes' *Leviathan*," said Miss Falconer. "What does that mean to you?"

"Nothing at all, Miss Falconer."

"And are you not ashamed?"

"You know," said Diamond, "I think I am a little."

"I'm delighted to hear it. Where are those plaguey glasses?"

"I think they are in that corner over there," said Diamond. She felt, suddenly, about ten years old. "Behind those books in red leather."

"Those books in red leather, as you call them, are an edition of Chaucer's *Canterbury Tales*. I suppose that means nothing to you either. I do not imagine you have ever heard of him."

"No, Miss Falconer," said Diamond meekly, then began to laugh. To her surprise the old schoolmistress joined her, waving the bottle as she did so. An onlooker might have assumed the pair of them to be entirely drunk.

Presently, when the wine was poured out—it was acid and bad, but Diamond did not even notice—Miss Falconer said, "Now tell me all about your life of shame."

Diamond, raising her dark eyes to the blue ones, asked, "Why do you think I lead such a life?"

"Oh, I do not suppose you are a wicked girl," returned Miss Falconer, "and the cat likes you, which is something to your credit. But it is a fair assumption when a young female with no money and a gypsy father runs away from a workhouse. I am not blaming you for that, do not misunderstand me—Where am I?"

Diamond said calmly, "You were talking of a young female with no money."

"Ah yes. Yes. When such a young woman returns dressed in the height of fashion, and has our local gentry falling over themselves to help her, what else am I to assume? You are not married. You must have some means of support. Women in our day and age can become only governesses or whores, unless they marry, and perhaps marriage is a combination of both. I chose to be a teacher. You, I can only believe, preferred the second choice, which is not surprising in someone of your appearance. Surely you find my assumption reasonable."

"It's entirely reasonable," said Diamond.

"You always spoke well. I remember I used to be surprised. I daresay your father taught you."

"But," Diamond went on, "I am not a whore. At least I don't think I am."

"You do not seem very sure."

"Well"—this was really an extraordinary conversation, yet somehow it seemed quite natural—"well, perhaps I don't quite know what a whore is. I don't ply for hire," said Diamond, "and I don't lift my petticoat at street corners. But I did take myself a lover—a rich old man who meant nothing to me, except that I was starving and cold and without a roof over my head."

"I find that very sensible," said Miss Falconer. "I daresay I might in such circumstances have done the same, but I never had any looks and I was always too clever. The gentlemen used to run like hares at the sight and sound of me. So I took to teaching instead. I have never regretted it. But then, you were always a handsome girl."

"I think I was a poor sort of thing," said Diamond with a sigh.

"Oh no. Whatever you were, you were never that. Why have you come back, Clary?"

"I have been cast off," said Diamond, her hand caressing the purring cat. "My old man grew sick of me. I daresay he wanted a change. But he came from some old pedigreed family that went back to the dark ages, like your books, and gentlemen of his sort don't ditch their whores, they farm them out. He decided to send me home. I didn't like that at all. I never meant to come back here. It's changed, Schoolmistress. It ain't as I remember it. They say there's some odd goings-on here nowadays, and the story of Mr. Wall is terrible. Would you know anything about all this?"

"There's nothing wrong with my eyes and ears," said Miss Falconer.

"There's nothing wrong with mine either," said Diamond.

"Have a care, child."

"Oh, so they all say! What do they think will happen to me? Do you imagine that one day I'll be found in a ditch with my throat slit open?"

"It is not," said Miss Falconer in her most pedantic manner, "beyond the bounds of possibility."

"Oh," said Diamond quite pettishly, "I am growing sick of being warned off. 'Take care, don't peer and pry, it's nothing to do with you, don't walk abroad alone at nights . . .' What is all this? What's going on? It's that Captain Ringham, isn't it? I always hated him and I still do, for all he's furnished my cottage for me. Why did he do that? I think you know a lot more than you're admitting." Diamond jumped up from the chair, spilling Hob as she did so, and flung herself on her knees at Miss Falconer's feet. She paid no attention to the small pile of books she had just knocked over, only said coaxingly, "Oh, do tell me. Do!"

"Those books you have just thrown to the floor are the collected poems of John Donne. Have you no shame, girl, no consideration? He is worth all the village put together."

"I've never heard of him either," said Diamond, but she picked the books up and arranged them in a neat pile. She looked down at her dusty fingers. "He's a dirty sort of fellow, isn't he?"

"He was a genius," said Miss Falconer.

Diamond shrugged. "It don't seem to have got him very far. Why don't you answer me? I think you know all about everything."

"The things I know wouldn't be good for you."

Diamond, rising to her feet again, said, "You must have known Parson Wall."

She saw Miss Falconer's face become blank, then shrunken, as if the eyes had fallen back in her head. But the schoolteacher only said, "I'm an old woman and I grow easily tired. I'm asking you to go, Clary. I think I've had enough excitement for one day. But I'm asking you to come back sometime. Will you do that, or are you too fine a lady these days to trouble yourself with a retired schoolmarm?"

"I'm not really a fine lady at all," said Diamond, smiling back at her. "I'm as common as dirt. And of course I'll come back. I'll be back every day if you wish. I always liked you, Miss Falconer. You were nice to me. You treated me like a real person."

She moved toward the door, trying not to knock over any more books. Miss Falconer said, "I suppose I mustn't ask you where you're going now."

"I'll tell you," said Diamond. "There's no secret in it. I'm going to have a look at my workhouse. They tell me it's gutted by fire, but I'd like to see it again. I think I want to lay a ghost, a whole legion of ghosts. There's no harm in that, surely? It must be quite empty. I shall not stay there more than a few minutes. Where does Mr. Vincent live these days? I'd like to see him too. Oh, how I want to see him—"

"It will do you no good," said Miss Falconer. "I suppose if I say don't go, you simply won't listen to me."

"No," said Diamond a little sadly, "I shan't listen to you."

"Then there is no use in saying it."

Diamond opened the door, then hesitated. She said suddenly in a rush of words, "Miss Falconer, will you teach me to read?"

The old woman looked at her for a while in silence. Then

she said, "You'd better sit down again. I see I'm not to be rid of you so easily. Why do you want to learn? I offered to teach you a long time ago. You refused. What has made you change your mind?"

"I do not know," said Diamond. She spoke in a soft, flat voice. Her eyes were clouded. "I don't even quite know why I said it. I think I didn't mean to. You remember my pa, Miss Falconer?"

"A wrong-headed man," said Miss Falconer. "We used to argue a great deal. Whenever he came here, as he sometimes did to do odd jobs for me, we always fell into a discussion. He liked the sound of his own voice. I must admit that I found him more interesting to talk to than most other people in the village. But his views were often quite opposed to mine. He was an interesting man, Clary, though his morals were deplorable. Why are you smiling? With education he might have made something of himself, instead of loafing about with you and existing on nothing. But no one is interested in education these days. They have even shut down the school. Why are you suddenly so interested?"

"My pa," said Diamond with apparent irrelevance, "had what they call the sight. He saw things that were going to happen. He had a kind of pair of glasses for the future, if you know what I mean. He knew he would be hanged. Oh, I didn't really take it in, and when you're very young you don't think about death, especially with people you love, but he did say once—" She broke off, briefly closed her eyes. "He did say once he'd die at the end of a rope. Like a rabbit in a snare. He did die like that. Do you remember, Schoolmistress?"

"Yes, child, I remember."

"Captain Ringham hanged him."

"Why do you think that?"

"I don't think. I know. He's a justice. He was there at the hanging. It was his rabbit. But I don't mean to talk of that. I only wanted to say that sometimes I have the sight too. And when I said that just now about reading— Oh, I don't know, I cannot explain it, but it's important, almost as if my life might depend on it."

She looked a little defensively at Miss Falconer, as if half expecting her to laugh. But the old woman remained grave and silent, so she went on, "Of course, I'm only half of Romany stock. My mother wasn't a gypsy. I asked my father once who she was."

And she sighed and laughed, remembering his heartless reply.

"You killed her off, Clary," he had said, and she had scowled at him, saying, "How could I? I was only a baby."

"She was a traveling girl," he had said gravely. "She worked on one of the farms, for a while, to earn a few pennies. She came from London town. I liked her. She liked me. But I'm not the marrying kind, I doubt I'd have married her. And you came, Clary, and she died of it. I was sorry. But it would never have worked out. I could never stay with one woman all my life."

"You're staying with me," she had said determinedly.

He had grinned at her. "Am I? I'd not depend on it too much." Then he spoke of other things, and she forgot about it all.

She said now to Miss Falconer, "Did you know my mother?"

"No," said Miss Falconer. "There were a great many women, Clary. You must know that. I remember seeing him with you when you were a baby. He never told me who your mother was. He was a strange man, your father. He had a great power over women. I think he came so often to talk to me because he knew I would never fall in love with him."

"I don't know how you could help falling in love with him," said Diamond.

"That is a foolish thing to say. I have never had much time for men," said Miss Falconer. "Perhaps it is a pity, but it's too late now. Though when I see what can happen—I had a friend once. Oh, I think I may call her a friend, though she came from a class above mine. No, Clary. I am not talking of your mother. I tell you, I didn't know her. But my friend was most unhappily married, and she met your father when she was so desperate she would speak of taking her own life. I suppose it was what you would call romantic—moonlight and all that kind of nonsense. She was a well-bred young woman, she had never behaved in such a way in her life. Afterwards she could hardly believe it. But she had to tell someone, and she told me. I think it was most reprehensible, but there was no point in saying so."

Diamond said softly, "My pa had a way with him."

"Well, he certainly had a way with her," snapped Miss Falconer, "and it was a terrible thing to have done. She could not really have loved him; it was like a fit of moon-madness. I think I shall never understand my own sex, but then, I have never had much patience with folly."

"I understand it very well," said Diamond. Her eyes were shining. "I wish such a thing could happen to me."

Miss Falconer said sharply, "Oh, stuff and nonsense. I hope you will never behave like that."

"I hope one day I will."

"Then you are a remarkably foolish girl, and you don't know what you are talking about. What good did it do her? It ruined her marriage, and even if she had not been married, your father would certainly not have wed her."

"Did her husband find out?"

"She told him."

Diamond thought this was very silly, but did not say so. She said at last, "What happened to her, poor lady?"

"She is dead." Miss Falconer's voice was briefly like the tolling of a bell, then she said in her normal harsh tones, "It's the best thing that could have happened."

"I think that's a terrible thing to say."

"Oh, stop squeaking at me like a rabbity little chit! You're not on the boards now, miss. You're putting on airs, Clary. Your father was the kind of man who took his pleasure where he found it, and it was no matter to him if other people were ruined. Though in the end— Well, never mind that. The one thing I'll say in his favor was that he took charge of you. Whether this was to your advantage or not, I would not like to say."

Diamond did not answer this. She had grown aware that Miss Falconer's harsh words concealed a most tender heart and that this kind of remark signified nothing. But she could not help asking, "Who was this lady? Was it someone I knew?"

"That I am not telling you. What good would it do you to know?"

"Then I did know her!"

"Clary, you're too clever for your own good. We will not talk about it any more. There's no point in it. It's done, and that's the way it is. I do not know why I mentioned it at all. I think myself it was disgraceful, though of course to you, your father, your pa, as you call him—why do you use such an uneducated word?—was God, which he certainly was not. He was just a lecher like all men. And it's no good your making faces at me, miss. I know what I'm talking about."

"Have you really never been in love, Miss Falconer?" asked Diamond.

Miss Falconer only said, "I shall expect you here at eleven o'clock tomorrow morning, for your first lesson. Kindly be punctual. I will not endure tardiness in my pupils. And if, for once, you will take my advice, you will now go straight home instead of wandering about a burned-out workhouse, which will do you no good at all. Good morning," said Miss Falconer, and virtually shut the parlor door in Diamond's face.

❧ VIII ❧

Diamond had no intention of obeying the schoolteacher. She walked slowly toward the gaunt outline of the workhouse in the distance. It was ugly and frightening, a great blackened ruin silhouetted against the sky. She brooded on what Miss Falconer had told her, for a brief, foolish moment wondering if the old woman were herself the lady in question. But this was ridiculous; even then she must have been about seventy. It was, in any case, impossible to imagine her in such a wild and romantic situation. She always, ever since Diamond remembered her, had been old and tiny and burnt-up, with a razor-sharp tongue, a most damnably observant eye—especially for delinquents in the back row who were usually doing what they should not—and a passion for the books that took up all her spare time. Even in her extreme youth, Miss Falconer could never have been tumbled in the moonlight. More likely she would have recited poetry to her would-be lover, and chastised him with her ferule if he spoke out of turn.

Diamond saw, without much conviction, that women existed who were not ruled by their emotions. She could not really understand it, for though she had never fallen deeply in love, she had always loved or hated, been up in the skies one moment, at the bottom of the sea the next. Everything she did, she did with passion, bursting into frantic tears or laughing wildly, fiercely up in arms against injustice or flung down on her bed in deep depression. The academic mind was utterly alien to Diamond, yet she could appreciate Miss Falconer's kindness and sense of justice, and knew that the silly lady, whoever she was, who had succumbed to Pa's blandishments could have chosen a far worse confidante.

Certainly her father had never mentioned the woman,

though as she grew older she became aware that there were always women wherever they went. Indeed, Romany Brown had a way with him, a gentle, loving, laughing way, that sent little farm girls falling flat on their backs, only too willing to do whatever he wanted. Sometimes she grew jealous when he came back late. But to quarrel with Pa was like building with water, it was not possible. In the end she came to accept it all as one of the laws of nature. She was even proud of his successes, and on the rare occasions when she passed in the street a girl who she guessed had been in Pa's arms the night before, she would bestow on her a kind of conspiratorial smile, as if to say, "Is he not a wonderful man, and he is my father too." After all, he always came home to her, and it was natural enough that so handsome a man should make all women fall in love with him. And it was, as he might well have said himself, none of her business.

Now she found herself facing the blackened walls of the workhouse, and for the first time she felt that Miss Falconer was right in telling her to stay away, for the horror consumed her, brought the sickness up in her throat.

A little girl—a dark, skinny little girl with a white, pinched face and huge, shadowed, wary eyes. Getting up at five in the morning, never enough to eat, scrubbing, washing, picking cotton, sprigging muslin, and sometimes grinding down bones from the local slaughterhouse, so hungry that she would suck the scraps of meat still adhering to them. Constant beatings and abuse and filthy language, always insulted and humiliated, as if she were an animal, not a human being at all. And a creature, who seemed to her like a gorilla, pushing her against the wall, shoving his hand up her skirts, trying to force her down on the floor. It was the cold and the dirt and the fear and the squalor that had given her the terrible feeling that her suffering must go on for all eternity, that there was no way out. The ultimate dream was not so much freedom or warmth or being able to do what one wanted, it was simply food, platefuls and platefuls of hot, lovely, delicious-smelling food, so that one could eat till one burst.

Diamond spoke a word aloud, a word she had learned from the Covent Garden gutters and which did no credit to her fine gown and admirably pinned-on hat. Then she gathered her skirts about her and stepped over the threshold of what had once been a forbidding, clanging door, into the blackened, roofless space that had been the dining room, Mr. Vincent's office and private rooms combined. But the inner walls were gone as well as the roof, and there was nothing left but a floor littered with charred remnants of furniture, the gaping windows like eye-sockets and the cold grey sky overhead.

Only at the back, where Lady Caroline's theatre had stood, was a wall left standing. However the blaze had started, there must have been little hope of escape for anyone in the front. Diamond, shuddering, icy cold, could picture the children running like mice, screaming, panic-stricken, with no one to help them. She whispered "Oh God," and felt so ill that she had to lean against a charred and splintered post. Then she realized that it was all that was left of the wall of Mr. Vincent's private apartment, where he had lived with his little daughter, Maria, and she could not bear even so small a contamination. She ran to the other side of the building, ran as the children must have run, in blind terror.

At last she recovered herself, and still a little dizzy, made her way toward the theatre. She thought as she went that it had not, after all, been so bad. Nothing was bad all the time. It was true that they had been half starved, overworked, wretchedly dressed, ill-treated, but they were young and resilient, they made friends with each other, lied like the devil to protect themselves, and like prisoners, learned to talk to each other without moving their lips. In the dismal crocodile they had formed when they walked to church, with Matron at the head, they moved stiffly, like little automata, staring down at the ground, saying rude things to each other under their breath, juxtaposed with respectable remarks: "Yes, Mr. Vincent, of course, sir, you bloody old bastard." Occasionally they would get the giggles, just like ordinary children, and their friends would try frantically to cover up for them, even sometimes pretending to lose their footing and falling flat on their faces so that the giggler was forgotten in the general crisis. There had been some toadies and tell-tales, for people such as Mr. Vincent encouraged spying, but there were still loyal friends. Diamond thought of a skinny little redhead called Rebecca, who sometimes, when life was unbearable, risked a beating by creeping into her bed at night, where they snuggled up to each other, pouring out their desolate hearts.

"I hope Rebecca escaped," Diamond said aloud. She really must stop talking to herself, but the smell of burning, the cold around her, the dreadful cold of an extinguished fire, made her feel so lonely that even the sound of her own voice was a comfort. "Oh, Becky," she said again, addressing the little ghost to whom she had said so tearful a goodbye six years ago, "I hope you escaped. I hope you are free and happy."

Diamond slowly walked through the filthy, blackened desolation into the theatre with its velvet curtains by the side door and the raised dais at the other end: a miniature theatre with small oval stage, the backless benches of the pit and the back boxes covered in green cloth.

Lady Caroline had persuaded Sir Francis to have the theatre built. "Let the children act," she had told Mr. Vincent, who, with his dish-clout face, was bowing and becking: Yes, my lady, of course, my lady, so generous of you, my lady. "It will keep them out of mischief," she had said, "and who knows but one day one of them will be a celebrated actress. Think how proud you'll be. You can say, 'She might never have been on the stage but for me.' "

The children had all listened. They knew it would not happen, but it sounded so wonderful. They huddled together, their eyes on Lady Caroline in her bright silky clothes, waving her ringed hands so elegantly, smelling of such lovely perfume. Mr. Vincent, the bloody old hypocrite, was smiling fit to burst his face, and Matron, who always looked like an ill-made pair of stiff stays, even patted one of the children on the head to show how she loved them all. The moment her ladyship was gone, she would be dealing out slaps and pinches as to the manner born. It was all a play, purely for public performance.

There never was any acting in that theatre, only once a recital in which Lady Caroline stood on the stage all by herself, speaking the words of someone called William Shakespeare. Nobody had heard of Shakespeare, nobody understood one word of what she was saying, but it was new and exciting, even though the only person on the stage was a poor little rich lady with a funny painted face who spoke so oddly and waved her arms about. When it was over, they all clapped like a volley of stones, and she smiled at them and made them a vast curtsy, her petticoats billowing out. Then there were little cakes for everyone, baked by the cook at Axenford. This was worth the whole show put together.

Sir Francis had sat with the children, watching his wife perform. Local gossip had it that after he had met Lady Caroline and fallen in love with her, he had told her—this was what Middleditch had said, nobody really knew the truth—that he could not have a wife on the stage; if she was to become mistress of Axenford, she must never act again.

Diamond looked about her now with love and longing. A passion of regret for Drury Lane swept over her. She would never act again, she had never really acted at all. She knew perfectly well that she had no enduring talent, but oh God, oh Christ, how she missed it. The memories crowded in on her as she stepped onto the stage—she could almost hear the audience, the wicked hooting that could damn a performance, the wonderful silence that was better than any applause.

She swept a curtsy to the empty auditorium. The stage was peopled with shadows. The young actor who always sucked his wrist as he spoke. Mr. Woodward, overviolent as Petruchio, hurling Kate to the floor, so that she badly bruised her leg. Kitty, with her air of infantile innocence and simplicity, playing the Country Wife, or strutting in her hose and trunks as Captain Wildair. The insolent young blade who slid behind the scenes and planted a kiss on Diamond's neck, for which he received a resounding slap across the cheek. The paid puffs who cheered and laughed and shouted, usually in the wrong place. The naughty Mrs. Abington, with her trick of turning her wrist and seeming to stick a pin inside her waistband. The lady who laughed loudly, while twirling an orange on her finger, during the poison scene in *Romeo and Juliet*. And the poor Cleopatra who caught half a kettledrum in the train of her dress during the asp scene.

Diamond began to speak, her voice shaking with nerves, as if she really were making some important appearance. She began, " 'Men have died from time to time, and worms have eaten them, but not for love,' " then broke off, it was too high. She started again on a lower key, but stopped after the first three words.

She was not alone. The shadows slid away, there was nothing there but dust and silence, but she knew she was being watched for all there was not a sound. She gave a gasp of fear and swung round, her eyes moving frantically over the empty benches, the unlit stage, that door still open, which led to what remained of the front building.

There was not a whisper. There was not a flicker of movement. There was nothing but Clary Brown, standing in the middle of the stage, speaking her lines, rather badly, to workhouse ghosts. Yet there was someone, someone silent and still, who watched and listened.

"Who's there?" Diamond called out in the clarion voice that was her one real acting asset; but she was terribly frightened, and it cracked into dissonance.

There was no answer. The silence hummed in her ears.

Diamond, shaking, called out again, hysterically, "Who is there?" Then, in the fury of panic, "I know you're there. I heard you. You're spying on me. Who are you? What are you doing here? What do you want?" Then, almost in tears, "Oh, why don't you show yourself? This isn't a game—"

And she began to run round the theatre, banging on the walls, looking under the benches, even reaching into the boxes. And there was no one, no one at all, only once it seemed to her that the cloth over the dais moved almost imperceptibly, and crying now in her fear, she sprang on it and gave it a violent tug.

There was nothing underneath but the flat wood. To the side, behind the velvet curtains, there was the little door that led into the woods, but Diamond, swearing at her own cowardice, could not bring herself to open it. She was standing stark-still now, her head a little on one side so as to listen more intently, and then she knew that whoever it was had moved away. She was alone.

Then she could bear it no longer. She gathered up her skirts and ran like a hare, banging the theatre door behind her, almost falling over the piled-up debris. She did not so much as pause for breath until she had leaped over the high front doorstep, and stood shaking and panting in the cold September afternoon of Middleditch.

The sweat was pouring down her, despite the cold. Her hat

was lopsided and she had torn her dress on a piece of splintered wood. She muttered "Oh God!" and put her gloved hands up to her eyes. The gloves were soiled from the charred walls, and left black streaks on her cheeks. She stood there, struggling for self-control, wishing that she had never come, thinking that never, never would she set foot here again, when a deep, rough voice smashed down on her, shot her hands away from her face, and brought her swinging round, scarlet and indignant.

"What the devil are you doing here?" demanded Captain Ringham, and indeed he would hardly have spoken to his dog in such a voice. Perhaps this was the way he addressed his servants, no doubt it was so that he had spoken to Pa when he had him taken away.

Nothing could have restored Diamond more. She could never endure being shouted at, and she was damned if she was going to be abused by this abominable man who represented everything that she detested and feared. She was perfectly aware that she was not looking her best, and she instinctively righted her hat and pushed back the damp wisps of hair that had fallen across her cheek. In doing so, she added another black mark to her face, this time on her nose, but fortunately was not aware of it. She looked haughtily up at Captain Ringham and could not help wondering why he was in such a temper, for whatever grand illusions he had of himself, he could not regard himself as her keeper. If she chose to visit a burned-out workhouse, it was surely no business of his.

His next words showed only too clearly that he considered it was. She wondered irrelevantly how he treated his half brother, Philip, who had so ill-used Sir Francis' race horse. The captain had apparently been out riding himself; she could see his horse tethered to the post that was all that remained of the original gateway.

"I thought," he said, his face black with temper, "that I told you not to pry. I knew, of course, that you wouldn't listen to me. Your kind never does. What are you doing here? You've been inside. I can see that. Your face needs washing." Then before she could begin to answer, her whole body now taut with rage, he asked, "Did you go inside the theatre?"

Diamond, too furious to adopt any airs and graces, answered

him in a most unladylike squawl of rage. "What I do is my affair. Yes, I did go inside the theatre. Why shouldn't I? What's it to do with you? You seem to have some strange idea, Captain Ringham, that you are responsible for me—"

"I am not, thank God," he said. He was actually smiling.

Diamond longed to smack the smile from his face, but restrained herself just in time. "Then I suggest you remember it and stop ordering me about," she said, managing at last to lower her voice. But by now, of course, it was too late, as his smile told her well enough, and she dug her nails into the palms of her hands in an effort to control herself. "I think," she said, "that this time you can listen to me."

"I'm listening," he said.

"I do precisely what I please. If I choose to go inside a ruined building, I will do so, and if I wish to take a look at Lady Caroline's theatre, I will do so. You seem to think that because you threw a lot of your castoff furniture at me, I owe you some kind of deference. Well," cried Diamond—oh, Georgy would be dreadfully upset, and perhaps it was true, she was hardly distinguishing herself—"you can take back all your damned furniture and everything else. And you can make yourself sick on rabbit stew, for all I care. I never want any of your horrid gifts again. Only leave me alone! I will not be followed around like this—" She broke off, painfully aware of the tears that were springing to her eyes, then said in a whisper, "It was you who followed me into the theatre. Wasn't it? Oh, it must have been . . ."

He did not answer. Instead he strode up to her and seized her by the arm. She gave an outraged cry and raised her hand, but he caught at her wrist, so that she was completely helpless, pinioned against one blackened wall. And suddenly the hideous memory that she struggled so hard to forget returned to her: it was no longer Captain Ringham's angry but undeniably handsome face that glowered down into hers, but another, a dish-clout face, with piggish eyes and a great wide, wet, lascivious mouth.

Diamond closed her eyes. From a remote distance she became aware that the hold on her arm had relaxed. A startled, rather muted voice said, "Miss Diamond, what the devil is the matter with you? If I have hurt you, I can only apologize, but you really are most damnably exasperating."

"I am perfectly well, thank you," said Diamond, opening her eyes. "I have no doubt," she went on, in impeccably ladylike tones, "that you do not know your own strength." She rubbed at her wrist as she spoke, thinking that all this gave her the advantage. He was now standing a little away from her. She could not see him very well, for her vision was still blurred, but she had to admit that it seemed as if he were laughing at her instead of being abashed, as any gentleman should be. She said, "If you will forgive me, I must now return home."

She tried to move, but he blocked her way. He said, "God knows what all this nonsense is about, but now you, madam, are going to listen to me."

Diamond exclaimed, "Oh, surely, sir, there's been enough of this. You—you knock me down, you bruise my arm, you frighten me to death—and after all that I am supposed to listen to you. I'm not going to be so bullied. What are you, Captain Ringham?" demanded Diamond, now well away, stamping the boards, waiting for the pit's cheering. "Are you lord of the manor or something? If you are, I refuse to recognize it. At least Sir Francis has good manners, and he has a bigger house than yours, and I'm sure he's more important, but he don't order me about. I want to go home. Kindly let me pass."

Captain Ringham, his voice very quiet, said, "In a moment, ma'am. There is just one thing, and you will kindly answer me, now that the barnstorming is done."

"*Oh!*" cried Diamond in a hiss of rage, and tried to push past him. But she might as well have hurled herself against a rock, for he did not budge, and she found herself almost pressed against him again, her face some six inches below his, her eyes moving wildly sideways, caught in his contemptuous gaze.

He said in the same quiet tone, "You asked me if I followed you into the theatre. That is what you said, is it not?"

Diamond was too confused with all that had happened to take his meaning immediately. She cried out, "Yes, I did. You accuse me of spying, but it seems that you are the spy—" Then, too late, she realized where this was leading, and fell silent.

He said very softly, "You saw someone in the theatre."

"No, I did not! If you will please let me—"

"Then you heard someone."

"No, I—" Then Diamond burst out, "It was probably a rat. The place is empty and horrid. There are bound to be rats there, especially after the fire. I didn't see anyone, I really didn't. I just had the feeling that someone was there, watching me. I daresay it was just imagination. It's not a nice place. It has memories—" She broke off, twisting her hands together. Then she went on in a more bright and social way, "I was curious to have a look at it. I've never been in a workhouse before, and it's odd to have a theatre in such a place. It's quite a natural thing to do. There's no door left, so I just stepped in, and then went into the theatre. I can't see any harm in it. Anyone would have done the same. Why does it make you so angry? Why are you asking me all these questions?"

"And you are sure you saw nothing?"

"I've just told you. May I go now, please?"

"I have already found you to be a liar, Miss Diamond."

"How dare you!"

"I can only hope that in this case you are telling the truth. Now listen, please. No. Don't make those damned silly faces at me. They don't impress me at all. For once stop chattering, and listen instead. This village is no longer a happy place. Things have happened here—"

"So I have already heard, several times," said Diamond, bright-eyed. "It is so strange the things one hears. It wasn't like this when I visited it last. People seem to die horrid deaths and graves are so untidy, and poor old Parson— Oh, this is indeed an odd place, Captain Ringham, and it interests me very much. I never expected so much excitement. And I like to know what's happening. There's no harm in that, surely?"

His face was so set that she grew frightened. Perhaps it was unwise to bait so bad-tempered a man. She wished now that she had held her tongue. She said quickly, in an airy fashion that she suspected was not convincing, "But of course it's probably just all talk. I daresay it's as boring here as anywhere else. Indeed, I hope that soon I shall return to London. My mind is still inclined to the stage, and London is really what I dote on. To be forced to live in the country is, so they say, the worst fate for women of fashion."

He brushed this all aside as the fantasy that it certainly was. He said harshly, "Listen to me, Miss Diamond. There is no time for all this theatre, and it doesn't impress me. For one who has been here a mere two days, you seem to have pried and spied most effectively. It must stop at once. For your own sake."

"Are you threatening me, Captain Ringham?" Diamond had by now recovered herself. She pushed a tendril of hair behind her ear and pursed her lips a little as she did so.

He said, "If you choose to take it like that—I would prefer to say that I am warning you. Go back to London, by all means. Nothing would please me better, and I would even lend you my carriage to get you there. But whatever you do, for God's sake stop sticking your dirty little nose into what doesn't concern you."

"My dirty little—!" began Diamond, outraged, but he cut across this impatiently, saying, "You have half the filth from the building on your face. Why will you not listen to me? You seem to realize well enough that there are strange happenings here. God knows, that's true."

"Nothing to do with you, of course," said Diamond. She was rapidly forgetting all the manners she had trained herself to practice, but then, not for a long time had she been spoken to in such a fashion.

He ignored this. He said sternly, "There is danger here." Then he added, as if he could endure it no longer, "And if you don't take that silly smile off your face, I swear—"

He broke off as if he were swallowing a bone, and Diamond, moving back now that she was no longer enclosed, said icily, "I really must be on my way, Captain Ringham. My maid will be wondering what has happened to me. She does so worry about me, the dear thing— So devoted, you know."

"When you talk like that," said Captain Ringham, who really had less manners than anyone she had ever met, "I want to shake you, and indeed, if it would force some sense into you, I would do so this minute. Why do you not listen to me, you stupid little bitch?"

"Good afternoon," said Diamond, but he caught at her wrist again, so that she could not move away without an undignified struggle.

"Do you not know what the word 'danger' means?" he said.

"I refuse to believe," said Diamond, "that there is the least danger in Middleditch. You just want to frighten me away. And," she said, forgetting all caution in her temper, "As I told you, I have every intention of going where I please, doing what I please, and exploring anything that interests me. May I go now?"

He said stonily, "I will accompany you."

"Oh, nonsense! Surely," cried Diamond, "I am permitted to walk the few hundred yards to my own cottage. Really, this is all becoming too absurd. I think you must be either mad or drunk."

And with this broadside she began to walk away from the workhouse, moving more swiftly than was entirely elegant, quickening her speed so that she was almost running. She heard the hound of horses' hoofs, and the next moment found herself seized round the waist and picked up as if she were a sack of potatoes. Then, before she realized what was happening, she was seated precariously in front of the saddle, her petticoated legs swinging helplessly against the animal's flanks.

She wanted to scream and swear as little Clary Brown would have done years ago. Before she could check herself, she hissed at him, "You son of a whore!" He burst out laughing, and she could have killed both herself and him. Tears of impotent fury sprang to her eyes, but she managed after that unhappy outburst to remain silent; indeed, she was so terrified of falling off, she was compelled to brace herself against Captain Ringham's restraining arm. She had never, after all, been on a horse in her life.

When they arrived at the foot of the path that led to the cottage, he deposited her on the ground. He was still laughing, and she longed passionately to crack her hand across his face. Her breast was heaving as she turned her back on him and began to walk up the path, so frenzied with temper that she tripped over a loose stone and nearly fell her length. He called after her, as he turned his horse in the direction of the Hall, "If you so dislike the furniture, Miss Diamond, you can dump it outside the door, and I will instruct one of my men to move it tomorrow morning. It will only be thrown away. As you have intimated, I myself have no need of it." Then he touched his hat to her with what was plainly a derisory gesture, and the next moment was vanishing down Middleditch's main street.

Diamond, her mouth as tight as a piece of string, stepped into the cottage, to be greeted by Georgy with a mixture of enthusiasm and disapproval.

"Miss Diamond!" she exclaimed. "What has happened to you? Your hat is all crooked and your face is filthy— Was that the captain I heard just now?"

"It was indeed," said Diamond, pulling her hat off so violently that all her hair came down. She hurled the hat to the floor. She wanted more than anything to throw herself after it and scream and drum her heels, for the temper was almost bursting her asunder, but she only walked to the window, where she stood, breathing heavily, her hands tightly clenched together.

"All the gentlemen are after you," said Georgy, then, in a conspiratorial voice, "Sir Francis called half an hour ago. I'm glad he didn't see you in such a pickle. Miss Diamond, are you listening to me?"

"Yes, I'm listening," said Diamond, without turning. She repeated in a tight voice, "Sir Francis called half an hour ago."

"He left a note for you."

"What use is that to me? I am just a poor ignorant girl," said Diamond savagely. "I cannot read."

"He told me it was an invitation to dinner. For tomorrow evening. He will be sending his carriage for you. Surely," said Georgy with some exasperation, for really, Miss Diamond sometimes behaved like a spoiled child, "you're pleased. I think it's quite an honor. I knew he was taken with you. I told you so at the time."

She picked up the maltreated hat and tried to smooth out the feathers, tut-tutting as she did so, for it would need a hot iron to restore them.

Diamond said, "I am going to put all the furniture out on the path."

"Oh, Miss Diamond, don't be so silly!"

But Diamond turned from the window, and to Georgy's

horror, seized one of the smaller chairs, rolled it to the door, and with all the strength that was in her, sent it hurtling down the path.

It landed with a flurry of pebbles and a great crash.

Georgy gazed at her speechlessly, and Diamond, after a feeble tug at the heavy table, burst into a howling flood of tears, fell into one of the armchairs, and buried her face in her arms.

This at least Georgy knew how to cope with. Thankful that the crisis was over, for she knew her mistress well enough to see that the fury was done, she at once brought her a glass of wine, patted her on the shoulder, and waited for the crying to stop.

Diamond said presently, in a choked voice, "I can't do it. It's too heavy."

"It's all the furniture we've got," said Georgy. She gazed out the window. She could just see a leg of the chair sticking up from the roadway.

Diamond exclaimed weakly, for the strength was gone from her, "Oh, how I hate him, hate him, hate him! I'll get even with him for this, if it's the last thing I do." Then she pushed back her untidy hair, which had fallen over her face, and said more cheerfully, "What's for dinner, Georgy? I swear my belly is aching for food."

✖❧ IX ❧✖

Diamond set off next morning for her first lesson with Miss Falconer, Sir Francis's letter in her reticule. She saw that the chair outside had disappeared. She did not mention the matter again, but she had to admit to herself that her behavior had been appalling. Her cheeks flushed as she remembered the gutter-term she had flung at Captain Ringham; it was the kind of thing a bully-boy would say in a tavern brawl, not at all an epithet to be used by a genteel young lady. She wished, too, that she had not thrown the chair out. It was stupid and childish, and as Georgy had remarked, the castoff furniture was all they had. No doubt it would amuse Captain Ringham to have everything carted away again, but Diamond knew only too well that she had by now been spoiled for luxury. She could not bear the prospect of living in the cottage as it had been when they arrived. She ignored, therefore, Georgy's inquisitive eyes and mouth half open to ask questions, and decided that she would tell some of her story to Miss Falconer, whose advice woulld at least be sensible. The old schoolmistress had lived in the village longer than anyone else, and certainly she could be trusted. It might be well not to consult anyone else, not even Sir Francis.

It seemed to her, as she turned up the little muddy lane that led to Miss Falconer's cottage, that Middleditch wore a faintly sinister air. She met no one, not even Mrs. Rigg, and it suddenly struck her as strange that she saw no children either; indeed, had hardly met a child since her arrival. In the old days the village had teemed with dirty red-cheeked children, playing in the gutters, scrambling over the walls, catcalling sometimes at the wretched little crocodile of workhouse girls.

But now the street was silent except for the occasional sound of voices within the cottages. Perhaps the children were at some school in the next village, now that the little schoolhouse was closed.

As she came up to Miss Falconer's door, she paused for a moment to smooth her hair and make sure that her gloves were buttoned. She smiled at herself as she did so, for this was Clary Brown, confronted with authority, wishing to make a good impression. Certainly there was nothing awe-inspiring about the cottage. The walls were flaking and one of the windows was cracked. The garden was almost overgrown with weeds; the only carefully tended place was a small plot of herbs in the far corner. I must ask her to dinner one evening, thought Diamond, overcome with compassion. The poor old soul probably don't bother to eat. And as she visualized herself and Georgy filling the old lady up with rabbit stew, she saw that she was being observed from the top of the lane.

She swung around, her heart pounding, then was furious with herself. What was the matter with her to be so afraid in broad daylight, just because Captain Ringham chose to spin her his witch's tales? She only had to call out once, and the whole village would come running. After all, it was nothing more alarming than a young boy of perhaps twelve or thirteen years of age.

He was a handsome, well-set-up lad, with a face that was vaguely familiar, and Diamond, noting this, the good quality of his clothes and the fact that he wore the air of one accustomed to having his own way, knew who he must be.

She said, "Good morning, Master Philip."

He did not answer. He did not move either, only stood there, staring at her. Certainly he had no manners. No doubt Captain Ringham had already referred to her as an interfering bitch, and the boy had been instructed to treat her with contempt. Diamond decided she was not going to be set down by this silly child. She took a step toward him. She said, "And how is your brother today? Aren't you going to speak to me? My name is Diamond Browne. I am living in the cottage on the hill." Then she added derisively, flickering her lashes at him, "Why don't you call in one afternoon? Georgy will bake a nice sweet cake for you."

He stepped up the lane toward her, saying sullenly, "I'm not a baby. And I know very well who you are, thank you."

Diamond heard Miss Falconer's voice calling out, "Are you not coming in, Clary?"

Philip said, "Why does she call you Clary?"

Miss Falconer must have been standing in the doorway; no doubt she had heard this ill-bred exchange. Diamond, a little disconcerted, and making no attempt to answer the boy's question, stepped quickly into the hall. As she did so, Philip rushed up the path, pushed a box into Miss Falconer's hands, and ran away again.

"I gather," said Diamond, very ladylike, "that that is Captain Ringham's brother."

Miss Falconer gave her a look that consigned her to the corner, preferably with a dunce's cap upon her head. "There is nothing wrong with Philip," she said.

"That is not what Sir Francis says," said Diamond, piqued.

Miss Falconer was opening the parcel. It contained a dozen eggs. She laid the box on the hall table, saying, "One of the advantages of an education is to teach you not to believe everything you hear, nor to judge entirely by appearances."

"I do not like Captain Ringham," said Diamond, following her into the book-lined parlor.

"So I understand," said Miss Falconer. Her bright blue eyes moved over Diamond's face, which began to color up.

"I suppose everything is talked about here."

"Villages always gossip."

Diamond could only hope that her quarrel with Captain Ringham had not been heard by everyone, but as they had both been shouting, she did not feel very hopeful. A lady screaming gutter abuse would be news anywhere. She sat down and said, almost pleadingly, "I have my reasons, after all. You know that. You of all people must know that."

"At least," said Miss Falconer, opening a book on her knee, "you cannot blame Philip for that. When all that happened, he was only a small child. He is a good boy. I have known him all his life. You have been here only a few days."

"I was born here!"

"Yes, so you were, Clary, but a great many things have changed since you left Middleditch. It was, after all, six years ago. You have changed too, but in some ways you are very much the same. You were always a know-all child, disposed to meddle in what did not concern you."

"Oh," cried Diamond in exasperation, "surely you are not going to start all that nonsense about spying. I have done nothing wrong. Nothing at all. Only, wherever I go, there seem to be odd things happening, and of course I become curious. I'm human, I want to know. You must realize that there is something odd going on. You said so yourself when we met yesterday. And I'm on my own here, I have not much to do. It is surely natural that—"

"You can spare me the oration," said Miss Falconer severely. "At this moment you have work to do. Your first lessson in reading and writing. May I suggest, Clary, that you stop talking and listen to me."

"But," began Diamond, "I want to ask you something—"

"When we have finished the lesson. Now. We will start with the alphabet, capital letters."

Diamond, once she had swallowed her resentment at being treated like a child again, found that not only was Miss Falconer an excellent teacher, but she herself had not lost her quickness in learning. She learned her alphabet within the hour, wrote it out to the schoolmistress' satisfaction, and even started her first piece of reading. It was true that it was simply an illustrated children's book more suitable for a six-year-old, but she was flushed with the excitement of it all, did not once look at the clock ticking away on the mantelpiece, and was delighted when Miss Falconer said, "That is very good, Clary. Very good indeed. You were always a bright child. I am glad to see that the London theatre has not impaired your faculties. Now, I wish you to do some homework for me. You will write out all your capital letters, and you will try to make a few simple words for me."

Diamond nodded, saying, "Oh, I am enjoying myself. How long do you think it will take before I can write and read a letter?"

"That depends entirely on you. If you work as well as you have done today, it should not take so very long. They say that children learn more easily than grownups, but I believe that when an adult person turns his mind to education, he can make quicker and better progress. A child learns like a parrot; an adult assimilates what he learns. Now I will give you a glass of wine, and you may ask me what you please."

"Well, first," said Diamond, a little pink in the cheeks, "I have received an invitation to dinner from Sir Francis Axenford. For tomorrow."

She believed that she saw Miss Falconer's countenance change, and looked at her, startled, breaking off her remarks. But the schoolmistress said nothing, so she went on, "Of course I can't read it. I have got it here so that you can read it to me. And I think it is the thing in polite society to send a reply. If it is not asking too much of you, would you answer it for me, and I will get one of the children to deliver it to Axenford."

Miss Falconer still made no comment, but took the note from Diamond's hand. She read out in her precise way:

"My dear Miss Diamond,

It would give me great pleasure if you would dine with me tomorrow evening at Axenford. It will be an entirely informal occasion, and, I trust, the first of many. I will send my carriage for you at eight o'clock, and will naturally see that you are conducted home at whatever hour you please. I was most touched by your kind remarks about my poor dead wife, for it is in such things that the departed live. I should be greatly honored if you could find time to accept my invitation.

"He signs it 'Your affectionate servant,' with his full name," said Miss Falconer, handing the note back to Diamond, "and you will see that the paper bears his crest. The Axenfords have lived here for a long time. They are, so I understand, of German origin, and came to Middleditch in the fifteenth century."

Diamond, aware of some undercurrent that she did not understand, said, "You think I am right in accepting? I very much want to go, and nobody has ever written me such a letter before." Then she laughed, and her voice became more natural. "I am not a lady, Schoolmistress. I am a charity child and a bastard. I've learned to act the lady—" She faltered as she said this, remembering that occasion outside the workhouse, then went on, "I've learned to dress like one, too. At least I hope I have."

"You dress with good taste."

"I do my best. The old man—my old man who made me his mistress—he trained me. He was always so angry when I chose the wrong things. I was very young then, you will understand."

Miss Falconer glanced at the beautiful face, but if she thought that it was a face men might desire with passion, she did not say so.

Diamond, unaware of the scrutiny, went on, "I would not be so foolish now, but I did so love bright colors. I remember how one day I chose a scarlet shawl, and he snatched it from me and threw it in the fire. It made me cry, but I never did anything like it again." She added reflectively, "He was generous to me in his own way. I never loved him, and he certainly did not love me. I think for him I was a new toy, and he liked to buy clothes and jewelry for me. You see," she said with a smile, "I have expensive tastes, Schoolmistress. I like silks and satins, so I shall have to find someone with a great deal of money."

"You are not, I hope," said Miss Falconer, "dreaming of marrying Sir Francis."

"Oh no. Of course not. My old Georgy, she would marry me off to anyone, but though I like him extremely, he is far too old. He's old enough to be my father," said Diamond. Then she said, "I do not believe I'll ever marry."

"Fiddle!" said Miss Falconer.

"Oh, I have reasons for saying that." Diamond hesitated, then decided against any further explanation. Miss Falconer was a wise woman, and doubtless she knew a great deal about human nature, but the story of Mr. Vincent was somewhat not suitable for her ears. She went on quickly, "Poor Sir Francis. He must feel so sad about his wife, and so lonely. You think I may accept?"

"You are become very conventional, Clary. Yes, you may accept. If I forbade you, I do not suppose you would listen to me. I will pen your little note for you and see that it is delivered. Does Sir Francis not know what a lazy, ignorant girl you are?"

"Yes. He knows my real name, too."

Once again that indefinable expression crossed Miss Falconer's face. She said sharply, "Did you tell him?"

"I think he recognized me, but yes, I did tell him. I wanted someone to know. It was somehow like being a character in a play. I didn't feel real." Diamond added, "but I've told no one else. And certainly not Captain Ringham. If he knew I was the daughter of the man he hanged— One day I'll tell him. But in my own good time."

"You are overswift in your judgments, Clary. You view everything with passion. Passion provides a poor kind of spectacles. You must learn to be more detached, and you should know by this time that revenge is useless."

"I think of nothing else!"

"Then you are very foolish."

Diamond's mouth set in a hard line. She was thinking that Miss Falconer was an old woman who had never had a man. She could not possibly understand. After a pause she went on, "I was so sad to hear about Lady Caroline. She was very kind to me. I loved her— Miss Falconer, I said I wanted to ask you something. I'd like to do so very much. You accuse me of prying, and so does Captain Ringham, but it's something that happened yesterday, and I wasn't expecting it, it frightened me. I am hoping you might be able to explain it."

"I will do my best," said Miss Falconer, "but you must remember I am very old, and nowadays I live with only my books for company. And of course my Hob." She stroked the cat, who was sitting on her knee, running her hand through the soft, silky fur.

"I was terribly afraid," said Diamond, and at the memory of it her voice quavered. "I am ashamed of my cowardice, but I couldn't help it. I think I was more frightened than I have ever been in my life. And it's all so silly, because nothing really happened at all."

"Next time you feel frightened," said Miss Falconer calmly, "I will prepare you one of my herbal drinks to soothe you. Now tell me about it. You should develop a more precise way of speaking. You have started at the end. Why not begin at the beginning? It is not customary to start the alphabet with the letter 'Z.'"

"I went back to the workhouse," said Diamond, looking down at the hands twisted together in her lap. "I know you told me not to, but somehow I had to. I know I was wretched there, but it was part of me, I lived there for quite a long time, I had friends there. I heard that the theatre was untouched by the fire, so I walked through what was left of the place. That was quite horrid, it was like being somewhere that's haunted. Then I came into the theatre. And it was just as I remembered it, only of course it was smaller, everything seems smaller when you're older. I don't know why. And— oh, how silly it sounds, but I couldn't stop myself—I stepped onto the stage and began reciting something. I think it was from *As You Like It*. It was like being back in Drury Lane, I could almost see and hear the audience. And then—" Diamond reached forward for Miss Falconer's hand. "Oh, ma'am, there was someone there. I know there was. Someone watching and listening. I was so frightened. I couldn't see anything, but one of the curtains moved a little, and there was no wind. There are no windows in the theatre, and it must have meant that someone opened the side door. I managed to call out. I said, 'Who's there?' But there was no answer, and then I think whoever it was moved away, because I no longer had the feeling I was being watched. You don't think I'm making this up, do you? I swear I'm not. Who could it have been? Do you know? Oh, I think by your face you do—"

For it seemed to her that Miss Falconer had grown pale, and she had suddenly closed the blue eyes. But she said firmly, "No, I do not know. I have not the faintest idea who it could be. But I do know this, young Clary Brown. You must never go there again."

"But why? I'm not hurting anyone."

"You may be hurting yourself. You must stop this investigation of yours instanter. Captain Ringham is perfectly right, you are simply running headlong into danger. And you can take that mulish look off your face, miss. I am talking good sense, and you know it."

"You are treating me as if I were a child."

"You're behaving as if you were a child."

Seeing Diamond's stubborn expression, Miss Falconer did not pursue the matter, and presently Diamond said, "I must go.

I am taking up too much of your time. But I would like to ask you one more thing. Well, two things, really. I had a friend when I was in the workhouse. She was my best friend, and we loved each other very much. I know she came from somewhere near here. Perhaps you know what's become of her. I would dearly like to see her again. Her name is Rebecca. I called her Becky. She had bright red hair. Oh, I do so pray she was not killed in the fire— Can you tell me, please, Miss Falconer?"

"I've no idea whom you are talking about," said Miss Falconer, and though it was something hard to believe of so upright a person, Diamond, her nerves so taut that they picked up any reaction, sensed that she was lying.

She insisted, "You must have seen her. The hair was so unusual, I thought you would remember. She wasn't pretty, but she was a clever girl. They said her father was a lawyer. I remember that. I don't know who her mother was, any more than I know my own. At least she was not burned to death— oh please, tell me that."

"No, she was not burned to death."

"Then you do know who I mean!"

"I was given a list. Some of them had been my pupils. The name of Rebecca was not on it. I know nothing more about her, Clary, and now, if you please . . ."

Diamond moved obediently to the door. There she stopped, saying, "There's the other thing—"

"Oh," said Miss Falconer impatiently, "what is it now? Child, I keep on telling you I'm an old woman, I'm tired. I shall write your little note for you, and then I wish to rest for a while. Whatever it is can surely keep till tomorrow."

Diamond said, "The children don't play here any more."

Miss Falconer, with one brief glance at her, answered. "You should not play here either."

"Why not?"

"It's a wicked world, Clary."

Diamond, opening the door, said, "I don't understand it. I don't understand anything. When I was here I was unhappy, and the workhouse was a cruel place for us, but the village was lively and happy, and the children played in the street. What has happened? Surely you can tell me that."

"I suggest you ask Sir Francis."

"Oh, I will, I will. There's so much I have to ask him. About Mr. Vincent, for instance."

"Can you never let anything be?"

"I won't let him be, the— I won't! I've always promised myself that I'd tell him just what I think of him, and he'll look at my fine clothes and he'll not dare to say a word. Why won't you tell me about him?"

Miss Falconer only said again, very wearily, "Ask Sir Francis. Or better still, ask Captain Ringham."

"I certainly will not ask him!"

Miss Falconer snapped, with great energy, "Go away, Clary. Or Diamond, if you prefer it. You're beginning to bore me. Go away at once. I'll see you tomorrow morning. And mind you do your homework."

Diamond sighed, shrugged, then smiled, for she liked the old woman very much. It was not fair to exhaust her with so many questions, to which she probably did not know the answers. She came out of the cottage. She did not see Miss Falconer bend forward to bury her face in her hands, not hear her whisper, "Oh, my poor, poor dear, why did you not tell me?"

Diamond, as she stepped into the village street, muttered to herself, "A, B, C," and penciled the outlines in the air with her finger. Then she saw that Philip was ambling along on the other side, kicking up stones as he walked, his brow furrowed as if in concentration.

He looked round at Diamond. He really was an extremely good-looking boy, but so far she had not seen him smile; like his half brother he seemed to wear a permanent air of bad temper. Yet he did not seem to her one who would leave an animal to die in agony. She began to walk beside him silently, and for a time he endured this, pretended not to see her. Then it obviously fretted him beyond endurance, and at last he rounded on her, saying in a shout, "Will you please go away?"

"It's my village as much as yours," said Diamond.

He quickened his speed, but so did she, then he stopped dead, opening his mouth to shout at her again, took a deep breath, and burst out laughing. "I must say," he said, "you're an odd sort of girl. Do you always tease people like this?"

"I always follow handsome men," said Diamond. "Besides, I want you to hear my homework."

He eyed her warily. "What sort of homework?"

"My alphabet. You see," said Diamond, "Miss Falconer is teaching me to read. I am sure you read very well, but I never had the chance to learn, and now I think it's time I did."

She expected him to laugh at her, but he just considered the matter for a moment, then said gravely, "Very well, Miss Diamond. What do you want me to do?"

"Just tell me where I go wrong," said Diamond, and began to recite the alphabet to him, outlining each letter in front of her as she did so. Her memory did not betray her except for the letter "Q," and when she had finished he said with obvious admiration, "I say, that's pretty good for a first lesson. You must have a splendid memory."

"I have to have," said Diamond. "I could not read my part, you see, so I had to listen and remember it. Mind you," she added, "they were all very small parts. I don't know how I would do if I was an important character. But then, I never was, so it was all right."

They were at the cottage now. She wondered if she should ask him in, then she thought that she could not afford to be too friendly. So she thanked him, then, seeing that he was grinning, demanded, "Why are you laughing at me? Is it because I can't read?"

He exclaimed indignantly, "I would never laugh at you for something like that. I'm laughing because you threw Will's chair out. He wasn't half in a bait too. He said he'd like to kill you. I must say, I thought it was pretty silly, myself."

"I'll trouble you to keep your thoughts to yourself," said Diamond sharply. For a moment she could not think who Will was. It was somehow absurd to think of Captain Ringham as Will—William, possibly, but Will, no. However, she was too curious to let the matter lie, so she said, "What did he do with it?"

"You'll see," said Philip. He looked as if he was enjoying himself.

"What do you mean?"

"You'll see!"

"I think you're rather a stupid boy," said Diamond coldly,

preparing to go into the cottage. She added, "Anyway, I'll say goodbye now. I'm dining out this evening, you know, so I must get myself ready. At Axenford. With Sir Francis."

His face changed suddenly, as if she had slapped him. He had been grinning, looking very young and entertained, but at these words the smile vanished. He gave her a glare of what seemed to her pure hatred, then without another word turned on his heel and strode away.

Diamond watched him disappearing down the path. She said to Georgy, "I believe he really did ill-treat that poor horse. When he looks like that, he's the image of his horrid brother. I want something to eat, Georgy, and then we must look through my wardrobe and see what I can wear. I want to look grand. I want to be beautiful."

And indeed she looked both grand and beautiful when the carriage came round for her. Diamond, prepared now to be Ophelia, Beatrice and Olivia combined, had spent a long time in her choosing, and decided at last on a cream satin, cut low but seemly enough not to shock Middleditch. Mrs. Rigg would certainly be shattered by a deep décolletage, and Mr. Armstrong would probably look down it. Diamond was finding that it mattered to her what Middleditch thought, and as she pinned one of Captain Ringham's roses to her breast, she studied her reflection in the mirror, and thought that no one could complain of her. She looked a lady like other ladies. She would surely do Sir Francis credit.

But she said sadly to the admiring Georgy, "I wish I had a necklace to wear. The rubies—do you remember the rubies, Georgy? They would look beautiful with this."

"I told you not to leave them behind," said Georgy.

"You'll swing me high on Tyburn yet!"

"But I expect Sir Francis will buy you something," said Georgy cozily, and at this Diamond had to laugh, saying, "I've become so respectable, old woman, that I daresay I'd not accept them even if they were offered."

The carriage called on the stroke of eight, by the church clock. The coachman came in for her, to help her down the path. Here there was no covert insolence, only respect and courtesy, and Diamond laid her gloved hand lightly on his arm as she stepped over the muddy stones.

The coachman remarked, "I believe, ma'am, Sir Francis has some idea of improving this path for you. This is no road for a lady. You might fall and hurt yourself, especially if there is snow."

Diamond, who was as nimble as a little boy, and who had in her time scrambled up and down far worse places, inclined her head in approval, though a faint smile flickered on her lips. And she permitted the coachman to hand her into the carriage and place a rug across her knees.

She looked out of the window as the horses trotted along, and thought of another time when there had been no rug, no carriage, no subservient attendant, when the horses would probably have run her down if she had not been fleet of foot. And it was as if Clary sat beside Diamond, and the two looked upon each other as strangers.

She knew the way to Axenford. She had walked there many times. The woods that lay between it and the Hall were full of small game, and her father had been there half the time, not saying a word of what he was doing, but sometimes returning with a pheasant or a fat rabbit, or even a hedgehog, which he would bake in clay on a stone. Diamond, washed and combed, in her fine cream satin gown, looked sideways at Clary, with her dirty bare feet, the black hair tossing over her face, a great rent in the side of her filthy dress. And she put out a hand, almost as if the gypsy child were there, to meet nothing but the side of the carriage. This shocked her so that she shivered, for all that there was a fur mantle about her shoulders, a rug snugly on her knees. This evening she would certainly not be eating hedgehog; no doubt she would be served some fine French fare prepared by Sir Francis' cook. A great loneliness possessed her, for she had moved into a new world, and it was not yet her world. The freedom that had once been hers was gone forever; she was bound down by pretty clothes, the need to be clean, smooth of speech, the obligation to do and say the right thing. She looked with longing into the face of Clary Brown, who had nothing, who was ragged, barefoot, often cold and nearly always hungry, but who had been happy because she loved and was loved.

She knew then why she was lonely. Pa was gone, Pa would never come back, and since his death there had been no love.

Friends, yes, good company, gaiety, often happiness, but it was love that Diamond longed for, and it seemed that this would be denied her forever. For even if she met someone who loved her, the consummation of that love would become dirty and repulsive, and all for a disgusting old man who was apparently still alive and who certainly did not care that he had ruined her life.

The tears of anger and self-pity filled her eyes, and she turned hastily to stare out the window; she must not arrive at Axenford with the marks of tears on her cheek. She gazed up —her eyes very wide so that the drops should not fall—at St. Joseph's Church. In the bright, white moonlight, she saw Mr. Revill standing outside the gateway, wearing his surplice, his arms crossed on his chest. She could not hear anything, but she thought he looked as if he were talking to himself, and somehow this reminded her of the strange chanting she had heard that first night, and she shuddered. Then, as the carriage turned the corner, she saw him stretch out his arm and make some strange gesture, as if he were invoking or repelling a demon. The next moment he apparently went back into the church, for there was no more sign of him.

Diamond, repelled yet fascinated, thought, Oh, how I wish I was Clary Brown again, for just ten minutes, so that I could creep after him and find out what he is doing.

But she was not Clary Brown. She was Miss Diamond Browne, late of Drury Lane, and she was going to dine with a baronet in a handsome house. Clary Brown would not even be allowed into the kitchens to scrub the dishes, but Diamond Browne would be an honored guest and treated as if she were a lady in her own right.

Now they were coming up the drive of Axenford, and there were lights in all the windows and the door was wide open to receive her.

X

Axenford, like most buildings of its kind, had been added to by successive generations. There was a Tudor wing and a Queen Anne wing, and a modern section built by Sir Francis himself. In the garden, to the left of the house, was what seemed to be a summerhouse, which no doubt the family used on hot summer afternoons. It was a strange, squat pagoda-like place, in the oriental fashion of the age and to Diamond's eyes not very appealing. No doubt that was due to the half-light, for even in the pale light from door and windows she could not see about her clearly. Though the garden seemed to be vast and well laid-out, she could discern little but its dark contours. To the right, the woods that separated Axenford from the Hall moved and whispered in the wind, so that she was relieved the door would soon be shut upon them. It was all doubtless very rich and very beautiful, but it was a trifle too magnificent for Diamond's taste. A faint oppression settled on her spirits that she could in no way account for, and she was thankful when she saw Sir Francis coming to greet her.

He stepped into the drive to help her down. By this time the excitement and novelty of it all had quite restored her, and she went into the hallway, only to stop in some apprehension at the sight of two vast dogs that lay there motionless and watched her out of opaque amber eyes.

She had never cared much for dogs unless they were small and pretty, and she took care to keep her distance. However, mindful of her social manners, she made little appropriate noises to them, to which they did not reply by so much as a flicker of their tails.

She looked a little ruefully at Sir Francis, and he said, smiling,

"Don't be afraid, Miss Diamond. Wod and Lok will not harm you now that they see you are my friend."

"Wod and Lok! What strange names."

"They are ancient gods. A friend of mine christened them so, and the names have somehow stuck. They are useful beasts. At night I let them loose in the grounds, to keep out marauders."

"I should think they would keep out marauders very well," said Diamond, noticing the bulk of them and the great teeth that one of them displayed in a yawn.

"Oh yes, indeed. There would be little point in my keeping a lap dog. I don't think there is anyone in Middleditch who would dare to set foot here. Since that matter of the race horse, which I believe I told you about, I feel that I have no choice. But at least I have made it known that I keep guard dogs, and no one in his senses would be foolish enough to trespass. The law is, after all, on my side."

"Would they really kill?" asked Diamond, stepping carefully out of their way as Sir Francis led her upstairs to the drawing room.

"That is what they have been trained to do. Oh yes, Miss Diamond, like you I disapprove of violence, but in the circumstances, I have to feel that I am justified in taking these precautions. Now, my dear young lady, you will repose yourself a little before dinner, we will talk of more pleasant things, and you will take a glass of wine."

Diamond walked sedately up the stairs. She felt, as she always did in such circumstances, that she was playing her part as a trained actress: She was outside herself, watching herself critically from the pit. She looked with interest at the portraits on the walls. The old man's mansion was grand enough, but not like this magnificent place. Here there was more space, everything was beautifully laid out, it all seemed to stretch into the distance, so that there was no end to it.

"Are all these your ancestors?" she asked Sir Francis.

"Sir Francis Axenford at your service," he replied. "Fifteen hundred, sixteen hundred, seventeen hundred—take your pick."

"You are all so much alike!"

"Give or take a wig or two, Miss Diamond, a change of dress, a different collar, we could shift from century to century, and no one would ever know. That is my father. He was also Sir Francis. We are all Sir Francis."

Diamond examined the portrait and found it rather unpleasant. Sir Francis Senior was indeed like his son, but the face was grim; he looked as if he could be cruel, and it was hard to imagine him smiling. Diamond made no comment, only thought it strange that none of these people bore any imprint of a Lady Axenford. Perhaps the wives had all been weak females with no character to impose on their descendants.

She had wondered with some trepidation if there would be other guests. She was not accustomed to the ladies of the *ton*; the old man had kept her well away from them. She was frightened lest there be someone who would see through her, perhaps even discern little Clary Brown huddling under the fine clothes. But there was no one there but herself, and so she sipped her wine, feeling shy and awed by all the beautiful things around her, so much so that on pretext of warming herself at the blazing log fire, she rose to her feet and stepped across to the mantelpiece. She exclaimed, "Oh, that is Lady Caroline." And as Sir Francis nodded silently, his eyes fixed on her, she looked up into the face that the artist had painted in its full youthful beauty.

Sir Francis said quietly, "That is how she looked when I married her. She was the most beautiful woman I have ever met in my life. I could almost say that I was glad when she died. For the last two years she refused to have a mirror in the house. I have kept it like that in her memory. Even polished surfaces had to be covered up, and once when she caught a glimpse of herself in a silver tureen, she fell down in such a swoon that we all believed it to be the end."

The words sent a shudder through Diamond, but she did not answer. She continued to gaze at the portrait, then, sighing, moved away. She saw that over the picture was a crucifix, and on the mantelpiece just below it, a beautifully painted porcelain ceruse box. She touched it, and Sir Francis said quickly, "I cannot bear to part with it, yet in all reason I should have destroyed it long ago, for I am certain it destroyed her. It is a memento mori, Miss Diamond. I see you do not wear rouge. Let me beg you never to do so. You do not need it, with your pretty complexion, and my dear Caroline did not need it either. But this beautiful box comes from France, and even though the sight of it chills me, I have never had the heart to throw it away."

Diamond felt that she could never have kept so sad a reminder, and turned away. As she did so she noticed that beside the box lay a letter, closely written in a beautiful copperplate, and she thought what a pity it was that she could not read one word of it.

Sir Francis, observing her, said, "That was written on your behalf by Miss Falconer. She writes at great length, as you can see, even though it was simply to accept my invitation. But I daresay the old lady has time on her hands, and so she wanders on—about the weather and her garden and the ill behavior of the village boys.

Diamond could not help finding this a little strange. Miss Falconer was not the kind of person to waste time, and it seemed extremely unlikely that she would write about her weed-ridden garden or complain about the village children. However, she only said, "I'm sorry I couldn't write myself. I'm afraid I have never been taught my letters. It is very ignorant of me."

"There are a great many ladies besides yourself who can neither read nor write. It is nothing to be ashamed of."

"Well, I think it is, and so now I have gone back to school again. I've decided that it's a shame to look at all Miss Falconer's books and not be able to understand one word of them. Perhaps next time, Sir Francis, I will answer you myself."

"Can you read anything at all of that letter?"

"Oh, not yet. I have had only one lesson. I am beginning to make out capital letters. I think," said Diamond, holding the letter in her hand and peering intently at it, "that she starts: 'Dear Sir Francis,' for I can make out the 'D' and the 'S' and the 'F.' And there's an 'R' there and another 'D'—would that be for me?—and oh yes, a 'G.' That don't help me very much, I'm afraid."

"I think you are a remarkable pupil," said Sir Francis, and at that moment the footman appeared to say that dinner was ready.

Diamond was to wonder afterwards what possessed her. As

no doubt Miss Falconer might say, ill-breeding must always out. As Sir Francis turned to speak to the footman, his face was averted for the fraction of a second, and in that moment she picked up Miss Falconer's letter and slipped it into her reticule. It was no excuse whatsoever to say, as she did afterwards to herself, that in a way it was hers, that it was quite unimportant, that he would probably not so much as notice its disappearance, and if he did, would simply assume it had fallen into the fire. It was still, from whatever point one viewed it, unpardonable behavior. Diamond, a little flushed, tried to calm her conscience by telling herself that it would provide a reading lesson for later on, and that Miss Falconer's precise copperplate would be easier to decipher than most. But the color was still high in her cheeks as she let Sir Francis escort her to the dining room, and once she almost confessed her misdeed, only at that moment some exotic dish was presented to her and her remorse was swallowed in greed.

It was indeed a splendid dinner, and so she said to Sir Francis, her face so rapt that he burst out laughing.

"You should have come back to us a long time ago," he said. "I think we need you, Miss Diamond. I think Middleditch has been the worse for your absence."

"I think," said Diamond sadly, as she selected an apple from the bowl set in front of her, "that Middleditch is the worse for everything." She raised her eyes to Sir Francis. By now she was feeling relaxed and at ease. She was still playing her part, but it was like being in a play that had continued for a long time. The table gleamed with the Axenford glass and the Axenford china; a big vase of chrysanthemums was set in the middle and the candles in their silver holders burned high. It was entirely beautiful and rich in the fashion of a world where riches were the norm; it was a million miles away from a place where little girls ate with their fingers off stones and drank water from a stream. Diamond, bemused, felt translated, almost as if she were a shadow. She was in no way part of this world, perhaps never would be, yet she was aware of a warmth for this strange, kindly man who was trying so hard to make her feel at home, who in no way patronized her, who seemed so enchanted by her company.

Georgy would be marrying them off any moment now. Poor Sir Francis! He would be utterly shocked if he knew of the old woman's matrimonial designs.

He answered Diamond in a strange, heavy voice, unlike his usual tones. The room was heated by a huge log fire, yet at that moment a chill struck her—the unaccountable presentiment that had overcome her on arrival was back once more.

He said, "That is indeed so. Middleditch has changed. You are very observant, Miss Diamond."

"Captain Ringham calls it prying and spying," said Diamond, and at that he rose abruptly to his feet, shooting a fork to the floor and saying quite sharply, "I cannot abide the mention of that name. Forgive me, Miss Diamond, I am not normally a hating man, but such things have happened— I think the time has come for us to talk in full detail. I regard you already as a friend. You are my friend, are you not?"

"Oh, I hope so, I do indeed."

"Shall we go back to the drawing room? Or would you prefer to remain here? This is not London town, and we do not always stand on formality. The carriage will take you home whenever you please, and I propose to do myself the honor of accompanying you, but if you would prefer to stay at the table—I must confess," said Sir Francis in his open way, "I so rarely entertain these days that I have forgot the proprieties and conventions. You are from London, ma'am. You must instruct me."

Diamond did not believe one word of this, thinking that Sir Francis had simply observed that she was now at her ease, and in his tactful fashion did not wish to spoil her pleasure. And certainly she felt happier at the table, for she could twirl her glass round if she chose, peel her apple, play with the silver ornaments around her. The drawing room had in some odd way frightened her. It was partly the portrait of Lady Caroline, though the sweet lady would certainly not be wishing her ill, and it was also the presence of that ceruse box. She could not understand how Sir Francis could bear to keep it on display, it was rather like treasuring a knife that had stabbed someone to death. And the dining room was smaller, there were no forbidding family portraits, simply a huge picture of some deer, and the velvet curtains at the deep bay windows reflected the light of the fire and kept the darkness out. There were no ghosts here, no crucifix—was Sir Francis perhaps a devout man?—no dead ladies with destroyed faces.

Diamond smiled secretly at the idea of her instructing her host. She could have said to him, if she had chosen, When I dined in a London house, we went to bed afterwards. But this was a side of her life he must know nothing about. Diamond did not share Georgy's simple views, and preferred that her past should remain a secret until the end of time, except from someone like Miss Falconer, who did not seem to care.

She said with her most innocent air, "Oh, I could never instruct anyone. You seem to have forgotten, sir, who I am. I am Clary Brown. I am used to eating berries and cupping stream water in my hand. I never had a dress worth the name—"

"Your present one is most charming."

She wished suddenly he would not pay her these old-fashioned compliments; she found it irritating, almost as if the remarks came out automatically. But she smiled and said, "Clary Brown would simply goggle at the sight of it." Then she added in a matter-of-fact voice, "Let us stay here. I want to hear these details."

He said, "I think we will have a glass of brandy first. Do you drink brandy, Miss Diamond?"

Diamond thanked her stars that the old man had not only taught her how to eat in a seemly way, but also how to drink, warning her of the signs that would indicate she had had enough. She had a very strong head, much to his surprise and a little to his annoyance. At the beginning he had encouraged her to drink, thinking this might thaw her, but he soon found that wine made no impression on her at all.

She said that yes, she would like a glass of brandy, and watched in fascination the golden liquid poured by the butler from a most magnificent decanter.

"You have such lovely things," she said in frank envy, adding, "That is a strange ring you wear, Sir Francis."

"It is a family ring." He did not offer to take it off so that she could see it more closely. "You have an eye for beauty."

"If I have, it comes from my father. He loved beauty. He never owned anything in his life, but he knew so much about animals and birds, and he could read the stars. He knew all their names and could even tell the weather by them." She added, "He loved beauty in women too. But then, he was such a handsome man."

She knew almost instantly that she had said something wrong. She had no idea why. It was a perfectly natural thing to say. Sir Francis presumably loved beauty in women too, otherwise he would not have married his Caroline. But his reaction was as violent as the snapping down of a bolt, and she raised her head, startled, dismayed. Sir Francis did not comment. Yet it was as if a rage and despair burned in him. However, he said nothing, and presently moved over to the fire and placed one arm along the mantelpiece.

Diamond waited. The alarm still pricked within her. She wished he would speak. And as he remained silent, she could endure the waiting no longer, and burst out, more violently than she intended, "There are so many things I cannot explain. Why are there no children in the street? I asked Miss Falconer, and she did not answer. Can you tell me? I suppose you think it a silly thing to notice, but I can remember the days when there were children everywhere. There are still children in the village. I know that. I hear them sometimes behind the curtained windows. I see them with their mothers. But they are hardly ever alone. They never seem allowed to play. They never sing their songs. When I was young we played and sang. Even in the workhouse we played and sang." She stared at Sir Francis, whose head was bowed toward the fire. She wished she could see his face. "Children like singing. I remember there was one silly song— will it shock your servants to hear a lady singing at the dinner table? Shall I sing for my supper?"

She wondered, even as she spoke, what was making her talk like this. The fear seemed to be impelling her to foolishness, for she had not the least desire to sing. When he finally answered her, her nerves were so taut that she jumped.

He said, still not raising his head, "I should like to hear you. I do not give a damn what the servants think. I pay them. I do not pay them to think." Then he remarked in an oddly slurred voice, "I had a footman once. He was addicted to thinking. I do not know what he thought, but one night he crept out into the grounds. Why? How should I know? He wanted to find out something. He thought— The dogs tore him to bits. We found what was left of him the next morning."

Diamond, horrified, exclaimed, "No! Oh, that isn't possible . . ."

"I'm afraid it is." He was looking at her now. He was smiling. He could have been talking of the weather. "I should never have told you. You have too tender a heart, Miss Diamond, and it was a long time ago. Let me hear your song."

Diamond had never wanted less to sing, but felt she could hardly refuse. She said a little faintly, "It is very hot here," and fumbled for her fan.

Sir Francis instantly went across to the window and pulled back one of the curtains to open it. The cold night air streamed in, then Diamond heard a low howl. She went white. She whispered, "What is that?"

He answered indifferently, as if it did not matter, "Oh, that is Lok. I always know which one it is. At least he gives marauders due warning. Sing, Miss Diamond. It would give me such pleasure."

Diamond closed her eyes. Perhaps Sir Francis thought this an artistic affectation. It was not. She was terrified. Not so much of him, for she could not believe he would harm her, but of Middleditch, where dogs tore intruders to pieces, where children no longer played or sang. She tried to think of a song, and could think of nothing, nothing at all. All that came to her mind was a silly bit of nonsense, a baby's chant, which sometimes she and Becky had sung. It was absurd to offer something like this to Sir Francis, but gripping her fan so tightly that it hurt her fingers, she sang:

> "Ring a ring of roses,
> A pocket full of posies,
> Atishoo, atishoo,
> All fall down!"

Then she said, as if bewildered at herself, "It was the plague song, you know. Someone told me that once. We didn't know. I suppose it's really rather horrid. but to us it was just a little game. I'm sorry. I should have sung you something prettier."

Sir Francis said nothing for a moment. Then at last he said very softly, "And the children no longer sing."

Diamond said with a sigh, "The children no longer sing."

"I see," he said, "that I really owe you a full explanation." He came back to the table and sat down. He poured himself another glass of brandy. "If I have not done so before, Miss Diamond, it is because I didn't want to frighten you. But I am beginning to see that a half-explanation is more alarming than a full one, especially to a person as sensitive as yourself. But you must believe that whatever happens, I shall look after you. Will you try not to be too frightened? If you do not know all the facts, you may inded run into peril."

"I am not so easily frightened," said Diamond, twirling her brandy glass. She had not yet touched a drop of it; now she did not dare.

"It is of course," he said, "about the Hellfire Club, though I suppose the name is not actually used here. Such a club meets in London and takes its amusement from violence, black magic and evil. But hellfire is appropriate, for we are infected. It is like the plague you mention, only worse. We do not even know who is responsible, though . . . But there is no proof. All we know is that there are people here—one, two, we are none of us sure—who go in for such devilish practices. It is in its evil way a cult of youth, which is why I am afraid for you, my dear young lady, with your innocently inquisitive eyes. The victims have all been young, defenseless. I myself," said Sir Francis, "am an old man, and I have no wish to be young again. When one is young, one is vulnerable, one is easily hurt. You will know that, Miss Diamond. When you grow older, things do not matter so much. But that, unhappily, is not everyone's view, and Mr. Revill and I— You have met Mr. Revill, I believe?"

"Yes indeed," said Diamond, looking down into her brandy glass.

"He is a good man. I think you do not like him very much."

"I hardly know him," said Diamond.

"You must take my word for it, he is not what he seems. He is a shy, reserved person who does not always make the best of impressions. But he has grown only too aware of what is going on. At the beginning graves were robbed, Black

Masses were said in the church, and there was at last a most wicked murder. Mr. Wall, our minister, was crucified in his own church. But I prefer not to dwell on that. The children you mention— It is not only the workhouse children, it never has been, though they were the easiest victims, since there was no family responsible for them. But children have vanished, even in broad daylight. They have never been seen again. It was Mr. Vincent's protest about the workhouse children that certainly provoked the fire."

Diamond said, her voice shaking, "But I still don't understand. Why have the children vanished? What has happened to them?"

"There is a wicked magic that claims to renew youth in older people through the living hearts of children. At one time I think these people believed that the dead disinterred from their graves could serve the same purpose. For a long time we none of us were really certain," said Sir Francis, not looking at Diamond, who had grown pale with shock, "but then the body of one of the children was found, in the woods by Captain Ringham's estate. It was hideously mutilated. It was only too plain that the girl was the victim of some kind of primitive sacrifice. The murder was hushed up. She was one of the workhouse children. No one was particularly concerned for her, and we were all anxious that something so ugly remain secret."

Diamond whispered, "Do you know who she was?"

"Yes. I naturally made inquiries. I know nothing about her personally, of course, but I remember she bore some Hebrew name. Yes. Rebecca. I remember now. I saw the body. Captain Ringham and I had to examine it. She had red hair. It was almost all that was recognizable."

Diamond began to cry, putting her hands to her face. Sir Francis at once rose to his feet and touched her shoulder. He said in distress, "I should not have told you. But I had to, I was too afraid for you. You see, it is not only children. The young and handsome have also been victims, as if there is a particular potency in them. There was a young dairymaid, and a farmhand— If I alarm you by warning you, you will understand. I could not endure that anything should happen to you. I fear I have caused you great distress—but you will

141

understand now why the children do not play in the streets, why the villagers look sideways at each other, and why Mr. Revill can find no one to work in the churchyard. We all— Some of us are convinced we know who is responsible, but there is no proof. No proof! My dear wife believed she knew, and I have sometimes wondered if her death was a natural one. Miss Diamond, will you not go back to London? This is no no place for you."

"No," said Diamond, "I have to stay."

"Why? Do you really think there is anything you can do?"

"I only know I have to stay."

"You are an obstinate young woman!"

"So my pa always told me."

He said, "Then let me escort you to the carriage. Only be careful, for God's sake. There is an evil spirit abroad, and we are not sure if there is only one. Everybody suspects everyone else. There is even a tale that your Miss Falconer is a witch."

At this Diamond recovered herself. She turned a tear-stained face on Sir Francis, saying angrily, "But that is simply wicked nonsense! Of course she is not a witch. Besides, there are no such things as witches. My pa always said that. He said it was stupid and cruel to burn poor old women who were just daft in the head. Miss Falconer is a good, kind person. You cannot possibly believe such things of her."

She thought he would agree at once, but to her vexation he said, in what seemed to her a pompous manner, "I no longer know what to believe. She grows strange herbs in her garden, she keeps a cat, she claims to be able to cure sickness. I think one day she will find herself in trouble. It will be partly her fault. Why, even the children are afraid of her."

"That is because she was a schoolteacher."

He said, "Someone must be responsible. I agree, it is unlikely that an old woman could do such harm, but we are all suspicious these days. You cannot blame us." Then he smiled at her. "Forgive me, Miss Diamond. I did not mean to spoil our evening. But you will see now why I had to tell you all this. Let me ask you again: will you not go back to London?"

Diamond said more calmly, "London is a far more wicked place than Middleditch. And this village is my home. I am not going to be frightened away from it."

"Well then, I'll ask you something else. If I dared," said Sir Francis, "I would insist. But you are a very fierce young lady, Miss Diamond, and I see that no one can compel you to do what you do not want to do. But all I ask, very humbly, is that if you come across anything that seems to you strange or alarming, you will tell me or Mr. Revill. And nobody else. Nobody at all. Oh yes, you can trust Mr. Revill, and I hope you think you can also trust me."

"I do indeed."

"The carriage will be brought round for you shortly, and I will accompany you. I want to make sure that you arrive home safely."

Diamond stepped into the hallway and let Sir Francis slip her mantle about her shoulders. She was grateful for it. She was very cold, and the cold was not due to the autumn air. As Sir Francis turned to summon his coachman, she looked around her and saw something gleaming behind the high hall table. She glanced furtively about her, then stooped down to see what it was.

It was a stack of mirrors. There must have been at least half a dozen of them, leaning against each other, all highly polished. Diamond quickly straightened herself—the accusation of spying was proving only too true—and turned to smile at Sir Francis, who said, "The carriage is waiting."

She did not mention the mirrors to him. But she thought of the poor lady who had suddenly caught sight of herself in the polished surface. Diamond's face twisted. The mirrors were simply one more inexplicable thing, and she had the feeling that it all added up to something she ought to have known long ago, yet she could not see the answer.

In silence, the two of them walked down the steps to the carriage. As the coachman started to open the door, Diamond turned to look at the dark outline of the summerhouse, desolate and a little sinister in the darkness.

Sir Francis said, "We often sat there in the summer. My wife was fond of it. One side is open to the garden, and sometimes we would take our midday meal there. You would find it cold and depressing now, but when the hot weather comes, I will invite you to luncheon. I would like you to see it. You and my wife seem to share many tastes."

As she climbed into the carriage she heard the baying of one of the dogs and saw his shadow slide behind a tree. It made her shudder. She thought they were far more frightening than any marauders. Sir Francis, now sitting beside her, began to speak of casual matters, neighbors whom Diamond might care to meet, people who lived outside the village, a few miles away and then, in country fashion, talked about crops and harvests and the possibility of heavy snow in a couple of months or so.

Diamond walked quietly up to the cottage door. Sir Francis held her hand for a moment, saying, "Be careful. You are so young and pretty. Do be careful."

"Oh, I will," said Diamond, then opened her reticule and produced the little pearl-handled pistol. "You see, I am prepared."

He looked down at it, then up at her again. There was bewilderment in his voice. "Do you know how to use it?"

"I do, yes. I don't think I am a very good shot," said Diamond, "but if you hold it close enough, you can't miss. I always carry it with me."

"You are a very disconcerting girl. I do not think," said Sir Francis, "that I have ever seen anything quite like you."

This made her laugh so that she briefly forgot her fear. But when the carriage had started back to Axenford, she shut the door very carefully, making sure that the latch, now repaired, was fastened and the key turned. She looked at Georgy, who, anxious to hear all the news, ran toward her.

"No," said Diamond, as Georgy opened her mouth, "he has not asked me to marry him, nor has he suggested I come to his bed. You would have found it very boring. He behaved like a gentleman, he gave me a gorgeous meal. I used all the right knives and forks and I did not become elevated. And I would like a hot drink."

"Captain Ringham called, Miss Diamond."

"What! What did he want? What did he say? He has no right to come like that without invitation. I suppose he bullied you, I suppose . . ."

"Miss Diamond, he only wanted to know if you were all right."

"And why should I not be all right?" Diamond set her arms

akimbo, and her voice rose in a fashion that Sir Francis had not yet heard. "It is no business of his. I do not expect Captain Ringham to act as my nursemaid. And he don't give a damn if I'm all right or not. He's just spying on me to make sure I'm not spying on him. I hope you did not let him in."

"Miss Diamond, you would never expect me to leave him standing outside in the cold, a gentleman like him."

"I would. And he's not a gentleman."

"He brought another rabbit for you."

Diamond burst out laughing. It was not so much the mention of the rabbit as at Georgy's genteelly reproachful face. She said, "I hope you threw it back at him."

"I certainly did not. It will do nicely for our dinner tomorrow. I think you must be foxed to talk so."

"I'm not foxed at all. And what about my hot drink, old woman? You're forgetting your duties, and I'm very cold. It's a bitter night."

But later, when she was in bed, with Georgy's hot drink beside her, she made no attempt to drink it. She lay on her back, sleepless, staring at the ceiling. She said aloud, "Oh, Becky, Becky," and she wept for the little girl who had never had happiness in her brief life and who had come to so terrible an ending. If anything were needed to keep Diamond Browne in Middleditch, this was it. You'll be avenged, said Diamond to herself. Oh, you'll be avenged, my darling Becky. I'll not leave here until I find out who the wicked murderer is. Then her exhausted mind wandered to other strangenesses: that stack of mirrors, Miss Falconer accused of witchcraft. Thinking of her old schoolmistress, she took the letter out of her reticule.

Diamond put it on the pillow and struggled to make some sense of it. It seemed desperately important that she should, though she could not imagine why. Perhaps it was because it was so lengthy, for what could Miss Falconer have to say beyond some silly politeness about Miss Diamond Browne being delighted to accept his invitation? Diamond traced the letters with her finger. She could see that Miss Falconer wrote a beautiful script, it was regular and straight and always in line, but to Diamond it could have been the hieroglyphics on an ancient tomb, for all it meant anything to her.

"I must learn," muttered Diamond aloud. "Oh, I must learn."

And bursting with powerful resolution, she took out the paper and quill pen Miss Falconer had given her, set the inkwell by her bedside, and with a great many blots, some of which fell on the sheet—Georgy would be very cross—wrote out all the capitals laboriously, ending up with her own name. It was not the scrawl that Kitty Clive had taught her, but DIAMOND written clear and large.

And then she lay awake for a long time.

❧ XI ❧

The lessons, for several weeks, progressed remarkably well. Diamond went to Miss Falconer's cottage punctually every morning, and worked with a fierce determination that seemed to startle the old schoolmistress, who remarked once, "I did not think you had such powers of concentration, Clary. You are an extremely intelligent young woman. It is a pity you did not show such interest when you were young. We might have made something of you."

"I have made something of myself," said Diamond proudly, and Miss Falconer raised her head, as if recognizing a fellow warrior, and smiled at her, almost for the first time.

She did not ask about the dinner, nor did she mention Sir Francis, but Diamond, drinking the glass of sour wine that always terminated the lesson, told her a little of what had passed. She did not go into details, nor did she mention Lady Caroline's ceruse box or the stack of mirrors. She did not wish to frighten the old woman, though it was true that Miss Falconer did not wear the air of one made easily afraid. But she herself was beginning to be very much afraid, and she had to notice that the village, once so friendly, so anxious to propitiate the pretty lady from London town, was now regarding her askance. Because this was incomprehensible to her, she was compelled to mention it one morning just as she was leaving.

"Do you understand it?" she asked Miss Falconer. "When I first came here they were all so kind to me. Mr. Armstrong sent wine over for me, and as for Mrs. Rigg, she was so humble, I wanted to laugh. I could not help thinking of the old days when she drove me away from her shop window. But now . . ."

It was only small things. There was no direct hostility. But

Mr. Armstrong, who had always doffed his cap to her and in his rather surly way made some comment on the weather or the crops or the new crate of French wine that had arrived, looked at her silently and retreated into the inn parlor. Mrs. Rigg, once so servile, seemed almost impertinent. She would look sideways at Diamond, then say in her high voice, "Oh, good day, ma'am. Fancy you coming out in such weather. I thought you London ladies never stepped abroad in the wind and rain." And the other women, like Mrs. Cowling, who did the cleaning and cooking for Mr. Revill, scuttled past her without a word, so that Diamond, back in her own home, began to feel like a pariah.

The children did not, as she had already remarked, play in the street any more, but the odd one whom she met scurried past her as if terrified, and this distressed Diamond more than anything, for she would normally have stopped to speak to them or play with them.

"As for young Philip," she told Miss Falconer, who had listened to all this in silence, "he cuts me dead. One day," said Diamond, her voice soaring up, "I shall box his ears. To stick his nose in the air and stride past me like that— Horrid boy! I swear he's as bad as his brother."

"You dined with Sir Francis," said Miss Falconer, stroking her cat.

"I dine with whom I please! What's that to do with him?"

"Captain Ringham and Sir Francis are sworn enemies. You should know that."

"Of course I know it. And I know whose side I'm on." Then Diamond, forestalling her schoolmistress's reproaches, said quickly, "I'll tell you something, Miss Falconer. I detest the man."

"That's hardly news, Clary."

"But I think he's evil. I think he's responsible for—" Diamond broke off, and Miss Falconer said quietly, "Responsible for what, Clary?"

"Oh, it don't matter. No, that's not what I meant to say. One day he'll know what I think, he'll know, too, that I am the daughter of the man he hanged for nothing. But that can wait," said Diamond. "Only, he does everything possible to infuriate me. That chair—"

"Child, I do not know what you're talking about."

"Oh well," said Diamond after a pause, "it don't really matter."

She found that she did not wish Miss Falconer to know that she had hurled the chair out of the cottage. It was not only ill-bred but excessively childish, and she did not want such a good friend to hear of her disgraceful behavior. Only a little while back, she had returned home to find Georgy, who at times was really extremely silly, convulsed in giggles, so overcome that she could not speak coherently—and the chair back again, just outside the door, so firmly dug into the path that despite her struggles she could not move it an inch.

She had yelled at Georgy, forgetting all decorum, "When did this happen? Of all the damnable impertinence— Oh, stop giggling, you fat old bitch! It's not funny. Answer me at once, or I'll throw something at your silly head."

But it took Georgy a long time to compose herself, and it was some ten minutes later that Diamond, now quite hysterical with temper, got the story out of her.

Captain Ringham had arrived with his young brother, the pair of them carrying the chair before them like a shield, and set it down on the path, digging it in so deep that no one without a shovel could possibly remove it. When Georgy, at that moment more scared than amused, asked what they thought they were doing, Captain Ringham replied calmly, "I gave this to your mistress. I do not care to have my gifts thrown back at me. In the summer you can now sit outside and admire the view. And you can tell Miss Diamond from me that it's high time she learned how to control her childish tantrums."

Diamond at that moment was giving an excellent demonstration of childish tantrums, but when Georgy told her this, she fell silent. She glared at the chair, saw that she could never budge it without digging up half the path, then, much to Georgy's relief, burst out laughing. She did not mention the matter again. She would have spoken about it to Philip had he not turned his face away and run past her.

She went on, to Miss Falconer, "I don't see why the village should mind my dining with Sir Francis. Oh, I can understand how Philip might, but he's behaved so disgracefully that I daresay he's ashamed of himself. But everyone else— Miss Falconer, do you believe in witches?"

Then she blushed scarlet, for she had not meant to say this. Miss Falconer raised the startling blue eyes and answered, "I believe in evil. There is great evil here. And, Clary, you are in some ways a foolish girl. Do you not see that you are running headlong into trouble? I am not afraid for myself, but I am beginning to be afraid for you."

"I am perfectly capable of looking after myself."

"That," said Miss Falconer sharply, "is a remark that has been uttered by everyone on the way to damnation. You will end by harming yourself. There are others here who are also trying to rid us of this black, wicked cloud that hangs over us all. They are stronger than you, more capable of looking after themselves. Leave it to them. I do not wish you to come to any harm."

Diamond's blank, smiling look answered for her. Miss Falconer saw it and sighed, remembering little Clary Brown, who had looked so when determined to go her own way.

Diamond said, after a suitable pause, "There is one thing I believe I have the right to know."

"The right!"

"Well, it concerns me very much. Mr. Vincent. Where does he live? There is some mystery about him. I wish to see him."

"Why do you wish to see him? I understand he did you great harm."

"Yes," said Diamond, and fell silent for a while, seeing once again the vast, ugly man. Then she said, in a puzzled voice, as if she did not quite understand herself, "I think I want to lay a ghost."

"You must ask Captain Ringham."

"Captain Ringham! What has he to do with it?"

"You must ask him," said Miss Falconer, adding, "Mr. Vincent lives in a cottage on his estate."

Diamond thought that it was utterly in keeping that her worst enemy should be sheltered by another enemy. She prepared to go, gathering up her belongings as if she were a little schoolgirl again, then, as she was at the door, she asked suddenly, "How long will it take for me to read writing?"

Today, for the first time, she had read the whole chapter of a book. It was true that it was a children's book, written in the simplest language, and it was true, too, that she had faltered over a great many words, but nonetheless she had read. Read! The black marks that had meant no more to her than the pattern on a piece of material were now words, they spoke to her, the page was at last a communication. Her face flushed with the glory of it, she had flung her arms round Miss Falconer and embraced her, exclaiming, "But I know what it means—I can read! Oh, Miss Falconer, I can read!"

Miss Falconer was not a person to show much emotion. She had disengaged herself amiably enough, patted Diamond's hand, nodded at her approvingly, then brought out the bottle of wine. As they drank to Diamond's success, she had said, "You must now learn to write," and it was with this in mind that Diamond posed her question.

"It is the most difficult part of it," said Miss Falconer. "It is always so with children, which is why, when one writes to them, one always does so in capital letters. You must be patient, Clary. I myself write, I believe, a clear hand, but nonetheless I form the letters in my own individual way. You must content yourself for a while in reading print where the letters are always identical."

"I am not patient," said Diamond, smiling, "and I will learn. Soon."

She thought, as she walked down the path, how astonished Miss Falconer would be if she knew why it had become so important to read handwriting. She would also be extremely angry if she knew where her pupil was going, for Diamond was about to return to the little theatre at the back of the burned-out workhouse.

She would have found it hard to give her reasons. She had been terrified that last time, though by now she had almost convinced herself that it was all imagination. For who could possibly have been hiding in the theatre? If there was really someone there, the person would have come forward and revealed himself. No, it was all quite absurd, and Diamond knew, as all actors know, that theatres are haunted places; there was no theatre that did not have its own private ghost. Certainly Drury Lane, with its long history, had plenty of them.

The truth, or at least part of it, was that Diamond, as she had to admit to herself, missed the theatre world most damnably. She could not pretend that life in Middleditch had so far been uneventful, but even so, it did not quite make up for the theatre, the first-night hush, the shadowy figures in the boxes who could make or mar a performance, the nervous tension of the players, the wonderful moment when one first stepped onto the stage.

Oh, thought Diamond, I am probably the world's worst actress, but how I love it, how I miss it, how I think of Kitty and Peg and that horrid little Bellamy who would upstage the world. The memories crowded in on her again as she made her way to the workhouse. She remembered the new actress who had lasted one day—a young woman who lost her hat, her cloak, her temper and her senses, more drunk and more angry than anyone could conceive, because she fluffed her lines. She remembered poor Peg, whom they had all liked and whom Mr. Garrick had more than liked, half paralyzed toward the end, a lifeless body with a long face. She remembered carrying halfpenny salads across to the theatre for their luncheon, thought with a wry smile of the poor prompter who spoiled a dramatic pause and was knocked down by the infuriated actor; of Mr. Sheridan Senior, known affectionately as "Old Bubble and Squeak"; of Mr. du Vall, the peruke maker. She heard again Mr. Garrick's paternal warning, "My dear girl, you are vastly followed. Men in general are rascals. You are young and engaging and therefore ought to be doubly cautious."

It was all too much. Diamond was nearly in tears. And now she was once more at the workhouse. She stood looking at it, feeling, as she had before, part of it, yet removed as if by a lifetime.

It was November now and bitterly cold. It had been a savage autumn. The Axenford woods stretched out bleakly at the side of the building. Perhaps they should be called the Ringham woods. The little girls from the workhouse had often stood on the fringe of them, touching the bark of the trees, soothed by the green foliage overhead. They had never dared go farther, not even Diamond. It was only Pa at his most audacious who stepped silently in, catching anything that would fill their bellies, and once, as Diamond remembered clearly, coming back with a deer, a vast creature with its antlers trailing the ground, which provided them with venison until it grew too high to eat.

She had asked—she was nine at the time—"Won't they be angry?" She had no idea if it was an Axenford or a Ringham deer. Perhaps Pa had no idea either. But she somehow knew that this was not just poaching, which normally no one troubled about, this was real, grand stealing, though the delicious meat was so good that she did not really care.

"Yes," he said, grinning, "they'll be angry, my darling. They'll hang me if they can."

They'll hang me if they can. They could indeed, and they did hang him, only it was not for a deer. It was for a rabbit that nobody wanted. Diamond had watched the hanging. It was the last time she would ever see Pa, and she knew she had to be there. It was something she would never forget, never. They said that criminals were wicked men who deserved to be hanged, but Diamond, after what she saw—it made her sick for a week, with a temperature that all but killed her—could not believe that. No one in the world, however bad, deserved to be slowly throttled—choking, retching, gasping, swinging in the wind.

Not even Mr. Vincent.

"Oh, Pa," whispered Diamond on a sob. "Oh, Pa, my darling, darling Pa."

Then she stepped into the workhouse. It was as if she could not keep away. God knows, apart from the theatre, there was nothing to draw her back, nothing but memories of cold and hunger and misery and fear. This time she did not pause to look round her. The place was as empty as a rifled grave, even death was no longer there. Only one ghost caught at her hand, the ghost of a red-haired little girl, plain, freckled and gat-toothed, who had crept furtively into her bed, whispered confidences to her that nobody else ever heard; they had plighted eternal friendship with a ring made of their hair, the black strand entwined with the red. Diamond still had that ring, with her old clothes in the portmanteau.

She turned her face away from the pleading ghost. She said aloud, her voice high, "There's nothing I can do for you,

Becky. You're dead. If you'd been still alive, I would have taken you to live with me. I would have given you plenty to eat and nice clothes. I would have done anything for you. But I cannot. What can I do? I can't even put flowers on your grave. There is only one thing left, and that is revenge. I swear I'll kill the man who killed you. But not now. Leave me alone. I'm alive and you are not. You smell of the grave. Go away. Please go away—oh, Becky, darling Becky, please go away."

But she believed she still heard the sobbing, saw a bright flash of carroty-red hair. Diamond pushed at her, pushed at nothing, then ran into the theatre. Uneasiness quivered her nerves as she walked onto the stage. Again she was aware of being watched. For a moment she was so afraid that her head swam, then her common sense came, if a little weakly, to her aid. If someone were watching her, that someone was a living person, not a ghost, and Diamond could not believe this creature, whoever it was, intended to harm her.

She swung round in a swirl of skirts, as if indeed she were acting a part. She threw her voice to the farthest end of the little theatre, as Mr. Garrick had taught her, and it pealed back at her with a shocking shrillness.

"You are a coward!" cried Diamond. "A scoundrel and a coward! Come out and show yourself. I'm not afraid of you, it is you who are afraid of me. Come out at once, do you hear? It is ridiculous to sneak behind the curtains—"

She stopped with a gasp. Her heart was pounding, her mouth gone dry. She could not utter another word. Her eyes stared in horror as the hangings parted. The person, whoever it was, did not step out as Diamond, paralyzed with fear, watched. But the face showed through, and it was such a face as Diamond in the worst of nightmares had never imagined.

It was hardly a face at all. It was like a living skull, the flesh all eaten away. The nose was two gaping nostrils, the mouth a slit of teeth, with the lips gone. Over cheeks and forehead was a kind of decaying fungus, as if some foul lichen had attached itself to the breathing flesh. Only the eyes were untouched, and Diamond, sick and faint with terror, met the gaze of two huge orbs, vast and beautiful amid the decay, fixed on her with a kind of despairing longing.

Then the person gave a sobbing moan, and instantly the hangings swung to again.

Diamond could not move. She stood as though struck by a paralyzing blow, and she continued to stand there, her hands upraised as if to ward off the apparition. She was unable to utter a sound, and the sweat of panic trickled between her shoulder blades. Then abruptly she recovered herself. She ran to the side of the theatre, and clenching her teeth in an effort to surmount her revulsion and fear, jerked the hangings aside.

There was nothing there but the small passageway and side door she had seen the first time. The door was unlocked, and Diamond pulled it open. It led to the Axenford woods. There was nothing to see but the bare trees and bushes, nothing to feel but the damp mold beneath her feet and the intense cold. She could see the winter sky through the leafless branches, leaden with the snow still to come. In the distance she could hear the baying of one of Sir Francis' hounds.

She paused for a moment, her hands clenched at her breast. Then she began to laugh in bitter self-contempt. The poor creature, whoever it was, had simply walked through the woods and used what would be an emergency stagedoor, planned perhaps for summer plays that could be performed out of doors, like *A Midsummer Night's Dream* or *As You Like It* or one of the masques that were currently the vogue. Perhaps it was some escaped lunatic who had crept in out of the cold; certainly it would be someone far more frightened than herself.

I should have given comfort, thought Diamond, but she knew to her shame that she could not have come nearer, and the thought of touching that appallingly disfigured mask, or even putting an arm round the person's shoulders, brought the vomit up in her throat, made her body go stiff with disgust.

She called out once again, but this time her voice was so choked with emotion that the person, probably already well into the woods, would never hear.

"Come back," whispered Diamond. "Don't be afraid. I won't hurt you. Oh, come back . . ."

Then she grew cold with panic lest the face should suddenly reveal itself between the branches. But there was neither sight nor sound, and Diamond, feeling that she could not bear to go into the theatre again, walked round the workhouse, through the damp, rotting leaves, and out into the main street.

She paused by St. Joseph's Church which, as always, looked cold and deserted. It was hard to imagine anyone coming there for help or comfort. She knew of course that there were Sunday services, so there must be some kind of congregation. Did Sir Francis and Captain Ringham sit on opposite sides, mouthing curses at each other between prayers? She herself had been asked to attend. The message was delivered to her from the minister by one of the choirboys. Georgy wanted her to go, though she was no more a churchgoer than Diamond; in fact, Diamond had never heard her so much as mention the subject.

But now she had the effrontery to tell her mistress that she should attend Sunday morning service. "It's expected of you," she said.

"Why is it expected of me? You're being perfectly ridiculous."

"I am not. You're a fine lady now, and you have to set a good example. The village will think very poorly of you if you don't go."

"I do not give a damn what the village thinks of me, and I have no intention of going. I don't like Mr. Revill. I'm sure he preaches a horrid sermon, and I'm not wasting my time on something that means nothing to me."

But she did not tell Georgy of the sad, bored crocodile of girls who had been forced into the church twice every Sunday, and she did not say, either, that the dramatic side of her nature tempted her to go all the same, complete with pretty hat, white gloves and demure expression. It would be amusing to sit there so devoutly, with everyone peeping at her and whispering behind hands; no one had peeped at the wretched little workhouse girls except to sneer at them and call them charity brats.

She had once asked her father about religion, but it was not a subject that interested him. She wanted to know if she would go to heaven when she died. He had laughed, saying,

"Why not, if that's what you want, Clary. But I shouldn't depend on it, girl. Parson don't admit there's a heaven for the likes of you and me. He would send us straight to hell, together with the papists and the Jews and all the other heathen."

She had no idea what he was talking about, but then, with Pa that so often happened. So she had asked him what hell was like, since apparently she was going there, and he spun her a long story all about beautiful woods and animals and birds and as much food and drink as one could manage, together with all the interesting people in the world, the poets and the poachers and the black people from Africa who swung on trees. After that Diamond was for a long time filled with a passionate desire to go to hell. It was only when she was in the workhouse that she heard she would go there whether she liked it or not, and that far from being a wonderful place, it was worse than the worst kind of prison, with devils to spear you with pitchforks and pour burning coals over your head.

Yet now, running from the workhouse, though God to her was irrevocably linked with Mr. Vincent, she felt so cold and shocked that she wanted to go into the church to pray, not for herself but for that poor lost creature with no face. She instinctively passed a hand over her own soft cheek, wondering what kind of hell on earth it must be to look so vilely repulsive that children would run screaming from you, that men would cross the road to avoid looking at you, and unkind people would jeer and mock and throw stones.

Oh, I could not bear it, thought Diamond, feverishly aware of her own beauty, I would have to kill myself.

But then, presumably this woman had once been like other women; it must be that some terrible disease had destroyed her. And this struck a chord in Diamond's shocked mind, for up till then she had been too overcome with the horror of it to think coherently. But before she could work it out, she saw that Mr. Revill had come out of the church door and was making his way toward her.

He said in accents of prim reproach, with the stifled giggle underneath, "This is no day to be abroad, Miss Diamond. And I see you have been walking through the woods, despite the inclement weather. My dear young lady, you should be at home by a good hot fire. I can see you are already chilled. You must come in for a while to warm yourself and let my Mrs. Cowling make you a hot toddy."

Diamond thought that a hot toddy would be most inviting, for her teeth were beginning to chatter; only it was a pity it had to be offered her by Mr. Revill. However, perhaps he could help her, perhaps he knew who this wretched creature was—he must surely know if she was a member of his parish. So she looked down wryly at her muddied skirts—he was an observant man, she had to grant him that—and agreeing to his offer, found herself once more in his study.

It pleased her even less this time, as indeed did Mr. Revill himself. She could not help thinking that Sir Francis's judgment was sadly at fault, but then, he was a kind-hearted man and no doubt believed that all parsons by virtue of their cloth must be good. She looked around her at the neat, cold, dark study, and her eyes lit once more on the crucifix. This, like the memory of that poor ravaged creature, stirred a thought in her mind, almost as if it reminded her of something she had seen before, but she pushed it away from her, sipping at her drink. She warmed her hands before the fire and wished most fervently that she were back home, for Mr. Revill's company in some way pricked the hair on her head.

He said, with his odd displeasing giggle, "I gather, my dear lady, that you are not a believer."

Diamond answered, quite indignantly, "No. I have never seen any reason to be so." And she wanted to add that if one saw the person one loved best in the world choking on the end of a rope, it was hardly conducive to faith and devotion.

But she checked herself in time. It struck her that he might have asked her in to scold her, to persuade her to come and listen to his horrid sermons. But she perceived to her surprise and a little to her unease that he merely looked amused. He certainly was the oddest clergyman. By rights he should be preaching to her on the terrors of hell or, like Georgy, pointing out that she should set a good example.

He said, "Have you had so hard a life?"

A sudden anger consumed Diamond, for she felt he was playing with her. After all, as a friend of Sir Francis, he must know something about her; he was plainly deriding her, play-acting that she was a fine lady.

She said coldly, "I have been very poor. I have near starved. I have learned that there is one world for the poor and one for the rich. When I was a child, sir, I came to your church, only you were not the minister. I had to come, it was my duty. But I cannot see that it will help your parishioners because I put on my best bonnet and gloves, and go through all the proper motions. Why should I come? It would mean nothing to you, and it would distract your audience—"

"My audience!" he repeated, then broke into a brief, sharp laugh.

Diamond flushed. It was a silly word to use. Clergymen did not have audiences. Then she realized why she had said it. It was not simply a slip of the tongue. Mr. Revill reminded her of an actor she had once known. She could not remember his name, and he had lasted barely a couple of months, but the company had called him the Teapot Actor, because his favorite pose was to stand in the middle of the stage, one arm akimbo and the other outstretched. He had proved himself a poor sort of actor, with the unpardonable habit of upstaging everyone about him. He indulged in idle gossip, spread wicked scandal about the entire cast, and was reputed to be as cold as ice and as conceited as the devil.

In the end Mr. Garrick dismissed him, for as the tale went, he had seduced a couple of young girls and later brought them to Old Kate in Covent Garden, for which he was paid a vast sum of money. Whether this was true or not, Diamond did not know. She was then new to the company and the Teapot Actor in no way interested her, except that Kitty called him a bad man, and Kitty was never quick to condemn.

You are an actor, thought Diamond, you are not a clergyman at all. You don't believe in God. If you believe in anything, it is the devil. And a shudder went through her, for perhaps this was the fiend who had murdered poor Becky, who was responsible for the black cloud of evil that lay over Middleditch.

She answered Mr. Revill as pleasantly as she could. "Oh," she said, "I have been on the stage. It is a word that comes naturally to me. After all, in a sense your congregation is your audience. It is not such a foolish word to use. But if I seem to have insulted you, please forgive me, it was not intended." Then, because she could not stop herself from speaking what was in her mind, she said in a flurry of words, "Is there perhaps some poor escaped lunatic in this place, who lives in the woods?"

His face grew so intent that she knew she should not have spoken. She had not specified the sex or referred to the dreadful disfigurement, but she suspected he knew what she was talking about. However, it was too late now, and she could only stare at the curious kind of glow that had spread over his countenance, as if this were something that engrossed him far more than sermons and congregations.

He said in a thin, vibrant voice, with, for once, no trace of a giggle, "Where did you meet this person?"

"Oh, I didn't actually meet him," said Diamond quickly. "I was in the theatre. It sounds foolish, does it not, but I do so miss Drury Lane, and I knew that Sir Francis's wife had built this little place, so I had to go there. I heard someone outside. When I opened the door there was no one there. But I heard a moan, and I thought— Oh, I daresay I imagined it. It could be some animal, or perhaps a strange bird—"

And you are overacting, girl, she told herself. He is a clever man. He knows perfectly well you are lying.

Mr. Revill rose slowly to his feet. He moved back nearer the window so that his face was in shadow. He had done this before, she remembered. His voice sounded perfectly ordinary as he said, "Did you not so much as catch a glimpse of this person?"

"No. Oh no."

"Are you so certain it was a man?"

"I am not certain about anything," said Diamond, her heart pounding. "I suppose I could not believe a woman would be wandering by herself in the woods on a cold November afternoon."

"There is no escaped lunatic," said Mr. Revill. "The nearest asylum is in the town some fifty miles away."

"Then perhaps it was a child playing some sort of practical joke."

"Perhaps. You must stop going to this theatre, Miss Diamond."

"Why?" She, too, was on her feet. In her heart was a panic-stricken urge to be away, though surely she could not be safer than in a vicarage, with Mrs. Cowling within call.

"Because," said Mr. Revill, in a voice she had never heard from him, "it is none of your business to visit such a God-forsaken place. The theatre is the work of the devil, and the devil is abroad in this village. It should never have been built. If I had been here, I would not have permitted it. I am only thankful that it is left to rot like the heathen thing it is. You will not go there again. I forbid it."

"I go where I please," said Diamond in a whisper. She was backing toward the door, but her head was held high.

"This is my parish," said Mr. Revill, "and you do as you are told, or it will be the worse for you." And suddenly he was on her, his hands gripping her shoulders. He said in a hiss, "You are beautiful. You are too beautiful to live. You preach the devil's gospel, Miss Diamond. You are my enemy, you should never have come here. But you cannot leave now. It is too late."

The nearness of him, the hot hands on her shoulders and the extraordinary contortions of his features, put Diamond in a panic of terror and rage. She raised her hand and clouted him violently across the cheek.

It made a sound like a pistol shot. He released her instantly. She wanted to run to the door, but her legs would hardly support her. The room was rocking about her, and it seemed as if there was a smell of incense in her nostrils that made her faint and sick.

His voice came to her from a long way off. "It will soon be Christmas," he said. "At that holy time the spirits will be exorcised. You will never leave here, Miss Diamond Browne. You will never see Drury Lane again. You have come here to spy on us, and Christmas will provide you with the heart of the mystery." Then suddenly his voice, high and vibrant, pealed out at her. "Soon the last king will be strangled with the entrails of the last priest. Behemoth, Astaroth, Incubus, Bael and Asmodeus, protect me! And you and your like, you will be tormented eternally by the words of the great key of

Solomon—Aglon, Tetagram, Vaycheon, Erohares, Retgrag-sammathon, Meffias, Adomai! Go while you can, you bitch of hell. Your time is short, the moment is almost come."

Then he made a strange gesture at her, which Diamond recognized, only the hand was held upside down. If the hand had been palm downwards, it would have been the warding off of the evil eye. Once it had been made to her father by a woman who called him gypsy and demon. He had laughed, and Diamond had not understood. "She thinks I am the devil," he said, then, seeing his daughter's frightened face, "Ah, never mind, Clary girl. There are no devils except in her mind. The poor soul is mad with her own fears, she does not know what she is doing."

But there were devils, and never had Diamond been more thankful than when her hand closed round the knob of the door, which, thank God, thank God, opened easily to her touch. Suddenly there sprang into her vision the crucifix over the mantelpiece, shining and clear as if it were a living thing, and then in the whirlpool of her terrified mind she knew why it had troubled her.

It was like the gesture. It was upside down.

She ran out into the passage, and beyond all pride or shame, hurtled herself toward the front door. She could hear Mr. Revill's voice. He seemed to be chanting some kind of gibberish, full of the strange names he had hurled at her. The chanting was the same that she had heard on her first night at Middleditch. She was crying with fear, and unaware of any-one else's existence, knocked against Mrs. Cowling, who was coming up from the kitchen.

The human contact shocked her back into her senses. She stared down into Mrs. Cowling's face, for she was a small, round woman, perhaps five foot in height, and tried to speak some form of apology, but her mouth was too dry and she could not bring out a word.

Mrs. Cowling said violently, "Go home, miss. We don't want your sort here. Go back where you belong. Go away! You're bad luck to us."

Then, as Diamond, amazed, began to stammer a protest, she shrieked out the one word "Gyppo!" and rushed back down the kitchen stairs.

No one had called Diamond such a name for over six years. She was too taken aback to say anything. For a moment she leaned against the wall, her eyes closed. Then she ran out into the blessed evening air.

✾ XII ✾

Two thoughts clung in Diamond's mind—one, that she must get back to the cottage, and then, that she must see Sir Francis. But she could not face the thought of walking through the woods alone; the dark was descending and the dogs would be abroad. However, company of some sort she must have, terrified as she was of whom she might meet, and when she heard the footsteps she swung round, shaking with fear, praying it would be someone kind and human who might escort her home.

It was Philip. He shot her one sullen look and would have stalked past her in grim silence, but Diamond was long past reason and she seized him by the arm. He tried to shake her off, but she clung like a burr, and short of knocking her to the ground, there was nothing he could do. He tried to pull himself away, but she shouted at him, "You stupid, cruel boy! Can't you see I'm frighted out of my wits? Hate me as much as you like, but at least walk beside me till I get home. I cannot and will not go on my own. You're only a little boy, of course," cried Diamond, almost beside herself, "but you're better than nothing, and I swear I'll not let go of you if . . . if I have to dig my nails into you." Then she whispered in a pleading voice, "Oh, please, please, don't leave me. If you do, I think I'll die."

He was utterly taken aback. But he was not stupid or imperceptive, and Diamond's face, white and shining with sweat, showed clearly that she was terrified. He thought she must be mad, but he could not ignore her distress, and she really was very pretty, so he said gruffly, "I say, what's all this about? Have you lost your senses? There is nothing here to frighten you. You're only a few minutes' walk from your home, and surely— Oh, all right. I'll come with you. Only let go of me, you've bruised my arm to pieces. I never thought a girl could have such a grip."

Diamond slackened her hold, but was still careful to cling to his coat sleeve. She walked beside him, and presently he said in an unsure voice, "You'd better tell me what's happened. Has somebody attacked you? Are you hurt? I'd better call my brother—"

"Oh no—no!"

It was the wrong thing to say, and she was instantly afraid that he would leave her. Her hand tightened once more, but he did not walk away, just said very stiffly, "Oh, of course, you are a friend of Sir Francis. I think you are a very stupid girl, Miss Diamond, and if I weren't a gentleman, I'd leave you this very minute."

"Yes," whispered Diamond, "I am a very stupid girl."

"Anyway," said Philip, "if you want to see Sir Francis, and I cannot imagine why you should, he's not here."

"What do you mean?" They were approaching the path that led to the cottage. The lights were all on. Georgy, thank God, would be there, and they could bolt the door and put a table against it as they had done the first night, and Diamond would take the pistol out of her reticule and see that it was always within touch.

"He's gone to London," said Philip indifferently. "I hope he stays there. We don't want him here. He's a swine and a bastard. I hate him. When I'm old enough I'm going to kill him. If Will don't do it first."

"Why do you speak so against him?" asked Diamond. She was at the door now. She wondered if she should ask him in, but suspected he would refuse the invitation without courtesy.

Philip looked at her without replying. There was such hatred in his face that Diamond was taken aback; it seemed extraordinary in so young a boy.

She said uncertainly, "You lamed one of his best horses."

His mouth opened in protest, then he turned violently on his heel and ran down the path as if devils were after him. Diamond, with a sigh of relief and exhaustion, opened the door, catching her skirt on that confounded chair as she did so. It was all absurd and childish. She really must get one of the villagers to remove it for her. As she opened the door,

Georgy, her face bright with excitement, came running toward her. Diamond said wearily, "What is it now?"

"You have a visitor, Miss Diamond," whispered Georgy.

"Oh no. Who can it possibly be? I am so tired, I just want to eat my supper and go to bed."

"It's him!"

"Him? Oh, you stupid old bitch, what are you talking about?" Then she looked into the sitting room as the visitor came slowly toward her.

It was the old man.

Diamond for a moment could think of nothing to say. This sudden reappearance of someone from a world she had left only a few months ago, yet which she had already almost forgotten, was like acting in one play and suddenly finding oneself in another. She looked at the old man in silence, then, when he took her hand, made him a slight curtsy, and still without a word, followed him back into the room.

She was aware that she was extremely disarranged. Her hat must surely be crooked; her hair was falling about her shoulders and her shoes and the hem of her dress were stained with mud and wet leaves. What she did not know was that she was looking so extraordinarily beautiful that the old man's breath was taken away. The color produced by her frantic walk back to the cottage was brilliant in her cheeks, the tangled black hair gave her a wild, dramatic look, and the quick breathing, which he believed was excitement at seeing him, stirred him as Fanny never had, as few women had in his life.

And Diamond saw a dried-up old man, immaculately dressed as always, the elegant long-fingered hands betraying the brown marks of old age. The voice in which he said "I trust, ma'am, this is not an undue liberty" was an old man's voice, impeccably well-bred but devoid—or so it seemed to her—of the smallest warmth or emotion. Yet it was emotion of some kind that must have brought him here, and she was filled with a strange pity that with all his wealth, his centuries of pedigree, his house filled with beautiful things, he still had to buy his women, still had to pay cash down for love.

She could not believe that she had ever been in bed with him. She had known him intimately, she had seen him stripped of his clothes and the corset he wore beneath them, she had received his body, she had accepted his rare kisses. But now it seemed remote and entirely obscene. She wished he had not come, could not imagine what they had to say to each other. She was, after all, no longer the little girl in the shocking clothes who had sat beside him in his carriage; she had grown immeasurably away from the person who had said *I have no choice.* This place she lived in he had bought for her, but it was nonetheless her own. She was the hostess, she was receiving him in her own home, on her own terms.

She said, simply, "Would you like a glass of wine, Harvey?" —and did not realize that she was using his first name for the first time, did not even notice the expression of astonishment that flickered across his face.

"I should indeed," he said, adding almost reluctantly, "Thank you."

He sat down on one of Captain Ringham's armchairs, and Diamond, now feeling so strange that it was as if she were floating above herself, walked over to the window and leaned against the sill. She could not help thinking—as Georgy, seething with suppressed excitement at the incredible drama of it all, brought in decanter and glasses—that in the old days the glass of wine had been a kind of official preliminary to bed. The thought made her mouth curve in an ironic smile, for if the poor old devil imagined she was going to lie with him, he had never been more mistaken in his life.

He saw that smile. He misunderstood it, taking it as an invitation, not recognizing it for the flattest of refusals. Certainly she was a lovely woman, lovelier than he remembered, and certainly she had changed in some strange way that he could not analyze, but she was still the little actress he had summoned to his bed, and he was not going to waste time in polite conversation.

He drank a little of his wine, eyeing her over the rim of the glass. Then he put his hand in his pocket and pulled out the diamond necklace he had once given her. "This is for you," he said. "You left it behind. I thought you might like it." And he held it out on the palm of his hand.

Diamond looked down at it. It was unwrapped. He had not even troubled to put it in a box. He held it out to her as if he were offering sugar to a horse. When he went on to say, "I want you to come back with me, Diamond," she continued to look at the necklace without so much as stretching out a finger for it.

Then he said, a little impatiently, "I believe I was mistaken in sending you away. It is true that you behaved in a very vulgar fashion, but I daresay you have now learned your lesson, and it seems to me only fair to give you another chance. My carriage is waiting in the street, just round the corner. Shall I tell your maid to pack your things? And I beg of you to take the necklace. It is, after all, yours. I was surprised that you left it."

"I gave it back to you," said Diamond. "Don't you remember, Harvey? I took it off my neck and gave it back to you."

He blinked at this persistent use of his name, but there was nothing he could say. She had always addressed him as "my lord." She was really no better than a servant, but he had made love to her, he had taken her into his bed. If she chose to be so familiar, that was something he could correct in due course. This was no moment to rebuke her.

He said, with his faint, grim smile, "You were in a temper. Women in tempers do foolish things. I knew at the time you did not mean it. Well, Diamond? Are you not coming with me?"

She said, "No."

At this he leaped to his feet, suddenly furious, and said, "What the devil do you mean?"

"I mean I am not coming with you."

"Why not, pray?" He looked about him, his mouth going down in contempt at the chintz curtains, the country furniture. "Oh, I can see you've made it pretty enough. It's the way of women. But you cannot pretend this is the kind of thing I've taught you to appreciate. You are not going to tell me, surely, that you like country life. I should imagine you are bored to death."

Then Diamond began to laugh. She had just been scared almost out of her wits, and whatever else one could say about life in Middleditch, it was hardly boring. Her laughter maddened him and all the surface courtesy vanished. He looked ugly and threatening, and took a step toward her, almost as if he would strike her.

But his voice was calm and cold as he said, "I think you've taken leave of your senses. I am not sure now if I want you back. I assumed you would have learned better behavior, but I see now you are precisely the same vulgar slut I was fool enough to take into my home. Now that you have finished with this unseemly mirth, I expect you to apologize."

Diamond said quietly, "I don't think I owe you an apology, Harvey." She saw his face tighten, and said, "Oh, but I am being overfamiliar. I am forgetting my place. My lord. Is that better?" Then she came up to him so that she almost touched him. She said, "I'm sorry. But I could never come back. You don't really want me. You just want a mistress who will not do you discredit. Perhaps I am a country girl, after all. I think I once said to you that I had no choice. Now I have the choice, and I've made up my mind. You were never unkind to me. You were sometimes generous—"

"Thank you," he said. He had grown very white. He was fumbling for his hat. No woman of her sort had ever refused him before; he could hardly believe his ears. He had been so sure that she would at once accompany him to his carriage, that things would be again as they had always been, that the little house in Highgate, now untenanted, would be hers again. And she had the impudence to use his first name, to refuse the necklace, to refuse him.

She went on—she had always talked too much—"But you never treated me like a person. Even now, when you want me to come back to you, you don't ask, you order. You take it for granted that I will follow you like a little dog. You could have said for instance that you loved me—"

"Loved you!" He was outraged. He was beginning to believe that it was he who was out of his mind, to hear such extraordinary, unbelievable words.

"Well," said Diamond reasonably, "you would not have meant it. But you could have said it. People do. I still would not have come with you, but at least it would have been friendly. I am not suggesting that you offer marriage . . ."

This was too much. He stalked toward the door, the diamonds still in his hand. He was positively shaking with rage. The cottage was hers, for it was bought and paid for, but if he could have smashed the roof down over her disgraceful head, he would have done so. And as he went he almost tripped over a small table. This was the last straw and his fury almost choked him.

Diamond went on, a little sadly, "Marriage would of course be ridiculous. But just to . . . to whistle at me and say, Come— Oh, my lord, I do appreciate a great many things that you have done for me, but it is all such a long time ago, such a very long time ago."

"Two months," he said with a snap. He had opened the door. He looked at her with hate.

"It seems like two years," said Diamond. She longed to ask about Fanny, but saw that this would be inadvisable. She said again, "I'm sorry. It was kind of you to ask me. Can we not part as friends?"

He had flung the door open. He forgot himself so far as to shout at her, "Friends! I do not make friends with cheap little whores!"

Captain Ringham's deep voice interrupted him. "Who is this?" he asked Diamond, who was standing in the passage, not knowing whether to laugh or cry. "Do you wish me to deal with him for you?"

He was sitting in the chair outside the door. He looked, Diamond thought, perfectly ridiculous, leaning back in a brocade-covered chair in the November dusk, with the temperature certainly below freezing. As he spoke he rose to his feet. He came up to the old man, towering over him, and moved his right arm back as if to knock him down.

Diamond cried out in dismay, "Oh no, no, don't! He's an old man . . ."

It was the final insult. The old man's face spoke murder, but he did not back an inch, though Captain Ringham stood a good head above him. He looked up into the dark, threatening face, and the contempt and disdain in his expression was such that his opponent burst out laughing and his arm swung back to his side.

There was a silence. Then the old man, after waiting a brief moment as if to see what would happen, turned on his heel and started to stride down the path. Halfway down, with both Diamond and Captain Ringham watching him, the one in trepidation, the other in amusement, he wheeled round and flung the necklace, still dangling from his fingers, back at Diamond. It landed at her feet, the diamonds sparkling in the light from the passageway.

She did not attempt to pick it up, only turned her head to look down at the waiting carriage, half concealed by the turn of the street. She looked at Captain Ringham, at the chair, then back at him again. She said very wearily, "You had best come inside."

Then she burst into tears and cried rather noisily for a while; she had never learned how to weep prettily. Captain Ringham, to hide his embarrassment, bent down and picked up the diamond necklace, then sat down, twirling it in his hand, and waited in silence for the storm to pass.

When Diamond at last finished her crying, she blew her nose, mopped at her cheeks, and glanced a little blurrily at Captain Ringham, who met her gaze with an almost compassionate look. As their eyes met, she made a sudden discovery. This was the man she had always believed to have hanged her father. This was her enemy. But she knew at the moment with complete conviction that whatever he was, he was in no way responsible for the strange, evil things that were happening around her. The face that now regarded hers was a stern, dark face, the face of a man who could be harsh in his judgments, who certainly had a violent temper, who could be intolerant, condemn too easily, but it was not the face of someone who would obscenely murder little girls. The idea of Captain Ringham conducting a Black Mass, chanting with Mr. Revill, or tearing hearts out of people to rejuvenate himself, was simply preposterous.

And as all this went through her mind, the dreadful urge to honesty, which had so often proved her undoing, came upon her. She stepped up to him, so that her skirt brushed against him, and stared defiantly down.

He held out his hand. "Your necklace, ma'am. I realize that you like throwing things out onto the path, but it seems a trifle reckless to cast away something that must be worth nearly a thousand pounds."

"If I keep it," said Diamond in a choked, snuffly voice, "he'll probably have me hanged at Tyburn."

"I should think that unlikely," said Captain Ringham, laying the necklace down on the table. "It would offend his pride. Besides, you have me as a witness."

"Would you testify for me?" asked Diamond unbelievingly.

"Certainly."

"Even though I'm nothing better than a cheap little whore?"

"I cannot see what difference that makes. In any case," said Captain Ringham, "I do not find that a particularly accurate description."

"It is perfectly true," said Diamond. She could not stop herself. "You must know it's true. That old man— His lordship was my lover. He kept me for three years. He treated me rather like a pet dog. I had a nice kennel and a bone to play with and . . . and his bed to sleep in. The dress I'm wearing now was one of his gifts. All my clothes are what he has given me. He simply whistled for me when he wanted me, and he tied big blue bows round my neck. He would probably have whipped me if I had misbehaved. And when he was tired of me, he threw me out. Only, he did buy this cottage for me, he always buys cottages for his castoffs. He said he would never see me again, he would have me thrown into prison if I dared go near him. But today he wanted me back—"

Diamond broke off. She was finding Captain Ringham's steady gaze unnerving. She said in a whisper, "I didn't want him. He'll never forgive me."

"I should not think he would," said Captain Ringham. "Especially as you called him an old man. Nobody in the circumstances could forgive that."

Diamond cried out hysterically, "You sit there like a hanging judge. Why don't you walk out? You shouldn't be talking to a woman like me. I am sure you are a most respectable gentleman."

"Why should you think that?" he asked, and to her amazement he produced a large pair of spectacles from his pocket and put them on, apparently to see her more clearly.

Diamond muttered, feeling that the situation was roaring out of all control, yet excited by the drama of it, "Are you wishing to see more clearly what a whore looks like?"

He said, with a sigh of exasperation, "I know very well what a whore looks like, and I know, too, that she would bear no resemblance to you. Besides," he added, his mouth twisting into a smile, "I am, according to you, the son of one, so we should do very well. Do you not think so?"

"Oh dear," said Diamond, the tears springing to her eyes again. "I should never have said that—Why you laughing at me? I don't like being laughed at."

"If I'm laughing at you," he said, "it's because you insist on dramatizing yourself. Stop making silly remarks to me, and for God's sake, stop play-acting. I am, as far as I know, a perfectly normal man, neither more nor less respectable than most, and I have no intention of playing the judge, hanging or otherwise."

"You hanged my father," said Diamond.

His face stiffened. There was no laughter in him now. For a while he did not say a word, and the remarks which Diamond would gladly have swallowed back burned between them like a Roman candle. He said at last in a harsh voice, "Yes. I have been expecting that."

"You knew who I was!"

"Of course I knew. Apart from that, my young brother heard Miss Falconer calling you Clary. I wish you wouldn't be so silly. In some ways you are an extremely intelligent young woman, and then you behave like a spoilt child, over-acting so appallingly that I am not surprised you preferred another career to that of the stage."

"How dare you!"

"I am only repeating what you have told me. May I suggest that just for one minute you hold your tongue and let me speak? I think I have been very patient with you, and I am not a patient man. Not only do you make dramatic scenes on the smallest provocation, but ever since you have been here you have been digging in the dirt, and from what my brother tells me, almost burying yourself in the process." He glared at her as he spoke. His face was dark and angry. "I have done my best to look after you, God knows I have. And you have scarce made it easy for me, going always to places where you should not go, consorting with—" He broke off. He said savagely, "What frightened you so today?"

173

Diamond's hesitation was brief, but she was convinced he noticed. She said in an airy fashion, "Oh, I wasn't really frightened."

"Philip said you were like a rabbit with a stoat."

"I think Philip imagines things. It was just that I went over to the little theatre—you know, the one at the workhouse—"

"I know."

"Oh, of course. Well, empty theatres are always haunted places, and I began to fancy I was seeing ghosts."

"And were you?"

"Of course not. There are no such things."

He said, his voice heavy and menacing, "What did you see?"

"I tell you, I saw nothing."

Then he roared at her, "Oh Christ, I could murder you!"

"As you did my pa!" cried Diamond, and she, too, raised her voice, so that she was almost shouting back at him.

He said more quietly, with an edge to his voice, "Applause from the pit! Most beautifully timed." He looked at her and gave a brief, bitter laugh. "So I hanged you father, did I? I knew him rather well, Clary. Or perhaps I should continue to call you Miss Diamond, if you prefer it."

"I do prefer it," said Diamond, tight-lipped. The horrid tears were back again, and she was determined not to cry; she could not stand before this extraordinary man and shed water like a fountain.

"Very well, Miss Diamond."

Then she had a wild desire to cry out, "Oh, please call me Clary, please, please . . ." but she knew she was preposterously overwrought, and would sound like the actress he accused her of being. So she said nothing, only sat down rather suddenly in the chair farthest away from him, her face averted.

He went on, "Your father and I used to talk together. He knew a great deal about plants and herbs and wild animals. I sometimes asked his advice. You will not, of course, believe it, but we did extremely well together, even when he plundered one of my deer."

"Was it yours?"

"It was indeed. I hope you enjoyed your dinner."

"But—"

"I owed him something. He saved the life of my favorite

sheepdog bitch, and he once cured my brother of a fever. He was in his way a good man. But he had one weakness—"

"You mean poaching?"

He gave her a grim smile. "No, Miss Diamond, I do not mean poaching. Poaching is a venial sin—"

"He died for it!"

"So you keep telling me. It seems that I am not only a hanging judge but an executioner in the bargain. But never mind. He— Shall we say he indulged his weakness, and died for it? He had to die for it. I knew it would happen. I told him so. He admitted I was right."

Diamond said faintly, "I don't understand you."

"No. You do not understand me. You do not wish to."

"But you . . . you did hang him. For that rabbit . . ."

He exclaimed, with the air of a man fighting to control himself, "Madam, in a minute I swear I'll— For God's sake, leave the matter. Very well. I hanged your father. For stealing a rabbit. I let him lift a deer, which is a capital offense in every country in the world, but I chose to hang him for a rabbit, one of those wretched animals that overrun my garden. And I'll tell you something more. If I could do it, I would this very moment take his daughter by the scruff of her damned stupid neck, throw her over my horse, and ride her back like hell to London. Miss Diamond. If I speak to you civilly, if I do not raise my voice, if I say to you with the utmost restraint, 'Will you please go away, will you please leave Middleditch, or will you at least accept my hospitality and come to stay in my house'—would you do so?"

"No," said Diamond, and she spoke sorrowfully, for at that moment there was nothing she wanted more than to be away, or at least under the protection of someone who would look after her.

"I thought you would say that." Captain Ringham rose to his feet. "Very well. There is nothing more to be said. God knows, I have done my best. Good day, madam. You are not, thank the good Lord, my responsibility, but may I entreat you not to return to the theatre and never, under any circumstances, walk in the woods unaccompanied? And I know I'm a damned fool to waste my breath, but will you please tell me what or whom you saw that frightened you?"

"I can't," said Diamond with a sob.

"Don't start sniveling again. Why not?"

"Because I'm not sure."

"What difference does that make? Perhaps I could tell you."

Diamond wanted to say, "I may be betraying her, I may be wrong, I shall not know until I've asked Miss Falconer—" but at last, with a wretched attempt at a smile, she said meekly, "If I speak civilly too, will you answer me something?"

"You refuse to answer me. I make no promises. Well? What is it?"

"Did you hang my father?"

"No. I did not. I daresay you do not believe me."

Diamond said, as if hardly believing herself, "I do believe you. I don't understand anything any more, but I do believe you. But . . . who did, Captain Ringham?"

He said, "It would serve no purpose if I told you."

"I suppose I must accept that," said Diamond, looking as if she did not accept it at all. Then she said, "I want to ask you something more."

"You certainly have a most damnable impudence!"

"Yes, I know. Are you very angry with me?" asked Diamond, and was amazed at the pleading tone of her own voice, for suddenly it mattered very much whether Captain Ringham was angry or not.

He did not answer, except with a smile that he tried instantly to suppress. But it encouraged her to continue, and she said, "I want to see Mr. Vincent. I understand he lives on your estate. It is very important to me, and as you know who I am, you must understand why. Did you know about me from the very beginning?"

He said impatiently, "Women are so vain. They imagine that if they dress differently or do their hair in some new-fangled style, nobody will know them. I have an excellent memory for faces, and fine gowns and fashionable curls in no way interest me." He gave her a look as he spoke. "I am so lacking in respectability, madam, that I am more concerned with what lies underneath. Besides, you are like your father, and as I have just told you, I knew him very well. I could not have missed you in a crowd of a hundred. Well, if you have so set your heart on seeing Mr. Vincent, you must do so.

It will do you no good, I can tell you that in advance. If you plan to speak to him in wounding words, to avenge yourself, you will be wasting both time and breath."

"Why?"

"Oh, you'll 'why' yourself into your grave. See him by all means. Then you'll know why, well enough." He turned toward the door, and Diamond, with a kind of mechanical memory of what a lady should do, said in a trailing voice, "May I not offer you a glass of wine . . . ?"

He laughed. "A glass of wine! After such a conversation it would be best to have pistols for two. Your necklace is on the table. You should not leave it lying around—even though I sat on guard outside last night, and may have to do so again."

"You sat on guard? In that chair!"

He exclaimed, "What in God's name else is there for me to do? There have been too many murders here already. I have so much evidence, so much, so much, yet there is still the vital piece of proof missing. I can only pray that that proof will not be you with a twisted neck. You'd have done better to go back to town with your old gentleman."

"Would you have liked that?" asked Diamond.

To her amazement he shouted out, "I'd have broken your back!" and with this, was away, moving so fast that it was like a tornado, and she had no time to utter another word. The door slammed behind him.

Diamond could only stare after him. Her color was high. Then, feeling that her last reserve of energy was gone, she continued to sit where she was, and presently she rested her head on her arms outstretched on the table. Georgy, coming in at this point, exclaimed, "Oh, Miss Diamond, what has happened now?"

"The world has happened," said Diamond, raising her head. She saw Georgy's open mouth, the eyes popping with curiosity. She knew she could not bear the barrage of questions so plainly due to come. She said, "Oh, you must make up your mind, my old woman. After all, I cannot marry the three of them. You'd best tell me which one you prefer."

Georgy answered without hesitation, "Captain Ringham."

"So do I," said Diamond in an astonished voice. Then she said wearily, "But he'll not have me."

"Why not?"

"Because I'm a whore."

"Miss Diamond!"

"Well, so I am. No, Georgy. I can't say anything more. Go away. I have to do my homework for Miss Falconer."

And indeed, after sipping a glass of wine she managed to do precisely that, as if somehow the pressure of all that was happening around her was released in the mental energy of writing out her letters.

❧ XIII ❧

On the way to her lesson the next morning, Diamond felt that
she had made progress; soon, surely, she would be able to read
writing, even write her own letters. But she was still exhausted
from yesterday's excitement, and it was only when she was
halfway down the village street that she was compelled to
recognize that the atmosphere around her had changed yet
again, and certainly for the worse. No one called her a gyppo,
yet it seemed to her that everybody knew who she was. The
people she passed stared at her with silent, unmistakable
hostility. Mrs. Rigg was too cowardly to display open enmity,
but she would have walked past without a word had not
Diamond, both upset and angry, asked how she was and said
perhaps on her way back she would look in at the shop to
buy some ribbons.

"Oh," said Mrs. Rigg, almost in a whine, "there'll be nothing
that will suit you, ma'am. You'll be used to the fine London
shops. You wouldn't want anything a poor old woman like
me could give you."

This kind of remark aroused the guttersnipe in Diamond,
but she managed to restrain herself, even smiled and said she
was sure that Mrs. Rigg's stock was excellent. If she had not
had her appointment with Miss Falconer, she would have
gone into the shop there and then, but it was already late, so
she hurried on. She saw that Mrs. Rigg was staring after her,
her face spiteful and sullen. Even Mr. Armstrong, leaning
against the lintel of the Rose and Crown, began to slide inside
when he saw her approaching, and when Diamond, still
resolved to be calm, called out to him that she would be
ordering some more of his excellent wine, he simply said,

"I'm afraid we're out of stock, ma'am," and retreated instantly into the inn.

"This is becoming absurd," Diamond said to Miss Falconer, and was so upset that she forgot her awe of the schoolmistress, ignoring her peremptory request to begin reading.

"You are being made the scapegoat," said Miss Falconer abruptly.

Diamond thought she looked very old and ill. There were pits of shadow under her eyes, and the wrinkled skin was yellow. She exclaimed, "What do you mean? I haven't done anything."

"When people are afraid," said Miss Falconer, "they always look for someone to blame. I daresay it has been indicated that since you came here, there has been more trouble."

"But that's nonsense! I know I'm curious. I can't help it. My pa was the same. He had to know."

"And look where it brought him," said Miss Falconer with an unexpected brutality.

Diamond flushed up, saying, "That's not fair. You know it isn't. Are you telling me that I'll be hanged?"

"I'm simply telling you, as I've always told you, to leave well alone." Then Miss Falconer reached out her wrinkled claw and took Diamond's hand in hers. "Child, I daresay you mean well, but other people do not. Christmas is coming, and it is always at Christmas that terrible things happen. If you do not take care, all the blame will be put on you, and then—" She broke off.

Diamond said impatiently, "What does happen at Christmas?"

"We are all praying that nothing will happen. They know who you are, Clary. They are saying in the village that the gypsy brat is bringing ill luck on them. They say you are allied with the devil."

"What have I done? Oh, Miss Falconer, you must tell me. What have I done?"

"I am too old," said Miss Falconer, as if she were speaking to herself. "I have seen so much, too much. I never believed you would come back, you of all people—"

"I don't understand you."

"You are your father's daughter. And here you are, running headlong into mischief, ignoring those of us who wish to help you. I can do nothing more for you, Clary, and if I could, you would not listen. I tell you, I am too old, there is no more strength left in me. I wish you had not come here. But now that you are," said Miss Falconer in her normal, brisk tones, "I suggest you do a little work."

"There is something very important I have to tell you."

"More interfering, no doubt."

"I suppose you might call it that," said Diamond sadly.

"Well, whatever it is, it can wait until you've done your reading. I thought you were so anxious to be able to understand handwriting?"

"Oh, I am, I am."

"Then you will certainly not do so by sitting there and talking. I have written out several lines for you, as clearly as I can. You will please read them out to me."

And so the hour passed, but Diamond, passionately longing to relate what she had seen, could not concentrate. For the first time she did so poorly that Miss Falconer grew angry, and scolded her as if she were a little girl again.

"This will not do," Miss Falconer said, and Diamond thought that if there were a ferule handy, it would be brought down on her palm. "This will not do at all. I believed at the beginning that you were an intelligent young woman, but any child in the first form would do better than this. You are simply not paying attention. You have made mistake after mistake. You have not done well in your homework. This lesson has been a pure waste of time. If you cannot do better than this, there is no point in your coming back. I have better things to do than try to teach an ignorant girl who does not even do me the courtesy of listening to me. Is that understood, Clary?"

"Yes, Miss Falconer," said Diamond meekly. Her dark eyes met the blue ones in desperation and appeal. After a pause the schoolmistress slapped her book shut and said abruptly, "Well, what is it? I see I'll get nothing out of you until you've told me. We'll have our glass of wine, though you do not deserve it. Now you had better tell me what all this is about."

"I have been thinking and thinking, and now I believe I have seen Lady Caroline," said Diamond.

Miss Falconer, normally so collected, dropped the glass she was holding. As it smashed to pieces on the iron fender, she muttered, "That was valuable glass . . ." Her face was chalk-white. She looked so ghastly that Diamond thought she would faint, and sprang to her feet to put her arms round her. But Miss Falconer pushed her hands away, saying in a loud voice, "You are talking wicked nonsense. Lady Caroline has been dead for two years."

Diamond began to cry at the horror of the memory; even now it made her dizzy and sick. She knew she would never forget the sight of that terrible face, and at this very moment it swam before her eyes. It was a little while before she could even speak, and Miss Falconer, too, said not another word. At last Diamond, stammering a little, managed to get the words out.

She said in a low, shaking voice, the country accent, as always in moments of emotion, thick and burring, "School-mistress, it had to be her. Oh, it was nothing I could recognize, it was . . . it was shocking. They say her face was destroyed, and so it was, so it was. I have never seen anything like it, I pray I never do again. Oh, ma'am, such a face—you could not imagine it in your worst nightmares. Like a corpse dug out of a grave after a long time . . ." Her voice shuddered down so that it was almost inaudible. "There was no face. It was eaten away. Sometimes on plants you see a kind of blight that devours everything. It was like that. It weren't no face at all. Just the eyes and . . . and bones and a mouth without lips. At first I was so afraid I thought I would die. And she gave a kind of moan and ran away. I didn't even speak to her. I am so ashamed of myself, I'll never forgive myself, but it was such a shock, I was nearly out of my mind. It must be Lady Caroline. It couldn't be anyone else. What is all this about? I don't understand any of it. Sir Francis said she was dead. He's just been lying to me. Why did he lie? I thought he was such a good man. Oh, ma'am," cried Diamond, the tears streaming down her face, "such things shouldn't happen to no one, not to a sweet lady like her. I want to help her, she was so good to me. She can't help her poor face. And perhaps if we talked I wouldn't think about it any more—it's like that sometimes, you just don't see people. Where is she living? Why does she have to creep about the woods like that? He's got plenty of money. He could make her comfortable. And if he really loved her, he could surely stay with her sométimes, just to comfort her. What has happened? You must know. I don't understand anything any more. Everything has become so horrid. And I think Mr. Revill is mad. And Captain Ringham—he is the one sane person. I hated him so much, but I was wrong. He is a good man, I think perhaps he is my only friend. Oh, Miss Falconer, please explain it to me. I can't bear it any more."

The old woman sat as if made of stone, silent, unresponsive. And Diamond thought suddenly of the mirrors, and then so terrible a thought came to her that she could not bring herself to utter it. She looked, almost frantically, at Miss Falconer, who began to mutter, "I knew it was her when you first mentioned there was someone there. But I did not want to believe it. We all believed her dead. Only Will Ringham once said he thought she was still alive. But nobody listened to him. She was a friend of mine. She used to come here sometimes. She said I was the only person she could talk to. Why didn't she come to me? Why didn't she come to me?" Suddenly her eyes fixed on Diamond, and her voice came out shrill and sharp. "Where did you see her?"

"I was in the theatre . . ."

"I told you not to go there."

"Yes, you did. But I didn't listen to you. I never listen to anyone," said Diamond sadly. "And I knew there was someone watching me again. And there she was. Why did that happen to her? They say she used too much rouge, and it destroyed her. But I used rouge when I was in the theatre. We all did, and it never happened to us." And she did as she had done before, put up a hand to her own unmarred cheek.

Miss Falconer had risen to her feet She was gathering her books together. She looked ghastly. There was no color in her face, and her mouth was twisted almost as if she had had a stroke, but she moved decisively, and her voice came out calm and cold.

"Go home, Clary Brown," she said. "You're a good girl, and a kind one. Go home."

"This is my home," said Diamond.

"Then go back to London. No doubt Mr. Garrick will offer you small parts."

"I am a terrible actress."

"Oh," cried Miss Falconer fiercely, "it is better to be a terrible actress than to be dead. I do not care what kind of actress you are. I do not care if you become a night-walker or go into a bawdy-house. All I want is to keep you alive. But you must get away from here. I will order a carriage for you, and then you and that maid of yours can be on your way. You need not pack. Just go. Now."

"No, Miss Falconer."

"Have you no sense at all? You can surely find yourself another protector. You have the looks. That is all men care about."

"For a schoolmistress," said Diamond, with a sobbing laugh, "you give me the oddest advice."

"I do not give a fig for your morals," snapped Miss Falconer. "I am only concerned for your neck. You are in terrible danger, Clary. What good are you doing by staying here?"

Diamond said again, "This is my home."

"It will probably be your grave. However," said Miss Falconer, still shuffling her books and papers together, as she had been doing for the past ten minutes, "I see there is no point in arguing with you. I really have no more time or patience. Go back to your cottage. I wash my hands of you. The lesson is over."

"I'll see you tomorrow," said Diamond. She looked steadily at Miss Falconer, who returned the gaze in grim silence. "It couldn't have been anyone but Lady Caroline, could it?"

"I'm afraid not," said Miss Falconer.

"I would like to see her again. To say I'm sorry. I would like to talk to her." There was no response, and after a moment's hesitation, Diamond said goodbye and left her old teacher.

She went straight back to the cottage. She met no one on her way except a farm boy with a load on his shoulders and a man driving a herd of cows to the milking shed, but the hate and hostility blew up from the stony road like an evil wind. And she knew what this reminded her of, and hunched her shoulders, desperate to be back within the safety of her own four walls.

The day they sentenced her father . . . She was only thirteen, but she went to his hanging, unable to bear it that he would suffer alone.

He had stood there, facing them all. A handsome man and tall. He towered above them, and for all the chains on his wrists and ankles, he somehow dominated them. He did not look afraid. His eyes moved from one condemning face to another, and his mouth curved in a smile. It was the smile he bestowed on his women: proud, insolent, victorious. Once he had said to her, "I'm not afraid of anything they can do to me, Clary. I'll not be afraid at my hanging. Why should I be? I'm better than they are. They can only kill me, they can't destroy what I have done and what I am."

But he had said that a long time ago. He had been proudly alive, striding along a little lane, with Clary at his side. The sun had been shining, the leaves green. Death was a lifetime away.

Clary, small, shivering, terrified, had smelled the hate on them all. She knew they longed for him to be dead, knew there would be no mercy for him. He was the stranger who had stolen their rabbits and chickens, taken eggs from the henhouse, picked apples from their trees. And he had plundered their women. It was these wives and daughters who plaited the rope that was to tighten round his handsome neck.

He had one weakness. And he died for it.

That was what Captain Ringham had said. Diamond had believed he referred to the poaching. Now she understood what he did mean. It was poaching of a kind. It was his roving dark eye, the animal attraction that brought them running. That was what had hanged him.

When the sentence had been pronounced, her screams pealed out, and they had all turned to look at her, the little gypsy bitch, with her dirty face, her greasy hair, her dress full of rents. Not one of them showed any compassion for her, not one woman came forward to take her in her arms. They simply smiled, seemed delighted with the double drama, and it was her father who spoke to her as they shoved him out of the courtroom.

His deep voice rang out so that her screaming stopped and they all fell silent. "Don't cry, my Clary," he had said. "There's nought to cry about. It'll soon be over." Then, as they kicked him through the door, "You should be ashamed of yourself, girl, to let them make you cry. They are nothing bastards, they are not worth a single tear. Spit in their eye, Clary. That's the only language they'll understand . . ."

Then his voice was lost in angry shouts, and presently the courtroom was empty except for Clary Brown, shriveled up in horror and grief, but dry-eyed now and silent. For Pa was always right, they were nothing bastards. They bloody well wouldn't make her shed one tear more. And she remembered now as Miss Diamond Browne, in her pretty dress, with her hair soft and clean—she remembered something that had not come back to her since that day, erased in the terror of it. Someone, she could not see who, for her eyes were blurred with unshed tears, someone—it was a man, she knew it was a man—came up behind her and put his arm about her shoulders. And she swung round, her bony little fists clenched, and spat straight in his eye. She never knew who it was, she did not even turn her head as she ran away. But it did not matter. She had done what her father told her to do. It had been a gesture of final defiance.

She arrived at the cottage, and the hate and anger made her head ache: the hate of the courtroom, the hate of the village, the hate that believed she was responsible for the evil around her. Perhaps wives were clutching at their stupid husbands, fearful lest they succumb to the wiles of this wicked gypsy slut. Diamond, rubbing at her forehead, longed to spit in their eyes too, longed to shout at them that they were nothing bastards. When she first came they had toadied to her because she wore fine clothes, because they believed she had money, but now they would gladly burn her at the stake. They would round upon her like a pack of hounds and drive her to her death, like one of Sir Francis's deer.

She saw from Georgy's face that she had a visitor again. She saw, too, that this time Georgy was not as delighted as usual. Indeed, the round apple-cheeked face looked quite worn and wan; instead of bursting out with the news, she clutched at her mistress and more or less dragged her into the kitchen.

Diamond, too distraught to placate her, said crossly, "Oh, what is it now, you silly old woman? Who is that in the sitting room?"

Georgy whispered, "It's Sir Francis." She still held onto Diamond's wrist, until it was jerked away from her. She was obviously in the midst of preparing a meal, for the table was littered with vegetable peelings and Captain Ringham's latest rabbit lay there, newly skinned and disemboweled. It looked disagreeably human, and Diamond, who preferred her meat cooked, averted her eyes. She said, unpinning her hat, "Then I'd best go and greet him." She added, under her breath, for this was not for Sir Francis to hear, "The village must believe I'm running a bawdy-house."

"Miss Diamond!"

"I am sure they are convinced of it." And Diamond, smoothing down her hair, turned toward the door.

"I must show you something, Miss Diamond."

"Surely it can wait . . ." But Diamond saw from Georgy's expression that it could not, and looked round at where the maid was pointing. In the middle of the kitchen window was an ugly, jagged black star.

"Someone threw a stone at us," whispered Georgy.

Diamond said nothing. She looked at the broken glass, almost without interest. Of course, it could be anyone. It could be a child playing with his ball. It could be Mrs. Rigg in a fit of uncontrollable spite, or anyone in the village who wanted the heathen bitch away. The hate, it seemed, was growing. Perhaps it was the nearness of Christmas, when dreadful things seemed to happen in the village. It began to look as if she might really end up roped to a stake, with the flames curling round her feet.

She shrugged, then, still silent, went into the sitting room. She wished her head would stop aching. However, she managed to smile at Sir Francis, who greeted her with his usual friendliness, apologized for inflicting himself upon her again, and assured her that if it was inconvenient, he would come back another time.

"You are always welcome," said Diamond without enthusiasm. She really felt most desperately tired, which was unusual in one who seldom indulged in the feminine vapors. She sat down opposite Sir Francis and asked if he had enjoyed his trip to London.

"My dear Miss Diamond, it was purely a matter of business.

Indeed, I found it excessively tedious. I am always so happy to return to the country. And how are you? I have come here for two reasons. One concerns an invitation. The other—the other is less happy. But I feel you are owed an explanation."

Diamond waited with a little, polite smile, and in the meantime her eyes moved over the amiable face confronting her. It was strange, inexplicable and a little frightening, but in that moment she knew with the utmost conviction that she did not like Sir Francis Axenford at all. She could not understand herself. This was the gentleman whom she had at once felt she could trust, in whom indeed she had confided almost instantly. It was surely not his fault that his poor wife was so dreadfully disfigured; perhaps the story of her death had been put about by Lady Caroline herself, shuddering away from being seen by people who had known her when she was beautiful and young. It was not fair to blame him until she knew the whole story, and perhaps one day he would confide in her. And it was the same countenance, kind, amused, a little boyish, rather plump now with the hint of a double chin, with laughter lines at the corner of his eyes and a scattering of wrinkles, to be expected in someone of his age. The voice was soft and gentle, the whole attitude that of a family friend.

And yet he chilled her. It was as if she had double vision, as if she were seeing him one way with her right eye and another with her left. She had the impression that within the charming exterior was someone else; for a second that someone slid out of the amiable body, standing at his side like a shadow, and that shadow was not amiable at all. The eyes were laughing, but at her, not with her, deriding her for a gull, making a mockery of her pretensions. The smiling mouth was loose-lipped, and the smile itself was like a muscular spasm, tilting up the corners, but with contempt and derision rather than with humor. The face was too fat, there was a lecherous air to it, and the hands— She had never really noticed his hands before. Her gaze fell briefly to them as they rested, clasped, upon the table. They were ugly hands, predatory, with fleshy, curved fingers, and for all their fine rings and the lace ruffle that half concealed them, they were not the hands one would expect from a fine gentleman.

Her eyes lit again on that strange ring. Suddenly she knew

where she had seen it before. It was in a play Mr. Garrick had put on about an alchemist. He hed been very proud to have found exactly the thing an alchemist would have worn. In such matters he was always precise, with a great love of accurate detail. Diamond could see it clearly now, for Sir Francis's hands were only a few inches away. Within the ring was an encircled triangle, the letters b, c and d at its corners, and in the center a small oblong with the letter a.

It meant nothing to her, but frightened her all the same. Then she realized that Sir Francis was aware of her scrutiny, and that he in his turn was observing her. As she raised her eyes to his, the color sharp in her cheeks, she thought that his face had grown wary and hard. The next instant he was his old, friendly self. He reached out one of the brutal hands and patted hers. He said, "I believe I have come at the wrong time. You look fatigued, my dear young lady. I fear you have been overtiring yourself with your lessons. How are they getting on, by the way? I hope that I shall soon be receiving my first letter from you."

"Oh," said Diamond, recovering herself a little, "I fear I do not work as hard as I should. Miss Falconer was very cross with me today. But I am making progress. I can now read a little of the printed word, and hope to understand handwriting very soon."

He asked her a few more questions about her lessons, and Georgy, still looking subdued, brought in some wine and a plateful of little cakes she had just baked. It was all perfectly friendly, but Diamond found herself shuddering with cold, as if she were in the presence of evil, and the sad, dreadful face of Lady Caroline was somehow between them. She sipped at her wine, wishing Sir Francis would go, and then he began to speak again.

He said, "I understand you saw Mr. Revill."

She raised startled eyes to him as he went on, "I am afraid I have to explain. Mr. Revill is a dear, good friend of mine, and we are lucky to have him with us, but since the loss of his wife some five years back he is afflicted from time to time with a kind of mental seizure. The doctors are unable to do anything for him, and you will understand that it is a most distressing thing in a man of his attainments and comparative youth, but he tells me that one of these fits overcame him when you were there. It must have been most disturbing for you, and he sends you his apologies."

Diamond was too taken aback to do anything but remain silent. Could Sir Francis really believe this was an adequate explanation? He said, "You will understand that we try to keep this matter a secret. If the village knew about it, he would lose his position, and that, coupled with everything else, would be disastrous for him. I can only assure you, Miss Diamond, that it will not occur again."

She said in a small voice, "I am sorry he is ill."

"I knew you would understand. The poor man has been desperately worried about this, and I promised him I would speak to you as soon as possible."

He waited, presumably for some sympathetic remark, but Diamond said nothing, and at last, with some signs of discomposure, he said, "Now we will discuss something far more pleasant. It will be Christmas within a few weeks. I believe, Miss Diamond, you and I are in the same situation. It is the family season, and neither you nor I has any family. This indeed has always been one of the bonds between me and Mr. Revill, for we have both suffered the most tragic loss. My dear wife— But I know how fond you were of her, and I must not continue to dwell on her death. Suffice it that she is gone, I am entirely alone, and you, too, are on your own. I am sure all your friends here will invite you, but may I ask if you will give me the great pleasure of dining with me on Christmas Day. We will be alone, but afterwards I always invite my tenants and staff, and if I am not imposing on you, I would like you to be the hostess. It would remind me of happier times. I realize I am asking you an enormous favor, and I shall quite understand if you refuse, but I sincerely hope you will come. It would give me so much pleasure."

Diamond knew that the reference to Lady Caroline was deliberate, for Sir Francis's eyes were fixed on her as he was speaking. She was afraid that when he used the phrase "my dear wife" she started, but hoped this was imperceptible; she might be a poor actress, but surely she had learned to conceal her emotion, especially when self-betrayal might prove dangerous. Still, she was almost choked by the anger that was rising within her, and she could not believe that these determined lies were to safeguard Lady Caroline. What sort of person was he? She obviously lived in his house, for she had fled through the woods in that direction, and yet he continued to speak of her as if she were dead, and in such a moving fashion that a stranger would have believed him instantly.

What sort of life was the poor lady living? Diamond thought again of that stack of mirrors, remembered how the furniture and silver in the house were polished until they were like glass, and the sick revulsion nearly overcame her, so that she shivered violently.

He said, with instant concern, "You are cold . . ."

"Miss Falconer does not bank up her fire. I am a little chilled. But the wine will warm me, and Georgy, I know, is making a wonderful dinner."

"Would you like to consider the matter? If you receive another invitation, perhaps with younger people . . ."

Diamond gave him a look, reflecting that Middleditch was hardly a hub of social activity. The only other invitation that was possible might come from Captain Ringham, but this so far she had not received. She was aware of an almost desperate longing for anything to prevent her going to Axenford. But it seemed to her that this was something she must do, and she answered quite gaily, "But I should love to accept. How kind you are to me, Sir Francis. I was quite unhappy to think that I must be alone on Christmas Day. Of course I will come, and I will play hostess to the best of my ability."

And now she had committed herself, driven on by the insensate curiosity that everyone from Captain Ringham to Miss Falconer deplored. God alone knew what was going to happen to her, for she was now stepping into the lion's den.

Only . . . he was not a lion, he was a rangy, ugly-jawed wolf.

It was true that as he stood up to say goodbye he looked like an amiable man. Diamond thought that fatigue must be blurring her mind, for even now she could not completely determine whom to trust and whom to regard as her enemy. She wished suddenly that she were back in London, even back to her shabby clothes, her dinners of mutton pies and porter, the cheap room for which she always owed her rent She felt cold and afraid and lost, and she longed for someone to look after her, to take this dreadful responsibility off her shoulders.

Sir Francis said, "I am so grateful to you. You can have no idea what a difference your coming here has made to me. Perhaps to all of us."

"It has made a great difference to me too," said Diamond, with perfect truth.

He said suddenly, "I understand you had a most alarming experience yesterday." Diamond, now fiercely alert, raised her head. He had opened the door and stood with his back to the light. His voice quiet and a little sad, he said, "Mr. Revill told me. Indeed, I believe the agitation provoked his seizure. He said you met some poor, mad creature. He thought you were badly frightened."

Diamond thought incoherently, You are frightened too, or you would never give yourself away in such fashion. And now that she knew, now that the indecision was done, she was no longer afraid. She said, with a nervous little laugh that she thought privately was very well done, "It was a trifle alarming. After all, I was alone. But I daresay he was more frightened than I was. I suppose in all villages there are such creatures. Poor soul. One should be sorry for him."

"You have no idea who it was?"

"No. I didn't really see him, and he vanished when I opened the door."

"I hope he is not dangerous."

"Oh no. I feel nothing but pity for such poor people."

"I think you have too tender a heart," he said, and then she was sickened by this hypocrisy and longed to bring the talk to an end. He went on, speaking very earnestly, "You will remember, will you not, that if anything further happens to alarm you, you must let me know immediately. I am never very happy about your living here alone with your maid."

"Oh, old Georgy would fight to the death for me," said Diamond, and extended her hand for him to kiss. Standing in the doorway, she watched him walking down the path, and though she now thought she knew what he was, though the thought of what Lady Caroline must have suffered, must still be suffering, appalled her, she still, with a small section of her mind, was bewildered that so amiable an exterior could hide so diabolical a heart.

She walked into the kitchen. Georgy might certainly fight to the death for her, but at this moment the old woman was in no state for battle. Worn out with excitement, she was sound asleep. A great pan of rabbit stew simmered on the stove. It smelled delicious, but Diamond hoped that Captain Ringham would sometime send down a plump chicken or a haunch of venison. She looked at Georgy with some amusement and a great affection. The old woman slept deeply, her head burrowed into her bosom, her hands folded in her lap. She was snoring gently. Diamond could not imagine a life without her. It seemed a century ago when they had met, almost knocking against each other, on the same landing. It was Georgy, coming back from her market stall, who had one evening, when Diamond was cold and hungry and depressed, asked her in to share her meal. After that she always managed to bring back fruit and vegetables, and presently she was mending Diamond's dresses, washing for her, tidying her room, and in the end coming to the theatre with her, as if she were her dresser. She had proved herself the best and most faithful of friends.

Diamond tasted a couple of spoonfuls of the stew, removed a carrot with her fingers, together with a piece of meat, then back into the sitting room to do her homework and try to push out of her mind the thought of Christmas at Axenford.

✎❧ XIV ☙✎

Diamond tried very hard before her next lesson to decipher Miss Falconer's letter. It still seemed to her important that she should be able to do so. She could manage to understand a few words, but not enough. At one point Miss Falconer seemed to have invoked her Maker, which was strange in a simple answer to an invitation, and Diamond assumed that the phrase was "for God's sake," which was even stranger, but after this she could read no more. The tails, dashes and curves defeated her. It was quite exasperating. She wondered at one point if she could ask Miss Falconer to read her own letter, but decided that this would seem both foolish and impertinent. The only solution was to work harder, and Diamond, full of good resolutions, pushed at the schoolmistress's cottage door.

The door was, as usual, on the latch. There might have been terrible happenings in Middleditch, but it was after all only a small village, and no one locked his door during the day. Diamond came into the hallway and called out Miss Falconer's name. She was carrying a small bunch of flowers, partly as a token of affection and partly in apology for her poor behavior the day before. Georgy loved to tend the small garden at the back of the cottage, and Diamond sometimes thought that in the summer it would be pleasant to recline there, but she had no interest in gardening and simply liked to see the result of other people's labors. She had picked a few bright-colored daisies. Miss Falconer, like herself, was no gardener except for her precious herbs, but no doubt she would enjoy the pretty orange and pink.

There was no answer to her greeting. Diamond, suddenly apprehensive, called again, more insistently. There was still no reply, and she moved hesitantly toward the sitting room, looking around her as she did so. There was nothing in any way different from usual in the hall, no sign of disarray. Miss Falconer could hardly be called a tidy woman, with her great dusty stacks of books, but such possessions as she had were orderly enough.

Diamond, feeling very cold, tapped on the sitting-room door and went in. There was no one there except Hob, lying in front of a briskly burning fire. Everything was in order, as Miss Falconer would see it, even to the saucer of milk in one corner. The old lady must have gone out on some unexpected errand and would doubtless be back within a few minutes. Diamond said, "Pussy, pussy," to the cat, which stretched itself out luxuriously. Then she sat down with her book on her knee, hoping to give a studious impression when Miss Falconer returned.

But she was too restless, and after a moment she stood up again. It was not in keeping with Miss Falconer's meticulous character to keep her waiting in such a fashion. She always insisted on Diamond's being punctual and would have regarded it as discourteous not to be so herself. In ordinary circumstances Diamond would have gone into the cottage next door to see if there was any message, but she was reluctant to do so now that the village was so openly hostile.

She paced up and down for a few minutes, stroked the cat, looked out of the window several times, then at last made up her mind. Without any further hesitation she went out into the street again and set off at a quick pace for the ruined workhouse.

She could not have said why she did this. There was no reason why Miss Falconer should be there, and it was extraordinary that she should choose to go just when her pupil would be arriving. But Diamond knew she was there, knew with a deep, irrational conviction, and she went as if she were driven: like her father she was sometimes compelled, like him she had premonitions of danger.

The day they came for him, he had said goodbye to her. They had been sitting by the stream and she was dabbling her bare feet in the water. There was no sign yet of the men with their dogs and their guns, the iron chains rattling in their hands. But he put his arm round her, gave her a hug, and said goodbye. "Goodbye, Clary girl, don't you grieve for me now. It will be all right in the end."

She asked, "Where are you going?" It was a fine day and she was happy. She thought it was some kind of joke.

"A long, long way, my darling," he said, and he gazed into the distance over the hill at the Axenford woods.

"But you're coming back again, Pa."

"No," he said. "No, my little love, I'm not coming back, ever again."

She was not afraid. She did not believe him. But it was true, for presently they came to drag him off to jail, shoving her away as she screamed and scratched and kicked at them.

She was never to see him alone again.

Diamond still moved as one compelled—the only thing for her to do was to go immediately to the theatre, which she had once so loved and which now terrified her. She walked as she had walked when a child, with speed, swinging her skirts. She was aware of no one. She passed Mrs. Rigg, who glared at her, and a handful of villager who looked sideways, whispering. She did not so much as see them, but when she came near St. Joseph's Church, she took the long way round, lest Mr. Revill be standing there, lest he ask her in.

And then she was at the workhouse; she went straight inside, looking neither right nor left.

She knew at once that she was not alone. For a second she closed her eyes, caught in a fear that convulsed her. She swallowed several times, for her mouth was dry, then called out in a hoarse whisper, "Lady Caroline!"

There was no answer, but someone was there, and Diamond's hands clutched at the reticule where the little pistol always was. She called again, this time with more determination, "Lady Caroline! Oh, please, do come out. I mean you no harm, and I do want to talk to you."

Then she gave a great gasp, and the words choked in her throat, for she saw what lay in the corner.

Miss Falconer sprawled on the small dais to the right of the stage, where the boxes usually were. It had been built for such occasions as the balcony scene in *Romeo and Juliet*, or in *Hamlet*, where Polonius hid behind the arras. There was nothing there now but a high step covered with a tattered, dusty velvet cloth. The whole bore an obscene resemblance to an altar, and on top of it lay the sacrifice: Miss Falconer, so huddled and small that she was like a shadow, a thin, frail, old woman as immaterial as a cobweb. Her throat was cut from ear to ear.

Diamond believed she would faint, but instead she moved forward with the calm of an automaton, amazed at her own detachment. She felt as if she were floating, no longer in her own body. She knelt beside the platform. She looked down into her schoolmistress's face. The slit throat was partially and mercifully hidden by the high lace collar that the old woman always wore. But it was red now, not white, and the blood had dripped down so that the velvet covering was brown and stiff with it.

Diamond knelt there for a long time. Once she put out her hand and touched Miss Falconer's icy cheek. She must have been dead for some time. The message must have arrived, and she would have gone out directly, meaning to be back in time for the lesson. Someone had been waiting for her. It must have been quick. The old woman could have put up no kind of fight. It would have been over in an instant.

Diamond continued to kneel there. The murderer might be waiting for her too, but she could not move. It was as if she were paralyzed. She did not cry. She felt as drained of emotion as Miss Falconer was of blood. She thought she would never be able to rise to her feet again. Only when she heard the rustle behind her did she raise her head and look round.

The face, now that she looked fully at it, was even worse than she remembered. It was no face at all; it would have been more bearable if it had been a skeleton. But Diamond managed to look straight at it without flinching, and somehow, in that steady gaze, the horror disintegrated. She no longer saw the rotting flesh, the battered frame of what had once been beauty, only the huge, desperate eyes and then the pathetic gesture of a hand suddenly raised in an attempt to conceal the destruction.

She said in a whisper, "Lady Caroline . . ." and hearing this, the disfigured ghost jerked aside as if she would run into the woods again.

Diamond jumped to her feet at last. She did not look again

at Miss Falconer's body. She said in a calm, brisk voice, the country accent strong, "Don't take on so, my lady. I am a friend. I am Clary Brown. Do you not remember me? You were so kind to me, I'll always remember you. Please don't go. I so wanted to meet you again." And she crossed the stage and took the battered creature into her strong young arms, patting and stroking her, then, without revulsion, kissed the ravaged cheek.

Lady Caroline at last pushed her gently away. Diamond saw that there was little left of her. She was nothing but bones, and looked as old as the dead schoolmistress. Her clothes were ragged and far too flimsy for the cold. Over her shoulders she wore a shawl such as countrywomen wear, and this she raised to bring over the lower part of her face as if she were some oriental woman in purdah.

When she at last spoke, it was the voice that Diamond remembered, the voice that had once recited from *Romeo and Juliet*. It was resonant, full and musical, and it came shockingly from this withered old woman whose beauty was so hopelessly ruined. It jolted Diamond back into horror as nothing else could have done, and for the first time her knees buckled beneath her. She had to lean against the wall until her head stopped swimming.

Lady Caroline said, "She was my friend. She was my only friend."

"She was my friend too," said Diamond, still holding onto the wall. "She was teaching me to read. Do you know who killed her?"

Lady Caroline seemed not to hear her. She said, "She's dead because of me. They told her I wanted to see her. She came at once. Of course she came . . ." Then the great eyes stared at Diamond. "I know you," she said. "You are the little orphan girl from the workhouse. You are his daughter. You had best take care. You are very beautiful. I was beautiful too. I daresay you don't believe it. It was a long time ago. You wanted to act like me. I was on the stage, you know. They say I did quite well. But he did not like it. He has always had to destroy. I wish he had killed me. But that would not suit him. It pleases him to keep me alive, looking like this. It is his revenge for what I did. He laughs sometimes when I see myself— He holds a mirror up to me. You must not let him destroy you. And now he has killed my only friend. I tried to prevent it. I never told her. I let her think I was dead. There are, after all, worse things than death. What did you say your name was, little girl?"

Then Diamond saw that her wits were half gone, that she was going back in time. She said in a shaking voice, "I am Clary Brown, my lady."

"I expect you are hungry, Clary Brown. I should like to give you something to eat, but then I have so little, myself. It is so difficult these days— So you wish to go on the stage. I would try to teach you, if I could. I come here often, you know. He doesn't mind that. He knows no one can bear to look at me, and he knows, too, that I couldn't bear it if they did. It's quite safe for him. I spend most of my spare time here. You would like to be an actress, wouldn't you?"

Diamond, not knowing what to answer, said faintly, "Yes."

"Perhaps you should try the part of Juliet. It was always my favorite. They all spoke quite highly of my performance. Why, I remember it even now. Let me see. Let me see."

And Lady Caroline began pacing up and down the stage, and it seemed she had forgotten her diseased face, for she tossed the shawl back over her shoulders in a dramatic manner, and began to declaim in that magnificent voice that was still so strong. It was like some dreadful macabre dance, with death playing the part of love.

> *"I would have thee gone;*
> *And yet no further than a wanton's bird,*
> *Who lets it hop a little from her hand,*
> *Like a poor prisoner in his twisted gyves,*
> *And with a silk thread plucks it back again,*
> *So loving-jealous of his liberty."*

The words pealed out, and Diamond listened, the grief choking her. The beauty of the phrasing was still there, if only one could shut one's eyes to that dreadful gargoyle of a face. Then there was a silence, and Lady Caroline suddenly knelt upon the stage and put her hands up to her cheeks, the thin grey hair falling over them. As Diamond started toward her, she held up her hand as if to stop her, then said very clearly, "Your father was kind. He was a gypsy. They said he was a thief, but he was so gentle and so kind."

"My father is dead, my lady."

"Oh no! He cannot be dead. He was so much alive. He put life into me. He gave me hope at a time when I believed there was nothing left. Why should he be dead? You are lying to me. I know he's alive. He was quite a young man."

"They hanged him, my lady."

Lady Caroline raised her head, and though it was hard to see how emotion could reveal itself in that massacre of a face, there was a terrible grief in her that left Diamond feeling helpless and hopeless. It was all over such a long time ago, but for this poor lady it was yesterday. She said in an exhausted voice, "Yes. Of course. He would have to die. It is a pity that I could not die too. I killed him, you know."

Diamond exclaimed, "Oh no! That is not true. Why do you say such things?"

"Of course. I have always known it. Such a kind man. I believe he loved me a little. I don't think he would love me now. Once, you know, it was wrong, I suppose it was wrong, but we met . . ." Her voice trailed away. "You are only a child. I should not tell you such things. Only he was kind, you see, and I was so starved for kindness. I lived my life being afraid, and Francis— However, I'm sure I'm boring you, my poor child, and really, it is not seemly of me to tell you such things. You are too young to understand."

Diamond said nothing. She was remembering what Miss Falconer had told her. She stood there very still. The smell of death was in her nostrils, and the pain of this poor, lost creature in her vision. She was so cold she felt she would die. And presently the beautiful voice began again.

"Such dreadful things have happened— To meet kindness and warmth and love, it was like coming out of a madhouse into a brief place of sanity. But I had to tell Francis. I do not know why, but somehow it was forced out of me. He never forgave me. He never will forgive me. I daresay he is right. What I did was very wrong. Only sometimes . . ."

Then the voice changed. It was as if she had suddenly

returned to the present. She came up to Diamond and said very loudly, as if she were throwing her voice to the back of the pit, "Go home at once. You are his daughter. You are the last person who should be here. You will be killed. Your only hope is to go now. You are young and beautiful, you are what he wants. You are in great danger. Go back where you belong, you silly girl. I have no patience," said Lady Caroline with sudden roughness, "with young women who think they know better than everyone else. If you stay here, you will be causing me great inconvenience. Go away at once. You are not wanted here. I don't want you. You are just a nuisance and a burden. I am sure your father agrees with me. I hope he scolds you. Parents are too indulgent these days. Do you hear me, little girl? I hope you are listening."

"Yes, my lady," said Diamond, for indeed there was nothing else to say, and it was only too true, she had never longed more passionately to be back in London town.

"Then," said Lady Caroline, moving away, "I hope I hear no more of this. I shall expect you to be packed and on the stagecoach by the evening. I shall be seriously cross if I find you still here. I shall tell your father at once, and I hope he will know how to deal with you. Goodbye, child. You may kiss my hand."

Diamond, trembling, came forward to do so. She felt as if she really were little Clary Brown, due for a whipping. She took the bony hand in hers and put her lips to it. It was as if she were kissing a corpse. She watched wretchedly as Lady Caroline moved slowly back toward the side door, a little like the Ghost in *Hamlet*, her eyes fixed on Diamond's white face. Only as she reached the curtains, she must once again have come to some realization of her appearance, for she put her hands up to her lipless mouth, wailed, "You should never have come here. Oh, why are people so foolish?"

The next instant she had slipped through the doorway to the woods. Diamond heard the faint crackling sound of her footsteps running through the wet leaves outside. Then she sat down on the stage because her legs would no longer bear her, and buried her face in her hands. Miss Falconer's body lay a few feet away from her, but she no longer thought of her, it was all more than she could bear. She only knew that she was alone, hemmed in by death and madness and evil, and she was too frightened to know what to do.

The deep voice shot her out of the nightmare and brought her struggling to her feet again. Then she saw that it was Captain Ringham, and he was plainly so furious that he could only glower at her, gasping for breath. Somehow this display of ordinary, common temper restored her more than anything else. The dizziness and despair vanished, and she said quite calmly, "I am glad you have come, but there is no need to shout at me. I am not deaf, and I have already endured quite enough this morning without people being horrid to me."

Her voice quavered a little toward the end. After all that had happened, to be roused with a roar of "Miss Diamond, what the devil are you doing here?" seemed the last straw.

But he had seen Miss Falconer's body. He looked down at it, up at Diamond, then walked silently toward it. Diamond, her arms clasped across herself to stop her convulsive shivering, saw him stoop over it, saw his hands move as if he were investigating the wound. When he stood up again, his face was as grim as death itself, and he said in a harsh, strained voice, "You see what your meddling has led to!"

Diamond cried out in a rage, "My meddling! You bastard! I am not responsible for this. It's not my fault—"

"Is it not?"

She fell silent. The angry, frightened tears were spilling down her cheeks. Perhaps it was her doing. If she had not told Miss Falconer about Lady Caroline, this might never have happened. She whispered, "I didn't know— Who could have done this? She was such a good person. Why should anyone kill an old lady? You like to blame me for everything, but—"

She broke off, too choked with misery to continue. She longed to tell him about Lady Caroline, but she had promised not to, and the knowledge might be dangerous for him. And there was also the thought that if he knew, he would somehow contrive to meet her, and this for the poor lady would be unbearable. She would not be able to endure being seen by a gentleman. It would be the final humiliation. Diamond said nothing more, and then Captain Ringham, who seemed beside himself, gripped her shoulders and began to shake her, repeating like the beat of a drum, "But? But what? Tell me immediately, or I swear I'll wring your neck."

Diamond looked up at him, outraged, then gave him a great push in the chest, which, since he was unprepared, nearly sent him flat on the floor.

He stepped back, regaining his balance. To her surprise he smiled. It was not much of a smile, but at least he had stopped shaking her. He said, "Well, this time you didn't spit in my eye."

"I didn't—! I don't know what you mean." Her voice tailed off. She said in a bewildered voice, "I didn't know it was you."

They're nothing bastards. Spit in their eye, Clary. They were the last words she heard from him. When they brought him out for his hanging, he only smiled at her, raising his manacled hands in a gesture of farewell.

Spit in their eye, Clary.

She repeated, ashamed, "I didn't know it was you."

He said gently, "You looked so small and helpless and afraid. I meant you no harm. I was going to offer to conduct you out of the courthouse." Then he said, "I congratulate you on your aim. For a moment you pretty well blinded me. And then you were gone. There was nothing more I could do." His voice returned to its normal roar. "I wish to Christ you were gone now. Oh, my dear damned idiot of a girl, I wish you were gone . . ."

"Take me away from here," said Diamond in a choked voice.

"With the greatest of pleasure. You should never have come." He looked down at the small, huddled body. "She didn't deserve such an ending. But she was old, and you are young. It would be a pity, Miss Diamond, if the same happened to you, and it could happen only too easily, I hope you realize that. Come. I'll take you home."

"But you can't leave her here like that . . ."

"I'll attend to it later. She is beyond all harm, and you are not. Come, girl. The sooner you are away from here, the better."

Diamond slipped her arm through his. They walked out of the theatre and through the ruined workhouse in silence. In the doorway she paused. She looked round her. She said, "I'll never come back here again. I could not endure it. I came to lay a ghost, and instead— Oh, Captain Ringham, we must collect her cat."

"What are you talking about now?"

"It was like her child. I couldn't let it starve. Everyone here thinks she is a witch, I'm sure nobody would go in to look after it."

He inclined his head, and together they went to the cottage. They passed a few villagers on the way. It seemed to Diamond that they crossed the street to avoid her. Hob was still there, in front of the dying fire. Diamond thought he would struggle when she picked him up, but he seemed to acquiesce, even purred as she cradled him in her arms.

As they came up the path to her home, she said, with a miserable attempt at a smile, "If we are still on speaking terms, sir, you had best come in." Then she said, "I'm so tired. I could lie down and die."

He answered, without sympathy, "I daresay that wish will be more easily gratified than you expect. You've run yourself into a fine hornet's nest. Now then—" They were in the sitting room. He looked about him. "You cannot really want to stay here any longer. I will lend you my carriage to take you back to London. I will even find you a lodging. I have friends who would be glad to help you. You will be back in your own world."

"This is my world. Why can't you understand that?"

"I understand nothing of what you say. Sometimes I believe you are half-witted. Miss Diamond or Miss Clary, or whatever you call yourself, do you want to die?"

"No. Oh no." And Diamond cuddled the cat as if she would seek warmth from his soft body.

"Well, you are well on the way to doing so. Oddly enough, I don't want you to die either. I understand you are invited to Axenford for Christmas. You could come to us. Philip would be delighted, but I am sure that would not satisfy you. Are you going? Oh, I am sure you are. You need not trouble to answer me. Of course you're going. If someone held a noose out to you, you would run your silly neck into it. I suppose I must wish you a Merry Christmas. I can wager that it will at least be an unusual one."

Diamond said in a dull voice, "You are quite right. I cannot stay here any longer."

He exclaimed in angry triumph, "My God, have you really come to your senses at last?"

"I am defeated," said Diamond. It was the first time in her life that she had said such words. "I didn't think I could be, but I am. I would like to accept your offer. But there is one last thing I must do."

"I knew it was too good to be true. What now, in God's name?"

"I want to see Mr. Vincent. I must see Mr. Vincent." She banged her fist against the palm of her hand, like a child in a temper. "You promised. You did. You gave me your word."

He was sitting on the edge of the table. He said, with an obvious effort at restraint. "Why do you want to see him? Do you want to spit in his eye too? He may have done abominable things, and I hold no brief for him, but he is nothing now but a poor old man. If it is revenge you want, you can consider that you have it. Nothing you can say or do will affect him any more."

"Is he mad too?" asked Diamond. The betraying words came out before she could stop them, and she flushed scarlet, trying to think of some way in which she could cover up. She added quickly, the words falling over each other, "Everyone here seems so strange. Someone threw a stone through our window. I think Middleditch has some kind of fever."

He looked at her in a way that kept the color in her cheeks, and said, "No, he is not precisely mad. If you want to see him so badly, I suppose you must do so. Only, it will have to be tomorrow. I have wasted a great deal of time looking after you, I have my estate to manage, and he lives a little way out. I should, of course, prefer you to leave for London immediately. But if you are absolutely resolved— Very well, ma'am. I will call for you tomorrow morning."

Then Diamond rose to her feet and came up to him. She put her hand on his. When he turned it palm upwards to hold it, she did not draw away. She said almost inaudibly, "I want to ask you this. Please answer me. I think you and Sir Francis are the only people who can, and I could never ask him now. It was Sir Francis who hanged my father, wasn't it?"

"Yes. He is a destroyer. He is a wicked man."

Diamond looked at him in silence, her hand still in his.

"He destroyed his wife, and I believe the same can happen to you. You are your father's daughter. Sir Francis will never forgive you for that. You have been marked for destruction ever since you came here. He hated your father with a passion, and that hate has been transferred to you. If I had told you that at the beginning, you would have laughed at me. Now you understand why it is so important that you should go away."

Diamond did not ask him why Sir Francis hated her father, for this she knew, this she should have known when Miss Falconer first talked to her. She said, "I really believed it was you. I'm sorry, but I was so convinced."

"One day," said Captain Ringham dryly, "I must show you my hoofs and my tail."

"You are one of the local justices here. You were present when they hanged him."

"Do you think I enjoyed that? It happens to be one of my duties."

"It was you who sent me to the workhouse!"

"What the devil else was I to do? I was terrified for you. Alone, you would not have lasted a year. You would have been at the mercy of Sir Francis, and such an unimaginable fate— I did not know things were so bad. Believe me, Clary. I did not know. I will never quite forgive myself for that, but we none of us knew. Do you believe me, Miss Diamond?"

She said, "I prefer you to call me Clary."

He looked at her in silence, and heaved a deep sigh.

Then she spoke again: "My father liked women very much. I always knew that. I think at the beginning I was a little jealous, the way children are, but when I grew older I was proud of him. It made me laugh to see how he just had to smile and look with his great dark eyes, and the women melted before him." She looked up at Captain Ringham. "That was why he died, wasn't it?"

"That was why he died."

"After all," said Diamond, "we are the same underneath, whether we are farm girls or . . . or ladies. That is so, is it not?"

"So they tell me," he said, his voice harsh.

"I mean," said Diamond, the absurd tears once again welling out of her eyes, "there must be times—there are times when we all feel lost and unhappy, and we want kindness so much, so much, and if there is someone . . . Of course," she said in a more bracing voice, "it's different for people like me. I'm what they call a bad girl."

"So you keep telling me," said Captain Ringham, adding in his deepest and most resounding manner, "It becomes confoundedly boring, but I gather it is a form of boasting, and doubtless it affords you some kind of pleasure."

Diamond said furiously, snatching her hand away from him, "I'm not boasting, and I don't know why it's supposed to give me pleasure, but it's true, and you know it's true. At least I don't think I'm particularly bad, but I'm sure Mrs. Rigg would think so."

"I cannot see what the devil Mrs. Rigg has to do with anything. You are surely not regulating your life by the opinion of Mrs. Rigg?"

"Oh, I don't give a damn for Mrs. Rigg. I was just trying to explain that whatever one is, there comes a time when one cannot stand anything any more, when one no longer cares what one does. I understand that so well," said Diamond. "And if you feel like that, if the world seems cruel and terrible, if you have really come to the end of your tether, and you meet someone kind— My pa was a kind man, Captain Ringham. There was no wickedness in him. People disliked him because he was a gypsy who wore earrings. They thought he was foreign, and they were afraid of him. And he just laughed at them, he never took them seriously. And in the end they hated him for being so charming and taking their women from them. But he didn't deserve to be hanged." Then she said, "I am so glad she had a few moments of happiness."

Captain Ringham said quietly, "I loved her too. I was only a young man, she was much older than I was, but I think I worshipped her."

Diamond thought bemusedly that the name had never once been mentioned, yet the sad, dreadful face hung between them, with its despairing eyes. She said, "It's a pity she couldn't have married you."

Then he smiled as she had never seen him smile, and the smile transformed his face. He said, "That is the most agreeable thing anyone has ever said to me, Clary," and before she knew what he was about, he leaned forward and kissed her on the mouth.

Then he rose to his feet, saying briskly, as if nothing had happened, "I will call for you tomorrow at ten o'clock." He looked at her very intently for a moment, then went on, "You will please not go out again in any circumstances, neither will you answer the door until I come myself. Is that understood?"

"Yes," said Diamond meekly. She thought privately that he had no need to say this to her, for she was very much afraid. She no longer had any confidence in herself; she felt defenseless. She wished Captain Ringham could stay the night in the cottage, but dared not ask him. She longed to be starting on her journey back to London at this very moment. Suddenly she hated Middleditch with a terrified hatred, and thought eagerly of the city with its dirty, crowded streets, its smell of sea coal, its noise of carriage wheels and signposts swinging in the wind. She no longer had the least desire to find out what Sir Francis was doing. Indeed, the thought of him appalled her. Let Captain Ringham deal with him, let poor Lady Caroline languish in her ravaged solitude. It was none of her business, it never had been any of her business; she was a fool to have meddled in the first place. But see Mr. Vincent she must, to lay his ghost, to prove to herself that she was free of him.

She went upstairs to her room, the cat still in her arms, the memory of a kiss still warm upon her lips. She lay on the bed. The cat, entirely at home, stretched himself against her, arching his body so that he fitted into the curve of her knees. Diamond stroked him absent-mindedly as she lay back with her head on the pillow. The images swam before her eyes, the images of what had happened a long time ago.

It was like a play, with the characters playing their parts. A sad, beautiful, exhausted lady stepped on the stage. And like the ballad, the handsome gypsy lover, who took his women as he pleased, who did not care if they were titled ladies, farm girls or anyone else. How did it happen? A chance meeting in the woods, the lady seeking the quiet and solitude, and he, oh, he would be poaching, of that there was no doubt, looking for next day's dinner, moving noiselessly as only he could move, the keen eyes searching and watching. How did it happen? Diamond saw them so clearly, both stepping into a clearing at the same time, seeing each other, stopping short, staring. And then she moved into his arms. It would be something past all coherent thought, a desperate urge for comfort, warmth and tenderness. And he—oh, he would respond as he might turn to dry his daughter's tears. He would never hesitate, it was not in his nature. He would love her as he loved all his women before he left them. He would for the moment give her his sweetness and strength.

I am glad, said Diamond to herself, that she had at least that one moment. What happened afterwards, God alone knew. For Sir Francis to learn that his wife—for all he had so cruelly misused her—had lain with a gypsy poacher would be something that he would never forgive to the end of his life.

Then Diamond saw the face again, that destroyed and hideous massacre of a face. This was Sir Francis's revenge, however he had contrived it. It was barely possible to imagine that anyone, however hurt, however angry, could be so diabolically cruel. Diamond turned toward the cat, trying to hide the memory in its soft fur, and presently, the tears still wet upon her cheeks, she fell asleep.

The next morning she rose early and quietly went downstairs. She opened the front door to let the morning air in, and stood there, pale after a restless night, staring out across the silent village. There was no sign or sound of anyone. The church clock was chiming the hour. She thought of Mr. Revill, who was certainly no minister of God, with his crucifix that was upside down—and then something strange clicked into place in her mind.

Sir Francis had mounted his wife's portrait with the crucifix underneath. That was upside down too.

Diamond went upstairs and dressed herself with the utmost care. She put on the richest dress the old man had ever given her, and she fastened on the diamond necklace, for, though she hated it and regarded it as a kind of slave collar, it was beautiful and expensive. Today she must look her best, Clary

Brown returned to see the demon who in a sense had spoiled her life, who had made it impossible for her to take a lover without remembering his onslaught.

She thought of last night's kiss. It had been sweet and warm. It had heartened her, made her feel alive again. But it was only a kiss, he had not even put his arms round her. If he had done so, she knew that the feeling of revulsion would have overcome her, for all that she now believed she loved Captain Ringham, would like to be with him till the end of her days. It was as if she were two people: one part of her desperately wanted his love, the other sickened at the thought of it. There will be no happiness for me, thought Diamond. I could not marry him even if he asked me. She saw herself haunted eternally by the dirty, ugly ghost who stood between her and everything she longed for. She could never explain it to any man; it would sound absurd and incomprehensible.

She longed desperately for Captain Ringham, thought of marriage with him, of bearing his children—and she tugged a comb savagely through her hair and wept for the happiness that she would never have. Today she would meet her incubus face to face, but there would be no miracle, there were no such things as miracles. It was simply something that she had to do. Cold with apprehension, yet fiercely pleased that at last she could have some kind of revenge, she went downstairs.

✄☙ XV ☙✄

Georgy, so unusually silent these days, made little comment when she saw her. This was strange, for usually she was enchanted by her young mistress' beauty. But now, as her eyes moved over the rich golden-brown velvet dress, the shining piled hair, the touch of rouge on the cheeks, she said nothing, not even about the diamonds that glittered and shone on the soft throat. She only petted the cat, who seemed to have adopted her, then brought out a bowl of hot chocolate, which Diamond drank thankfully. And then she sat by the window, waiting for Captain Ringham. He arrived on the hour, as he said he would, and she could see through the curtains that the carriage waited in the street.

He took her arm as she came down the steep path. She spoke in her quietest, most genteel voice. "He attacked me," she said. "He tried to rape me. He made it so that I can never love any man; he is always between us. He didn't want me as a person. I was just a young girl, like any other young girl. But he was there in power, he could do what he liked. He was a big man. He was like an ape. I fought back. I managed to get away. But now—"

He said quietly, "Do you not think I could make you forget?"

Diamond looked at him. She had never in her life longed so for anyone. She could not bring out the words, only sighed and looked away. What was the use of talking? She should not have told him. He would never understand. He might love her a little, even though she was a whore, but he would never understand. But when his hand moved to meet hers, she clasped it and was in an odd way a little comforted. And hand in hand, like two children, they walked to the carriage.

Presently they were driving out of Middleditch, past the woods, past Axenford, out into the countryside. Diamond sat very upright and still, on her knees the reticule with the little pistol inside. Captain Ringham said nothing, but held her hand firmly. As they were traveling along, she realized that St. Joseph's bell was tolling. Then she saw the small procession. The hand in Captain Ringham's stirred. She said in a whisper, "What is that?"

He answered briefly, "Miss Falconer's funeral."

There were four men carrying the coffin. It was a small coffin, as if for a child. There were only three mourners following after, villagers who perhaps felt it was their duty to attend the schoolteacher's death.

Diamond said in a sudden, loud voice, "Stop. Please stop."

As the carriage slowed down, she jumped out into the street and joined the procession, keeping in slow marching step with the mourners. After a while she realized that Captain Ringham was walking beside her. At the graveside, barely aware that the captain was holding her hand, the words flowed through her: "He cometh up as a flower, and never continueth in one stay." And she cried bitterly for Miss Falconer, though she was old and her life would soon have ended. She wished she had flowers to lay on the grave.

When it was over, she walked away without a word, but as she climbed back into the carriage, she said, "She should not have died that way. She deserved better. I loved her very much."

Captain Ringham said, "You shouldn't cry when you are wearing rouge. You don't need rouge. I am going to take it off." He took out his handkerchief and gently rubbed at Diamond's cheek, ending up by blowing her nose for her, which drove the last tears away. Then he said, "I imagine you prefer to see this gentleman alone."

"Oh yes. I must see him on my own."

"That is as well, for I have still a great deal to do. I shall leave you the carriage, and Tom will take you home. Unfortunately, I have business to attend to some distance from here, which will take me most of the day, but I can ride there, so you can have the conveyance." Then he said, "I should like you afterwards to go straight back to London. I am sorry I cannot see you off, but I shall be up to visit you."

Diamond said, "Last night I was very silly. I was so frightened. I don't know what was the matter with me."

"You had every reason to be frightened. You still have."

"Ah, but today I feel more sensible."

"That is only because it is morning. Things always seem better in— For God's sake," exclaimed Captain Ringham, "don't tell me you are starting all this nonsense again! Last night for the first time I believed you had come to your senses. I cannot tell you how relieved I was. Do you imagine I enjoy this kind of responsibility? You've seen what happened to Miss Falconer, simply because she, too, poor soul, was a meddler. Women are the most confounded meddlers, the whole damned lot of them. If she had not gone to the theatre, she might be alive today. Why did she go? Do you know? Of course you know, you interfering bitch." He shot her a savage look and said more quietly, "I can guess well enough. Are you telling me that you propose to stay on in Middleditch?"

"Only for one day more."

"Why?"

"Well," said Diamond a little faintly, "there is all my packing to do— No. Of course that is not true. I do not have so many possessions, and all the furniture and linen is yours. I could pack what I have in half an hour, and Georgy will be only too delighted to get back to London. Will you try to understand me and not be angry? Today I am doing something that I have dreamed of doing for six years. I don't know what will happen, not much perhaps, but in a sense I shall for the first time be free. And I want to—I must—walk round Middleditch as a free woman, as Clary Brown."

"No! No, no, no!"

"Well, I'll drive if you prefer it. It won't be quite the same, but if it pleases you— Oh, Captain Ringham, please try to understand. I shall be seeing my home without—oh, how I hope it is without!—something that has haunted me ever since it happened." Her voice trailed off. "You don't understand, do you?"

He said fiercely, "Listen to me, Clary Brown. This place

for the past few years has been infected with a kind of plague."

"Sir Francis said that. He used the very phrase."

"Did he now! That must have appealed greatly to his sense of humor. I hope soon to rid us of this infection, which has destroyed our way of living, made us all look sideways at each other, murdered our children. I have been waiting, and the death of your old schoolmistress will, I believe, at last give me my opportunity. You do not imagine, I hope, that I have really buried her. She lies in her grave, but for me she is still very much alive. Also, I believe we now have an actual witness. You know, presumably, whom I mean?"

"No," said Diamond, "I have no idea."

"I think you are a bloody liar, and a fool into the bargain." He met her injured expression, and suddenly grinned at her. "It doesn't matter, ma'am. In a little while I hope and pray we can all live in peace again." Then he said meditatively, "The Axenfords have a strange history. They said of the old man, Sir Francis's father, that he was a warlock. I do not believe in such superstitious nonsense, but there have always been ugly stories. One thing is certain: less useful members of society or more profligate and licentious characters than Sir Francis and his father have never disgraced this shire. And when Caroline— However, all that is past, and I am concerned with the future. Only . . . it will not be easy, even now. Sir Francis is a very dangerous man, entirely devoid of compassion. I want you out of the way. You have certainly stirred everything up, and it will not be forgiven you. Besides, you are your father's daughter, and you are young and handsome—it is a diabolical combination. It is the young and handsome who die here."

Diamond was growing frightened again. To change the subject, and because this was something she genuinely wanted to know, she demanded, "What is this about your brother's laming Sir Francis's horse? It was one of the first things he told me."

"And naturally you believed him?"

"Well, yes I did. After all, I found him charming and agreeable. I didn't find you charming or agreeable at all," said Diamond, and rather to her own astonishment, flirted her eyes at him.

He received this onslaught in silence.

She said, more pacifically, "What did happen? I cannot imagine Philip leaving an animal to die."

"It was an attempt at murder," said Captain Ringham briefly. "Francis knew that Philip went riding through the woods, and set a trip wire across the path. Philip might indeed have been killed. It was only by a miracle that he escaped. The horse had to be shot. But it was mine, not his— Here we are. I will leave you. Just tell me this. Are you still resolved to stay one more day?"

"I have no choice," said Diamond.

I have no choice. An echo of other words, a frightened girl in a carriage, a century ago.

I have no choice.

He did not press the matter. He gave her an angry, half-despairing look, then handed her out of the carriage in front of a small cottage, a puff of smoke coming out of its chimney. Diamond stood there. She was beginning to shake. The years were sliding away; she was back in a long, dark, cold corridor, hemmed in by fear.

Captain Ringham said quietly, "You look very handsome, ma'am. That is a very fine dress, and the color suits you admirably."

She gave him a wan smile. She wished he would put his arms round her, whatever happened then. She said, "My old man give it me."

"Then he had excellent taste," said Captain Ringham.

"You—you think that for a workhouse brat I look reasonably well?"

"I think, Miss Diamond Browne, you are the most beautiful woman I have ever seen in my life."

Then she knew that she loved him with all her heart. The color returned to her cheeks and the trembling began to subside. She whispered, "Thank you for calling me Miss Diamond Browne," then turned and walked up to the cottage door. She did not look round again, but she heard his retreating footsteps. The horses stood there, with Tom patiently holding the reins. She could at least run away. There was no wall to prevent her. It was a comfort.

She knocked on the door, and an old woman opened it.

Diamond saw that she was expected. The old woman said, "Mr. Vincent is in the parlor, ma'am. He says he is sorry he cannot come out to greet you, but will you please come in."

Diamond followed her. At last, after six long years, she would face her enemy.

She had remembered him as huge, a monster, a vast, hairy man with great hands. She had described him as an ape. In her mind he was six feet high and gross in proportion. Now, before her, she saw a tiny, wizened old man with snow-white hair, a face fallen in with lines. He sat in a chair with a rug across his knees. A pair of crutches leaned against the wall. He did not attempt to get up, but he raised his head, unsmiling, and said in a cracked, quavering voice, "The captain says you were one of my girls."

"I am Clary Brown," said Diamond.

She saw that the name meant nothing to him. He inclined his head, then extended his hand. It was a thin old hand that shook like an aspen. His hands had gripped her cruelly, forced her down. This could hardly push a blade of grass out of place. She could not bring herself to touch it, and he looked at her, almost in surprise, then let it drop to his knee.

He said vaguely, "It was good of you to come and see me."

Diamond had been prepared to rail at him, to reproach and abuse him, to say, "You were wicked and cruel and you've made it impossible for me to love any man. You treated us all shamefully. You made prisoners of us. You tried to rape me, a young girl in your charge. I've long wished you dead and I hope you die in agony." And she looked at the sad, old face, the face of a man who had long since lost hope, who had no wish to live, who would scarce have noticed if she had struck him across the cheek.

She made a hopeless, resigned gesture. He said, in a vague, remote way as if he hardly knew what he was saying, "Will you not sit down? Mrs. Slade will be bringing you a hot drink. They say it is a cold day. I don't know. I never get out now. I have lost the use of my legs, you see. I tried to save her. Maria. My little girl. You will doubtless remember her. But she cracked her head against the paving. She is dead. It is my great regret that I did not die too."

It should have been a great moment of triumph, but Diamond could only feel exhausted and wretched. She sat down in the chair opposite him, not knowing what to say. She did not really remember Maria. Mr. Vincent had had his own private rooms; his wife was dead and his child was cared for by a nursemaid, seldom allowed to mix with the rough workhouse girls. Diamond now had no memory of what the child had looked like. She said, her voice coming out so strangely that she hardly recognized it as her own, "What happened?"

At this moment Mrs. Slade came in with a bowl of soup. She set it on a table beside Diamond, who looked down at it with revulsion; she could not have touched one drop.

Mr. Vincent seemed to be away in his thoughts, barely aware of her presence. He repeated her remark, said, "What happened?" Then after so long a silence that he seemed to have forgotten, he said at last in a monotonous voice, "There was a fire. He started it, of course."

"He?"

But he went on as if she had not spoken. "He killed two or three of the girls. I do not remember their names. And I was afraid for Maria. She was a lovely child. I spoke to him. Then there was the fire, and I jumped out of the window with her in my arms. I killed her. What did you say your name was?"

"Clary. Clary Brown, Mr. Vincent."

And you did dreadful things to me, you did dreadful things to all of us, why should I mourn for your child? You didn't care for us, and we were children too . . .

"I don't remember. There were so many of you. I fear my memory is not what it was. Thank you for coming to see me." He looked at her, and for the first time it was as if he saw her as a person. "You look very well. I trust that life has treated you kindly."

She longed to scream at him; the words were like vomit in her mouth.

But at once his attention wandered again, he no longer saw her. "She was such a lovely little girl. She was all my life. I ran to the window, you see, with her in my arms. The flames were roaring behind us. I jumped out of the window. She cracked her head against the paving. I wish I had died too.

But God willed otherwise. He took away the use of my legs, but I am still alive. Captain Ringham has been very good to me, but I am afraid the other one is still at his mischief."

"What other one?" demanded Diamond, her voice rising in hysteria.

He looked down, shaking his head. "I tell the captain to be careful. He has a young brother. *He* likes them young, and he hates the captain. One day he will take him away. It is very wicked. What did you say your name was?"

"Clary, Mr. Vincent. Clary Brown. Do you not remember me? You were so cruel to me."

He said, "Oh yes. I'm afraid I do not recollect you. I daresay I will in time. I killed my little girl you know. My daughter . . ."

Diamond rose to her feet. What was the use? He was too ill, too old, he no longer cared. The only person he had ever loved was his own child, and he believed he had killed her.

He said vacantly, "Oh, are you going? Thank you for coming. And will you tell the captain to be sure to keep an eye on Philip? He is a good boy, and I would not wish him any harm. If he is taken to the summerhouse, it will be the end for him."

"The summerhouse, Mr. Vincent?" Diamond came up to him. She wanted to hammer him, to force him to see her, but it was no good. He lived in his own unhappy world. It was a miracle that even Philip should impinge on him.

He said, "That is where it happens. There were two or three girls— I really do not remember. Thank you so much for coming, Miss . . . Miss . . ."

"Clary Brown!"

"Oh, of course. You must have known my little Maria. You see, I had no choice. If I hadn't jumped, we would have been burned alive. But she cracked her head against the paving . . ."

Diamond could take no more of it. She walked quickly out of the room, and he seemed not even to notice her departure. He was still mumbling to himself as she closed the door. Mrs. Slade was waiting for her in the hall. She said, shaking her head, "I'm afraid this is one of his bad days, ma'am. Sometimes he is much better. But he does brood so on his little girl. I daresay he told you about it."

"Yes," said Diamond, "he did indeed."

"It was a great tragedy. Poor old gentleman. You must come again, ma'am, when he's better. He's always so pleased to see people. Have you known him for a long time?"

"All my life," said Diamond wearily.

"I daresay the captain will let you know when to come. It makes such a difference for him to have visitors."

Diamond knew that she would never cross this threshold again. She had met her monster, and a poor, sad thing he had proved to be. She was consumed with a mixture of disgust and pity— Pity for Mr. Vincent! Pity for this creature who had spoiled her life, who had made her childhood such a misery! Yet the angry pity stirred within her, and as she went thankfully toward the waiting carriage, she felt herself followed by a confusion of ghosts: a tattered, hungry little girl, an inhuman monster of a man, indissolubly entangled with a poor creature in a chair and a girl with diamonds round her throat.

As they drove back toward the village, Mr. Vincent's words about Philip weighed oppressively on her mind. A sudden curious idea came to her. She opened her reticule, and saw Miss Falconer's letter neatly folded inside, the pistol beneath it. She wanted to talk to Philip, and he of course could read the letter to her. It seemed more and more important that she should know its contents. Besides, though she had not entirely followed Mr. Vincent's rambling remarks, she was aware of a growing apprehension. It would be dreadful if anything happened to this young boy.

She said to Tom, "Could we perhaps call at the Hall? I would like to have a word with Master Philip."

Tom answered placidly, "The young master won't be there, ma'am. He goes to his tutor always on a Friday, and he stays there till the late afternoon."

"Then," said Diamond, "we will call in at his tutor's."

This seemed to her as urgent as it was unreasonable: she had no right to disturb his lessons, and probably, being the kind of boy he was, he would be furious. But as they were approaching Middleditch, a sadness and weariness overcame her. It was strange how at this moment the prospect of leaving the village and going back to London gave her little pleasure, even the joy of revisiting the theatre and seeing Kitty again. She sank back in the seat, closing her eyes; pictures knocked inside her head; her old enemy as a wretched, crippled creature; a lady with no face; a schoolmistress who died in violence.

Then she thought of Captain Ringham and that image restored her. When they arrived at the tutor's house, she had recovered her spirits, and she jumped out of the carriage, prepared to meet Philip's fury.

A young man came to the door. Diamond thought she had seen him once or twice walking round the village. He was obviously impressed by her appearance, and this restored her spirits even more.

"I wonder," she said, with her most engaging smile, "if I might have a word with Philip. I do realize," she added, fixing her large dark eyes on him, "that you are giving him his lessons, but I have a message for him from his brother."

The young man, after begging her to come in, said in some surprise, "But Philip never came today."

Diamond stared at him. She felt suddenly very cold. "I thought," she said, "that Friday was one of the days for his lessons."

"Why, so it is, ma'am. I was surprised that he did not come. May I not offer you a dish of tea, or perhaps—"

"No. No, thank you. I have the carriage waiting for me. Did he send no message?"

"None at all. It is most unusual," said the young man, who plainly did not take the matter seriously but wished to keep this charming young lady talking. "Captain Ringham is most insistent on his attending punctually, and on the rare occasions when he is ill, a message is always sent. A most polite gentleman . . ."

Diamond thought the young man was rather stuffy, though possibly good at Latin and Greek, or whatever it was that the boys had to learn. She said, "Captain Ringham is away today. Perhaps Philip just played truant."

"Oh, no. He wouldn't dare do that. His brother would be very angry. He always comes on time and he works very well. He is a most intelligent boy."

He thought the young lady looked oddly distracted; she did not appear to be paying much attention to him. He knew who she was, of course, but had never so far spoken to her. It was all quite a pity, because she was so very pretty, and there were few pretty ladies in Middleditch. He said, trying hard to keep her there, "Perhaps he has gone riding. Now I come to think of it, I believe someone saw him in Axenford woods."

"Who saw him there?" demanded Diamond sharply.

The young men thought her color changed, which was extraordinary. Why should it matter to her if a naughty boy chose to go riding instead of reading his Virgil? He said, "Oh, I mentioned the matter to Mr. Revill. At St. Joseph's Church. I daresay you know him."

"Yes, I know him," said Diamond in a soft, chill voice.

He went on to say, "Mr. Revill kindly offered to go after him, to remind him of his lessons. He did not seem to take the matter very seriously. He was laughing. But I suppose boys will be boys. I shall give him a great scold, I promise you. It is very wrong of him, though it has never happened before."

Diamond said, "Thank you," and climbed back into the carriage. She looked at Tom, who was waiting for her instructions, and wondered what he would say if she ordered him to drive to Axenford. But it would be quite ridiculous. Philip was only twelve, and his brother was away. Perhaps he really had decided to go riding instead of going to his tutor, who did not seem to be very inspiring. The worst that would happen would be a severe scolding from his brother. Why should she assume that Sir Francis had abducted him, or that there was something sinister about Mr. Revill's laughter? Mr. Revill was always giggling: he was a little mad. Perhaps he had simply found it amusing that Captain Ringham's young stepbrother should misbehave himself.

She said to Tom, "When will Captain Ringham be back?"

"Oh, not for several hours yet, ma'am. He has to travel some twenty miles, and the business takes up quite a bit of time."

"There's no chance that he might be home now?"

"None at all, Miss Diamond."

"Then you'd better take me home, Tom. If," said Diamond, struggling to repress the unreasonable panic that was consuming her, "Captain Ringham has come back, will you please tell him that I must see him immediately."

She saw the calm country eyes focus shrewdly upon her.

Tom, as she could plainly see, was adding up two and two and making it a dozen. But she was long past caring about such things. Let him imagine her wildly in love with his master, it did not matter a damn.

And of course she was. He was perfectly right. The blood raced to her cheeks so that they became scarlet. The fear by now was pounding within her, and this coupled with an emotion she had never yet experienced was so violent that she scarcely knew how to control herself. She thought, I love him so much. Then: Oh God, oh Christ, I pray that nothing has happened to him or to Philip.

Tom saw her into the cottage. It was obvious that he had instructions not to leave her alone in the village. She said as she opened the door, "You'll give my message to the captain, won't you?"

He answered soothingly, the laughter in his eyes, "Yes, ma'am, of course, ma'am," and stood there watching her until the door closed behind her. He had not missed the hand-holding, nor the look in his master's eye. Head over heels, the pair of them, and very nice too. She was a pretty lass, and it was high time the captain married and settled down.

Diamond came slowly into the kitchen. Georgy, the cat on her lap, looked happy again. It was obvious that she had needed company, and it was obvious, too, that Miss Falconer's ghost had no need to worry about Hob. He was being looked after as if he were a baby, with cream in his saucer and a pile of carefully boned breast of rabbit on his plate.

She said, "Did you have a good day, Miss Diamond? I hope you had a nice dinner." For she had naturally no idea where her mistress had gone, only knew that she had gone out driving with that nice Captain Ringham, presumably for dinner at the Hall.

"Yes," said Diamond, wandering distractedly round the kitchen. She realized that it was long past dinnertime, but for once, was not hungry. She was trying to still the panic that was increasing every minute, and wondering what the devil she should do.

"That clergyman looked in," said Georgy, caressing the replete and purring cat.

"What clergyman?" demanded Diamond, her voice suddenly shrill.

"Him from St. Joseph's. The one that giggles. I don't go much for him myself," said Georgy, "though he was civil enough, I must say."

"What did he want?"

"He wanted to know where you were."

"And did you tell him?"

"I said you were out with Captain Ringham. He seemed quite pleased," said Georgy. "He was laughing away." She looked up at Diamond, then her face suddenly twisted. "Shouldn't I have said that? Oh, Miss Diamond, I never thought . . ."

Diamond rubbed fretfully at her forehead, trying to understand why Mr. Revill should come to see her.

Then Georgy said suddenly, "I'll forget my own head next—there's a note come for you. I hope it isn't urgent. Of course I can't read it, but after your lessons, perhaps you can. I don't know who it's from. It just dropped through on the mat. I'd have asked that Mr. Revill, but it came five minutes after he was gone."

Diamond was to thank God for that, but she did not at that moment take the note seriously. Almost certainly she would not be able to read it. She opened it and saw that it was on a rough piece of paper, without any heading. It was written in capital letters and was very brief. She stared down at it. And then the miracle occurred: it made form and it made sense; she could actually understand it. She could hardly believe her own eyes. She read it again, almost gasping with amazement, and the words came out to her like a voice. Then she fully took in what she was reading.

It said: PHILIP AT AXENFORD. TELL WILL. There was no signature.

Georgy saw her color vanish as if a sponge has passed over her face. She at once jumped to her feet, spilling the cat to the floor. She cried out, "Oh, Miss Diamond, what is it? Is it bad news?" Then, bewildered, "But you could read it!"

"Yes," said Diamond in a clear, cold voice, "I can read it." She went up to Georgy and crouched before her, looking

223

steadily into the uncomprehending face. "Listen, my darling old woman. Listen as you've never listened before." She took the rough, chapped hands in hers. "I'm going out now—"

"But the captain said—"

"I don't give a damn what the captain said. I'm going out. But he will be calling round soon—oh, I hope it's soon—and you've got to give him both this note and a message. Are you listening to me, Georgy? It must be only to Captain Ringham. Not anybody else, anybody at all, whatever they say to you, and even if they spin you some kind of story. Especially that giggling bastard of a clergyman."

"No, Miss Diamond," said Georgy; then, as if she were not quite sure, "Yes, Miss Diamond."

Diamond looked up at that honest, stupid face, and wanted to scream at her hysterically. But rising to her feet again, she controlled herself, only gave the hands a little shake. She said, very carefully, "You do understand, don't you? Only Captain Ringham. Nobody else at all, even if they try to persuade you. You'll give him this note, and you'll tell him I've gone to the summerhouse at Axenford. Oh, Georgy, please don't look so silly. Repeat it after me."

And in a moment, you daft old bitch, I'm going to shake the life out of you . . .

But she managed to keep her voice down, even managed to smile. If Georgy became frightened, she would forget everything. She might even hand the note over to Sir Francis or Mr. Revill.

Georgy said obediently, "I'm to give the note to Sir Fran— I'm sorry, Miss Diamond. You've got me all confused."

"Georgy! Oh, Georgy, it's so important."

"I've got it now. I'm to give the note to Captain Ringham, and nobody else at all, and I'm to tell him you've gone to the summerhouse at Axenford. Are you dining with Sir Francis, then, Miss Diamond?"

"In a manner of speaking," said Diamond, "I suppose I am." She gave Georgy a bitter smile as she turned toward the stairs. "Don't wait up for me, Georgy. I may be back late."

I may not be back at all. God knows what all this is about, but he will have his dogs out, and he is a very wicked man.

&✺≺ XVI ≻✺&

Georgy did not see Diamond go out. Indeed, she did not even hear the door shut, and for some time believed her mistress was still upstairs, preparing herself for the dinner party. Diamond crept out as if she were an intruder in her own home, for she could not risk Georgy's peering from the window. She was dressed, for the first time in four years, as Clary Brown. It was essential: the village must not know that Miss Browne was going to Axenford. Mr. Revill might see her, or someone might inform Sir Francis. In her fine clothes she would be as conspicuous as a sunflower in December. Nobody else dressed like that in Middleditch, and it would not take a minute for the gossips to be whispering about her. Besides, she was going through the woods, and her handsome dress would be torn to shreds. She stepped barefoot down the path, looking furtively to the left and to right. Once she was out in the street she would be comparatively safe, for no one would connect her with the cottage. It was a long time since she had walked without shoes, but the soles of her feet had been hardened since childhood, and she enjoyed the feel of the rough gravel, the dampness of the grass, the plants brushing wetly against her ankles.

A darned grey skirt. A washed-out silken blouse. But she did not wear the tawny scarf, for there was no warmth in it; she had filched a thick woolen shawl from Georgy's room. *I could scarce call them clothes.* That was what the old man had said. *Burn those things you are wearing*, he had said. Until now she had never so much as touched them again, but burn them she could not. They were part of herself. Now, in the pocket of her skirt, she carried the pistol he had given her: a gypsy girl with a lady's pistol, cold and hard against her thigh. On her finger she wore Becky's ring, the red and black hair intertwined.

She had looked at herself in the mirror before setting out. Her hair was falling down and she did not trouble to pin it up. She whispered "I am Clary Brown." And she spoke the name several times: "Clary Brown, Clary Brown, Clary Brown." Then she had said, "Look after me, Pa. Please look after me, and send Will soon." She was not aware that she called him Will.

But again she had to say *I have no choice*.

Perhaps that will be my epitaph, she thought. Presently Diamond was running along the village street, making for the Axenford woods. It was late afternoon and already dusk and very cold. She passed one or two of the villagers, and nearly knocked into Mrs. Rigg, who had just closed her shop and was going home. She was moving too fast for her face to be seen. Mrs. Rigg would simply notice a slatternly country girl, too much in a hurry even to wish her good evening. Diamond caught a brief glimpse of her face. It expressed curiosity and irritation at her bad manners; that was all. It was plain that she had not the faintest idea that this was the uppity London miss from the cottage.

It was only when she was in the cold, wet dark of the woods that Diamond discovered she had forgotten to take off her necklace. The stones were, fortunately, hidden by the shawl, but they gleamed most inappropriately on her throat. She broke into half-hysterical laughter. To walk into danger, perhaps into death, with a thousand pounds' worth of jewelry around her neck— But why not? The absurdity of it in some way pleased her. She patted the diamonds before wrapping her shawl more tightly about her, and continued to push her way through the trees, the fallen leaves and the branches crackling beneath her feet.

One hand stayed in her pocket, clutching the pistol which she had never used. It was the thought of the dogs that terrified her. She remembered Sir Francis's account of the poor, inquisitive footman, and she screwed up her eyes in panic, wishing with all her heart and guts that she could turn back, sink into the safety of her own home. She went on, her teeth chattering, expecting any moment that one of the hounds would leap at her throat. But there was no sound, no padding of remorseless paws, only the rustling and murmur of a forest in the wind and rain.

Just before she reached Axenford, she came to a clearing and paused to regain both her breath and her courage. At this moment she almost turned about and went back to the cottage. What, after all, was she expected to do? Sir Francis would certainly be more adept with a pistol than she was. Besides, he was a man and a big one; she would have no chance if he seized her in those powerful arms. And it was possible that all this was some figment of her imagination: Philip was probably safe and sound, eating his supper by the fire, his only worry a guilty apprehension about what his brother would say and do to him for playing truant.

Then she saw the shadow on the mossy ground. She gave a thin shriek of terror. It was one of the dogs. He was dead. From the twisted attitude and the foam on his mouth, it was plain that he had been poisoned. Diamond, clinging to a tree trunk, praying that she would not faint, understood that the person who had sent her the note—she knew now who it must be—was, as much as was possible, protecting her. No doubt the other dog had been served in the same way. Diamond could feel no pity for the animals who had terrified her, and the faintness left her, taking with it all indecision.

She walked on, her arms folded across her, and presently she came to the drive. She could see Axenford before her, ablaze with light, as it had been the night she had dined with Sir Francis. How courteous he had been, how flattering, how gentle. And how he must have laughed—

Turning sideways, she saw the little summerhouse. The lights were on there too. She crossed the grass and walked steadfastly toward it, cold with purpose now that the fear at last had left her.

She came up to the house. A hand descended on her wrist. She looked up into Sir Francis's face. "Why," he said, "you have come to join us in our little celebration, Miss Diamond." His eyes moved over her. He was smiling. "In fancy dress, too. Is this a masquerade, ma'am? I vow you make a most pretty milkmaid."

"I have come to fetch Philip," said Diamond.

It was strange how at this moment, when most certainly her life might be near its end, she grew entirely calm. Her face, illuminated by a flickering fire within the summerhouse, was composed and cold, her voice steady. She studied Sir Francis's face. She marveled that she had ever thought him a kindly man. It was a wicked face, debauchery and hate and cruelty in every line of it. The eyes were opaque, like those of his hounds, the wide mouth curved. She saw that she could expect neither pity nor mercy. This was what poor Lady Caroline had lived with. The thought of it chilled Diamond more than anything else.

She said nothing more, but waited for his next words. The grip on her wrist was ruthlessly strong. It would be both useless and undignified to struggle.

"Then you will tell him so yourself," said Sir Francis, still smiling. "I have no doubt he will be delighted to see you. You can join him at the little party we have prepared for him. If you remember, Miss Diamond, I have always wanted you to see my little summerhouse. I had thought your visit would be later on, at Christmas time, but since you are here, let me conduct you inside. My friend, Mr. Revill, is also with us. I know he will be equally pleased to see you."

He dragged her inside, up two small steps and into a large room, empty except for a burning brazier in the middle of it, some strange signs on the wall, with a crucifix below them. The signs were the same as those on Sir Francis' ring. The door, wide open, took up almost half the outside wall.

Sir Francis released her. He stepped back a little so that he half blocked the entrance. "Welcome," he said. "This is what my dear friend and neighbor, Captain Ringham, has always wished to see. It is a pity that you will never be able to describe it to him. Naturally, I keep the door locked and padlocked, but tonight it hardly matters, as the dear captain is out on his household errands. Were you not asking about Philip, Miss Diamond? You will see that he is here, as you no doubt expected. And of course, Mr. Revill you know . . ."

Diamond stared about her. She saw that Philip stood a little way from the brazier, which gave out a monstrous heat. His hands were bound but his feet were free. She could see that this did not matter—he was frozen with fear. His face was tallow-white and his eyes stared at her, wide and despairing. She could see that he did not even recognize her, perhaps thought her to be yet another tormentor. He was, after all, only twelve years old, and he was facing death—and he knew it. Despite this, he did not utter one cry, and the appalled eyes were tearless. Diamond was consumed with pity and a sheer, blinding rage. Her eyes moved to Mr. Revill, who was giggling wildly, and she thought she had never in her life seen such a couple of monsters. Her right hand crept into her pocket, but Sir Francis, who was watching her eagerly, saw the movement. In an instant his hand was on hers and the pistol was flung to the floor.

He burst out laughing. She remembered that boyish laugh. "Why," he said, "this is a real amazon. Are you planning to shoot me, little Clary Brown? I suppose you have the right. It's a pity you will not also have the opportunity. I hanged your stealing lecher of a father, and I can see you are spawned from the same stock. I can only hope that you were not also proposing to shoot Mr. Revill, who is a minister of God. You should have more respect for him. In any case, I fear you are too late." He kicked the pistol away as he spoke. It clattered down the steps and lay on the grass outside. He said, "You are not to be trusted. I regret having to do this, but you are a dangerous young lady, Clary. We have to make sure that you do not in any way prevent what we are about to do, especially as you yourself are now part of the sacrifice."

And with these words he seized her by the shoulders so that she could not move, while Mr. Revill, seeming to be enjoying himself vastly, leaped forward and bound her wrists tightly together with twine, so that they were clasped before her, almost as if she were praying.

Diamond stood there, leaning against the wall, and looked at Philip, trying silently to speak to him. The terror of this young boy seemed more important than her own, and she tried to say, through her mind to his, "It is all right, boy. Your brother will be here soon. He will have had the message from Georgy and he'll be here like the wind, once he knows." She nearly spoke the words aloud, in her desperation, but knew this might prevent the slight, so immeasurably slight, chance of rescue that still remained. She looked wretchedly at Philip's ashen face, the eyes still wide and staring, not meeting hers. He was over the threshold of reasonable fear, the fear that was now shuddering through her own body as her eyes moved to the nearly white-hot brazier. Yet his legs were untied. If only there was some way of arousing him, if she could only bring him to his senses, he might make a dash for freedom, with her body between him and his persecutors. Her mind began turning over possibilities, and meanwhile Sir Francis was speaking again.

"I think," he said, "you deserve a little explanation. You have made quite a journey to see me, and I appreciate the preparations." His eyes moved briefly to the little pearl-handled pistol lying on the grass. "What a pretty thing. I have never seen one quite like it. And you told me, I remember, that you know how to use it."

Diamond cursed her stupidity in letting him knock the weapon from her hand, but there was no point in brooding on that now. The only thing to consider was how she could possibly contrive to get Philip away. Physically there seemed to be nothing she could do. If she attempted anything, her feet would undoubtedly be bound. Besides, what chance could she have against two grown men? Somehow she must play for time, praying that Captain Ringham would soon arrive. She had no idea when he was expected home, was not even certain that Tom would give him the message to go to her cottage. Perhaps, even if Tom did, he might ignore it, regarding her as a temperamental female trying to assert herself, to show that she had some claim on him. The one real hope was that Sir Francis, a vain and wordy man, who plainly loved the sound of his own voice, would keep talking. She would pretend to listen attentively and, perhaps, retain his attention while the minutes slipped by.

She turned her face, streaked with mud from the woods, with the black hair hanging over it, and tried to smile at Philip, but he was too shocked even to notice. This again aroused a fury in her that helped to break the panic. She had never been able to endure bullying; that was one thing the workhouse had taught her. The thought of this child so frightened that his brain might well be turned so angered her that he became in her mind confused with the other children she had known, who had been bullied and starved and ill-treated. For the first time a dim idea of a plan of campaign began to stir in her mind.

"I believe you have now met my wife," said Sir Francis amiably, as if they were at a tea party. "The poor creature is so sadly disfigured. Of course, the world believes her dead, but I find it entertaining to keep her alive, so that she may see herself and remember that elegant little affair in the woods. With your pa, as I believe you call him. You pa, Clary. I daresay he needed a whore, and my wife served as well as any. I have a little attic room made specially for her, with mirrors on every wall. She is delighted to hide herself from the world, so I let her comes and go as she pleases. No one could endure to look at her without vomiting, which I consider so amusing. How did you find her? A trifle changed, I imagine. I understand you met her in that little theatre she was so fond of."

Diamond saw that this man was a monstrous egotist, who could not resist displaying his own wickedness. She did not answer him, hoping her silence would provoke him to speak on.

Mr. Revill, who had so far said nothing, remarked, "She was once a beauty. Do you not remember? I hope you admire her beauty now."

And he fell to giggling again, but Sir Francis held up an admonishing hand, saying, with amusement glinting in his eyes, "Come, sir, this is not worthy of you as a man of God. *Vanitas, vanitatum*, as they say, and the poor soul was indeed destroyed by her own vanity. Naturally, there was a little—how shall I put it?—assistance. But I do trust, Miss Clary, that you do not overindulge in make-up. The lead in it is vastly dangerous. Not that it will affect you now, one way or the other, for I fancy your days with the ceruse box are over, but it always grieves me to see young women bringing about their own damnation."

Diamond was so enraged that he could speak in such a fashion of his suffering wife, she forgot discretion and addressed him as she had once, to her shame, addressed Captain Ringham. "You son of a whore," she said. "How can you speak so? The poor lady must be tortured out of her mind, and all you can do is make mock of her—"

He stepped forward and struck her on the cheek with his clenched fist. The blow sent her reeling back, knocking her head against the wall, but she had endured a great many blows in her lifetime, and she did not faint or fall, simply shook her hair back and glared at him. He said savagely, "She deserves everything. She lay with your father. Is that not enough insult for any man?"

"And all good luck to her, the poor lass," said Diamond, tilting up her chin and contriving somehow to produce a derisive smile.

She saw that this astonished him, and she was so pleased that she forgot the smart of her bruised cheek and ignored the salt blood that was trickling into her mouth. Her plan might just conceivably work, if only Captain Ringham had returned, gone straight to the cottage and received her message.

Surely he would go. He must go. He must—

Sir Francis cried out shrilly, "To be my wife, *my* wife, and to fornicate with a thieving gypsy poacher— I would have killed her, only then I thought of a better way. And you, his bastard daughter, a workhouse brat, to come back here— Did you enjoy his hanging, Clary? I hope you did. It took a long time. It takes some twenty minutes to throttle a man, and I made sure that there was no one there to pull his legs or in any way help him. You saw every minute of it, didn't you? I daresay you still remember it. You are going to die yourself in a little while, and I doubt you or the boy will find it much more pleasant. It will at least settle my score. Nobody insults me and gets off scot-free."

Diamond remained silent. She looked at him with a steady contempt. She longed to move near Philip, to comfort him by pressing her body against his, but she knew that she must not. Any demonstration of humanity would only incite these two devils to further cruelty. And at least his attention was now on her, not on that poor child.

Sir Francis was disconcerted by her silence. He shouted at her, "I do not like meddlers. That old parson and then your old bitch of a schoolmarm found that out. When she wrote me that impertinent letter, she signed her death warrant. It is true that I did not expect her to find out about my wife, but that served my turn. I knew it would bring her to the theatre.

That was your doing too, no doubt? Yes, of course. It must have been. Who else?"

"Yes, it was my doing," said Diamond in a loud, clear voice.

Mr. Revill at this point interrupted. She saw suddenly that he was the more dangerous of the two—he was madder, less human, and therefore less likely to be distracted. He cared for nothing except his own evil purpose. He could not lose his temper because so much emotion did not dwell in him.

He said in his giggling way, "I am loath to interrupt you, Sir Francis, but I think it would be best if we proceeded. After all, there is always a possibility we might be interrupted, and at this juncture . . ."

Diamond saw that if she did not put her poor, weak plan into operation immediately, it would be too late. She felt her knees giving way beneath her, and began to swear silently at herself in such language as Middleditch would never have believed possible, with the crude, raw obscenity of the London gutter that she had heard many times in Drury Lane. She told herself that she must think of this as a first night. She managed to remain upright, though what Sir Francis was now saying was so unspeakable that she could only pray that Philip, still away in his anguished terror, could not really take in what was being said.

"You are perfectly right, Mr. Revill," said Sir Francis, then made him a little bow. "As always. We will proceed immediately. There is no point in delaying things any longer."

He swung round to Diamond. She did not immediately look at him, but turned her gaze on Philip. *Come back, Philip. Listen to me. Your legs are not bound. I am going to take up all his attention. I am going to behave like a lunatic. I am going to disgrace myself by screaming and crying. And you are going to slide nearer the door. The moment will come when you can jump out. Philip. Philip, damn your eyes, pay attention. Listen. Oh, my boy, come back to us, listen . . .*

She let herself totter perceptibly, and began to cry. Thank God, she had always been able to summon tears at will, but in truth it was not now so difficult, and the tears rolled down like a fountain.

Sir Francis was delighted. He came up to her. He said softly, "I think you are beginning to realize what is in store for you.

I believe I mentioned it to you when you dined at my house."
He turned toward the brazier, making a little gesture. Diamond saw that Mr. Revill had laid a great iron rod across it,
already red-hot, and that a pan was suspended underneath. "I
fear," he said, "we have to use living sacrifices, otherwise the
whole business would be quite useless. This time I believe we
may at last succeed. We have tried so many times before, but
with so young a boy and so handsome a female, it is possible
that the experiment may prove worthy of us. It is in a way
a compliment, Miss Diamond. You may not realize it, but you
are advancing human discovery by perhaps a thousand years.
Future generations will thank you, for Mr. Revill and I believe
we have discovered the secret of eternal youth. Now—"

Diamond thought despairingly, It is too late, then, No, it is
not, it is not, my pa will never let this happen— She gave a
great scream. It was one of her best efforts. Kitty used to say
that her screams almost broke her eardrums. Then she flung
herself on the floor at Sir Francis' feet and groveled and
writhed there, trying to snatch at him with her bound hands.

He began to laugh. He ignored Mr. Revill, who was plainly
annoyed by this distraction. "Why," Sir Francis said, "we are
frightening the poor lady." He looked down at her, trampling
on her entreating hands. Then his eyes narrowed. "You are
wearing diamonds!" he said. And he reached down his hand
and wrenched at the necklace, badly cutting Diamond's neck.
The stones rolled all over the floor. He said, "We must not
waste such beautiful things. Would you not like to make a
farewell present of them to my poor, dear wife, to compen-
sate for her unutterably disgusting appearance?"

Diamond held out her bound hands and began to howl. The
words tumbled from her memory, words out of all the plays
she had ever seen, ever acted in: indiscriminate, violent, hysterical words, yelled out at the full pitch of her lungs. She saw
through a kind of mist that Philip was at least stirring, at last
emerging from the deaf-and-dumb nightmare that had encased
him. He was actually paying attention to what she was shrieking out. Mr. Revill, outraged, had put his hands to his ears,
and Sir Francis was backing away from her, staring at her in
a mixture of fury and astonishment.

I now have my audience. Help me, Pa. Help me.

She not only had her audience, she was deafening it. And as she bawled, clutching first at Sir Francis and then at Mr. Revill, she squirmed her way toward Philip, who was gazing at her, the reason back in his eyes, a kind of dazed understanding in his ashen face.

"O never say that I was false of heart," shrieked Diamond, digging into her memory. "Though absence seemed my flame to qualify, *boy, move nearer the door slide a little.* My only love sprung from my only hate. *An inch at a time don't look at me.* For you and I are past our dancing days. Gallop apace, you fiery-footed steeds, *oh, gallop apace, an inch more for God's sake*, there's small choice in rotten apples, *it's your only chance*, but you know we must return good for evil, *he's on his way*, as if a woman of education bought things because she wanted 'em. See how love and murder will out, *slowly, slowly, don't look at me, look at him.* Music hath charms to soothe a savage breast, rise to meet him in a pretty disorder, *oh, rise to meet him another inch.* I never pin up my hair with prose, I have been toiling and moiling, *toil and moil.* Go to your business, I say, *go to your business, slow, slow, only go.* How sweet the moonlight sleeps upon this bank, on, on, you noblest English, *on, on,* I cannot fly, *but you can, you must.* They have tied me to a stake, *good, good, a little more, you're nearly there*, a king of shred and patches, they fool me to the top of my bent, *I'm fooling them*, you take care or the charming little devil will save all, *you're almost there*, give me the daggers. *Look like the innocent flower*, but be the serpent under't, *run, run, run . . .*"

Her voice, the celebrated voice in such contrast to her slender body, reverberated through the woods. Captain Ringham, riding like the devil, almost at Axenford, heard it across the grounds, thought of such horrors as almost made him frantic, leaped off his horse and started to run toward the inhuman shrieking. Sir Francis and Mr. Revill, who had never heard anything like it in their lives, and who were too astonished to make out a wailing word of it, took it as pure raving, but Philip, convulsed with a terror that at last restored his senses, understood, and as Diamond, still screeching, though her voice was almost gone, clutched at Sir Francis's ankle and flung herself across Mr. Revill's feet, he suddenly leaped up and dived toward the door.

There for one second he hesitated, but Diamond, swinging round like a top, raised her two bound hands and brought them with a crack upon his bottom. She gasped out, "Run, you little bastard, for Jesus Christ's sake, run!"

Sir Francis realized one second too late that he had been fooled. He made a grab at Philip, but his foot skidded on the diamonds, and he fell flat on his face. Diamond, almost voiceless now, burst into wild hysterical laugher, then collapsed in a huddle on the floor, too exhausted even to try to do anything to save herself, almost resigned, accepting the appalling things that were going to happen to her. Her face was streaked with tears and sweat and blood, her black hair wild, her hands cut and raw with her scrabbling. She raised her head and saw that a figure stood in the doorway, and she knew from Sir Francis' indrawn breath that he had seen it too.

Mr. Revill, who was facing the other way, said fiercely, for once without the giggle, "Throw this bitch on the brazier. Let her burn. Never mind the heart. Just kill her—"

"No," said Lady Caroline. She had picked up Diamond's pistol. She held it very steadily, for all her hand was so thin and frail. As Mr. Revill started to move toward her, her finger touched the trigger, and he halted at once, his mouth going down, his eyes dilated. Sir Francis was also motionless.

She said again in her beautiful voice, "No." Diamond, who had managed to raise herself to a kneeling position but who was too exhausted to stand, looked full at her, at the ravaged face clearly revealed in the flickering light of the brazier. Sir Francis, despite the hate that consumed him, the hate that had made her what she was, flinched at the sight of her, while Mr. Revill suddenly made a retching noise and turned away.

The face in that red light was straight out of hell. The bone hollows where the flesh had been eaten away were black pits, the skull-teeth gleamed as she opend her mouth, and her eyes, the beautiful monstrous eyes, were set in craters of darkness, shining now with a hatred that matched Sir Francis's own.

Only Diamond looked at her steadily, and said, "Thank God, my lady. Oh, thank God—"

Then she spoke. Her eyes were fixed on her husband. "You don't care to look at me, do you?" she said. "But you shall. You shall see at me for the last time. I am what you have made of me. You put poison in my rouge. You turned me into something so monstrous that no one can bear me. And for what? Because once, when I was so sick with unhappiness that I felt I could bear life no longer, I found a few moments of peace with a kind and harmless man. You never loved me. You made my life a misery. And yet you cannot forgive me because someone else took from you what you never really wanted. He was good to me. He was gentle and loving. I had forgotten what such things were. And for that you had to murder him, as you would murder his daughter. You turned my existence into hell. You spared me nothing, did you, Francis? You knew I couldn't bear to look at myself, but the house was filled with mirrors, the furniture so highly polished that I had to see myself everywhere, wherever I turned. And you enjoyed every minute of those years. But this is the end, for you and for me. This is the end of your murdering, your wickedness. You say you want eternal youth. Why? You have never been young. You have always been dead. Our marriage was always evil. And now, thank God, the play is over."

Sir Francis's face was undergoing an extraordinary transformation. Suddenly he appeared again as the kindly gentleman Diamond had met by the banks of the stream. Diamond, turning her head toward him as she still knelt there in her torn and filthy clothing, saw that the mask had come down; even the voice was gentle and amused.

"Caroline," he said, "my poor, dear Caroline, you are imagining things. You must have a fever. Miss Diamond has been acting a little play for us. Now be a good girl, give me that pistol and come and join us. Miss Diamond is certainly a most remarkable actress—"

Her gaze did not waver, nor did the pistol in her hand. She said again, "No." Then, without turning her head, she said sharply, "Run away, little girl. Will should be there by now. I think you will find him waiting for you. Do what you're told, child. Leave us. We do not want you here."

Diamond managed at last to pick herself up. She did not believe she could make the few steps toward the door. She was shaking from head to foot, her knees felt like boneless things that would never again support her, and the three terrible faces shimmered before her vision: the ruined mask of Lady Caroline; Sir Francis, now with his mouth dropped open; Mr. Revill, sickly white at the prospect of death, death that he had been about to mete out to her.

"Oh," said Lady Caroline, in the pettish voice that Diamond had heard before, "why don't you do what you are told? Children these days are so disobedient. Go away at once, or I'll have you whipped. You're only a little gypsy girl, after all. Surely you are not impudent enough to argue with me."

Then Diamond, summoning up the last dregs of her energy, ran, and as she half fell down the steps, she heard the shots. There were two of them, with only a slight pause in between. She did not turn back, only tried to run on, her steps beginning to totter. She almost knocked against Captain Ringham, running to meet her.

She whispered, "Lady Caroline . . ." but could get no more words out. Her throat was parched, and she only had strength to fall into the enclosing arms.

Captain Ringham said, in the voice of a man who had been through every hell of terror and rage, "You bloody, meddling little idiot, I told you— You've saved Philip's life. What am I to do with you? What can I say to you?"

Diamond only whispered again, "Lady Caroline . . ." and made a faint, weak gesture in the direction of the summerhouse, a few yards away. But even as she spoke, there was a flare and an explosion, and the flames shot out of the door, scarlet and wicked against the black night sky.

She heard him swear. He dropped her to the grass, saying savagely to his brother, "Stay with her. If you dare to follow me, I'll break your back."

But the flames were roaring now and the place was an inferno; and not only could Captain Ringham not get near it, he was compelled to retreat, dragging Diamond with him. The three of them watched helplessly as the little summerhouse burned. So great was the din of crackling wood and falling stones that not a cry was heard, and presently, as they stood there, aghast and staring, their faces red in the glare, the whole edifice crumbled to pieces, a heap of white-hot ashes, with the flames licking across and a pillar of smoke in the sky.

From the house, the doors flung wide open, came the staff of Axenford: the cooks, the maids, the footmen. They huddled together, their faces alight with a kind of terrible joy, as if they knew that the nightmare was over, that the devil who had owned them was dead and his poor lady released from her torment. Not one of them took a step toward the summer-house, and in the passage behind them the flames were reflected in the mirrors that covered every wall.

Diamond pulled herself out of Captain Ringham's arms and stared at the ruin. She was no longer seeing the men who had wished to murder her, or Lady Caroline who had saved her life, but ghosts that were at last liberated—the ghosts of children. It seemed to her that a little carrot-headed girl stood before her, smiling and stretching out her arms.

"Becky," she whispered. "Oh, Becky . . ."

There was a deep voice that seemed to come out of a tunnel, many miles away. It said, "Let me carry you, Clary. Let me take you home."

She turned toward the voice. She saw nothing but flames and blackness. She said in a hoarse, choked manner, "Oh, I can walk, thank you. I am not, thank God, of the swooning kind."

And saying this, she fainted dead away and collapsed at Captain Ringham's feet, her grimy, bloodstained face buried in the soft, sweet grass.

She came at last to her senses, dragged up from some deep pit of weakness and exhaustion, in a bed that was not her own, in a room that she did not recognize. She sobbed a little as she swam to the surface of consciousness. She was aware of her chafed, bruised hands, of her sore throat, and indeed her whole body felt as if she had been beaten, she could hardly raise her head.

But she did at last do so, turning it a little to one side. She saw that Captain Ringham was sitting by her bed, both his hands holding her own. There was a wet cloth on her forehead, and as she stirred, he put his arm beneath her shoulders and held some drink to her lips. She tried to push it away, but he silently persisted, and presently she swallowed something hot and sweet that soothed her aching throat. She clutched the bowl from him and drained it.

Then she looked at him and managed to smile, while the tears of weakness trickled down her cheeks. She whispered, as she had so often done to Kitty Clive after her performance, "Was I good? Oh, please tell me, was I good?"

He had no idea what she was talking about, but he said at once, "Yes, yes, you were wonderful," and at that Diamond sighed in relief and fell quietly asleep.

She woke up at last, to find Georgy bustling round the room, Georgy overcome as usual—and this time she might well be so—with the drama of it all, yet quite shocked and drawn-looking and clucking round so persistently that Diamond suddenly sat up and said in a rousing voice, "Oh, do be quiet, you silly old woman. You're making a fuss over nothing. Help me to dress, and tell Captain Ringham I would like to see him. You can send one of the village children—" Then she looked round her and said in a bewildered voice, "Where am I?"

For she had assumed she was back in the cottage, and this room was strange to her. It was a small, plain, comfortable room, with wide windows, a good fire burning in the hearth and a great bowl of flowers by her bedside.

"Captain Ringham thought you should not be moved," said Georgy importantly, "and I must say, I agreed with him. I thought it most sensible. He has been so worried about you, a really kind gentleman. He looked in at least a dozen times, and I am to tell him at once when you are awake so that a meal can be brought you. I am to ask what you would like to eat, then I will go down to the kitchens and tell the house-keeper—"

"I am quite capable of going downstairs myself," said Diamond, then, rather dazedly, "How long have I been asleep?"

"Nearly ten hours, Miss Diamond."

"What! But then, it's evening, it's the next day . . ." Diamond jumped out of bed, but had to clutch the bedpost, for the weakness was still in her and the room danced about her. However, by the time she had drunk a glass of cordial she felt better and did not object when a tray of food was brought in to her. Then she dressed carefully, with Georgy's help. Georgy had brought her clothes. The old woman remarked, "I don't know what those things were you were wearing, Miss Diamond. They didn't look your kind of clothes at all, but certainly you'll never be able to wear them again."

"I shall never want to," said Diamond slowly. "They have served their purpose."

The bruises showed clearly on her face, and her cut neck was covered by a scarf. There was still no color in her cheeks, and she had to hold onto the banister.

But Diamond looked contentedly round her as she went slowly downstairs. She could see on the first floor the open door of what must be the drawing room. The lamps were burning and it looked warm and inviting. She thought the house was an agreeable one. The Hall was not half the size of Axenford, and there were hardly any family portraits, but it was all neat and clean. Everything seemed a little worn but good, and the maidservant who came forward to conduct her into the drawing room was smiling and friendly.

Captain Ringham, who was pacing up and down, came instantly to greet her. He saw her white, bruised face, and for a moment his tightened in rage. Then without preamble he took her into his arms. Diamond made not the faintest protest. She held her face up to be kissed. Yet her body stiffened a little as she waited for the shudder of revulsion to go through her as his arms tightened. The tears pricked her eyes, for she loved him so much, more than she had ever loved anyone in her life, it seemed so sad that she must pass the rest of her life denied what she so desperately needed.

He stood murmuring endearments, of a kind that came oddly from so violent a man, and Diamond drank down the kisses and sweet words like someone dying of thirst in the desert. She found herself unable to move away from him, pressed her body closer, as if she would mold herself against him. After a time the extraordinary truth struck her: not only was there not the faintest feeling of revulsion, but she was filled with a warmth and joy and excitement that she had never believed she could experience. Indeed, she could have spent the rest of her life in his embrace. She gave a little cry of disbelief, and managed to move away from him, staring up at him in a kind of bewildered ecstasy.

He said quickly, "You must be utterly exhausted. Forgive me. I did not mean to be so thoughtless, but when you came into the room just now, I could not stop myself. I've made you cry again. My poor, darling girl, what you must have endured —I cannot bear to think of it. I am only sorry the devil is dead. I would have liked to murder him. I'll bring you a glass of wine. Tomorrow Philip will thank you in person. He is in bed now. Like you, he has slept the day round. Don't cry so, Clary. Dear little Clary, please don't cry. You make me feel a brute."

"I am so happy," sobbed Diamond. "Oh, I am so terribly happy!"

He stared at her. The ironic look that she knew so well had returned to his face. He put the glass of wine in her hand, then knelt beside her. He said, "Do you always cry when you are happy, you impossible girl?"

"Oh, I can't tell you—" She was sobbing convulsively. "Please hold me again. Please go on kissing me. I want you to put your arms round me tight, really tight, tight enough to hurt. Oh, please, Will, you don't know, you'll never under-stand what this means to me."

"I don't think," he said, "I'll ever understand you at all." But he did as he was asked, without any noticeable protest, and Diamond, her face pressed against his, saw for the last time through her closed eyes the ghost of a stupid, bad old man who now could never again touch her, who had receded into the distance as something of no importance. It was true that Will would never understand; it was not the kind of thing that men did understand. But it was over, and the delight and happiness within her was such that she wanted to dance and sing, to say foolish, ridiculous things, to shout her joy to the world.

In the end, it was he who moved away. They sat by the fire, holding hands, and at last, shivering even now at the memory, she told him what had happened in the summerhouse.

He listened, his face black and grim. "Philip says he was snatched up on the way to his tutor." He added, rather savagely, "I suspect he was playing truant, but it scarce matters now. As for you, I don't think they expected you to come. Your turn was to come at Christmas."

"I'll never know what happened in there," said Diamond, "but I'm glad they're dead. They were terrible men. How could they do such things? Do you understand?"

"I don't think it matters any more, except that a plague has been lifted from the village. Now, thank God, we can go about our normal lives again, and the Axenford line is done. As for my poor Caroline, she had nothing to live for, and I cannot believe she was sorry to die. I'm thankful she at last summoned up the courage to kill them. I always believed he was responsible for her—her illness, though I didn't know about the poisoned rouge. She must have suffered unimaginably. I cannot understand why she did not come to me. I would always have helped her."

Diamond thought that she understood very well. Lady Caroline had once been a beauty, and Will had known her in her prime. She could never have borne for him to see her as she was, but again, that was something even the most intelligent gentleman would not fully understand.

He went on, "I wonder how the fire started. Perhaps one of them fell against the brazier—" Then he made an angry noise and turned his head away. "Good God! That any man could do such monstrous things. If you hadn't come— Why did you go, my dearest idiot? What made you run into such appalling danger?"

"Lady Caroline left me that note. She wrote it in capitals, especially for me. And I could read it! Oh, Will, don't you see what a miracle it is that I can read? I don't think you know what it means to me."

"I know very well what it has meant to me and my young brother."

"Will you do something for me, please?"

"Anything. Anything in the whole wide, bloody world."

"That is a little rash of you, isn't it?" said Diamond with a smile. The color had come back to her cheeks. Her eyes were shining like the lost diamonds.

"I don't give a damn what it is." Then he asked suspiciously, "What is it?"

"Will you read Miss Falconer's letter to me, the one she

sent to Sir Francis? I think it made him very angry. I think that's why he killed her. It's in handwriting, which I can't read very well yet. Perhaps Philip will teach me."

He said, "I think Philip will do anything you want. He told me you were the bravest person he's ever met, and he didn't know anyone could scream so loudly. He says he will never despise girls again."

"That is very kind of him!"

"Well, he's only twelve, my love. At that age we all look on women as inferior creatures. Where is this letter of yours?"

Diamond took the crumpled letter out of her reticule and put it in Captain Ringham's hand. He read it through to himself, then read it again, aloud:

"Dear Sir Francis,
Miss Diamond Browne has asked me to write this letter for her. She will be dining with you tomorrow night, and is pleased to accept your invitation.
I am less pleased, sir, for I know, as you know, that she is the daughter of Romany Brown. For God's sake, let me entreat you not to harm this young girl. You and I have known each other for a long time, and during that time I have grown aware of the evil you have done, the crimes you have committed. I cannot prevent her from going, though I would do so if I could, but I must warn you that if you do her the least harm, I will see that she is avenged. I may be a weak old woman, but I know those who are neither weak nor old.
Sir, if you have any decency left in you, leave her alone. She is such a dear, good girl—"

He broke off. "Clary, you are crying again. You should not have made me read this."

"He said it was her death warrant," sobbed Diamond. "And I loved her so much."

"She loved you. And she was perfectly right. You are a dear, good girl, and I owe you more than my life. I could not pay back my debt in a thousand years."

"Well," said Diamond, recovering herself, "if you really do so much want to pay it back, I can tell you how to do it."

He gazed at her, beginning to laugh. "You never fail to astonish me. You are the most extraordinary girl. Well, what can I do? You may count it as done."

"You really mean that?"

"Yes, God help me. What do you want? The Hall? My estates? My head on a plate?"

"Oh, Will . . ."

"Well, I'm waiting. What is it"

"You'll remember," said Diamond, her voice faltering a little, "that I told you I was really a bad girl—"

"Oh, not again!"

"But I am. Perhaps it don't matter, but—but I should like to spend the whole of this night in bed with you, Will. I think," said Diamond, her voice growing even fainter, "that would pay off all the debt. If, of course, it doesn't inconvenience you."

She could not quite bring herself to look at him. The pause that followed seemed to her of an hour's duration. The color began to burn in her cheeks, for she had never said such a thing to anyone, and the words, now that they were out, seemed extraordinarily immodest. Perhaps he was angry. Perhaps he no longer loved her. Perhaps he would now walk away and leave her. She screwed her eyes up tight and waited for the blow to fall.

He said at last, in a voice that sounded improbably as if he were struggling not to laugh, "I daresay that could be arranged. Though I should be pleased to know what you would say to a little church ceremony in addition. If that—if that doesn't inconvenience you."

Diamond exclaimed, in what was nearly a shout of the purest astonishment, "You mean you are asking me to marry you?"

"For Christ's sake, what do you think I'm asking? I've wanted to ask you to marry me for a long time, only you talk so much, it is almost impossible to get a word in edgeways."

"But, Will, you don't have to marry me. I don't mind, you know. I mean, marriage would be wonderful, but I never expected to marry anyone, and I suppose it's not so important. Why? Please tell me why."

"It must be because I want to, Clary Brown. If I'm not too old for you. I must confess that I am thirty-five, which is a great deal more than you."

"I'm an old man's darling!"

"No. You're my darling. You always have been, and you are

going to remain my darling until the end of your days. If you imagine there will ever be anyone else, I shall wring your pretty little neck."

"There will never be anyone else," whispered Diamond, "except, of course, three children. I want three children. And none of them will ever go into a workhouse." Then, as his arms came round her, she muttered into his shoulder, "I think I'm going to cry again. Georgy will be so happy. You were always the one she preferred— Oh Will, you're laughing at me. Why are you laughing? I don't think I've said anything amusing."

"Oh, Clary," he said, "I've loved you from the first moment I saw you, though God knows why, for you did little else but insult me— You accuse me of laughing at you. You're laughing, yourself. I think you ought to be more serious. After all, I've never said anything like this to anyone before."

"I'm glad you love me," said Diamond, grave again, "even when I spit in your eye, or call you the son of a whore."

"Well," he said, in the abrupt, businesslike voice that she had once so disliked, "I think we should now be more formal."

"Yes, Will. I should like to be formal."

"Will you marry me, Clary Brown? Will you become Mrs. William Ringham?"

Then Diamond gave him a wide and lovely smile. "Oh, Will," she said, folding her arms about him and raising her face to his, "I have no choice."